Deryn Pittar writes and is published in sci-fi, fantasy, futuristic and contemporary romance, loves writing short and flash fiction, and is an occasional poet. She belongs to Spec.Fic.NZ, and the Romance Writers of N.Z. She reads and critiques for fellow authors and listens to their advice in return.

In 2020 she gained fourth equal place with her sestina 'Australia' in the Frank DiBase International Poetry contest.

Her dragon novel 'Lutapolii – White Dragon of the South' is a prize-winning fantasy, winning a Sir Julius Vogel Award at Geysercon in 2019 for Best Young Adult published in 2018. She also won the short fiction contest at Geysercon with 'Hendrik's Pet'.

In 2016 she won a steam punk fiction prize with her short story 'The Carbonite's Daughter' which became the inspiration for her novel of the same name.

T0288540

THE CARBONITE'S DAUGHTER

BY

DERYN PITTAR

The Carbonite's Daughter

All Rights Reserved

ISBN-13: 978-1-922556-46-2

Copyright ©2022 Deryn Pittar

V1.1

Printed in Palatino Linotype and Drakoheart Leiend.

IFWG Publishing International
Gold Coast

www.ifwgaustralia.com

For my family. Thank you for your unfailing support and belief in my ability.

Chapter 1

Calista kept a tight grasp of her mother's hand as they hurried down the sloping passage, deeper into the mountain. Each footfall made her small breasts bounce and tingle. They hurt and she wished she had enough boobs to wear a bra. She probably would soon. The walls were warm and her heavy coat made her hot. She wanted to stop and take it off but they had a train to catch.

"When will we see Father?"

Her mother stopped and put her arm around Calista's shoulders, whispering into her ear, "Shhh, remember, the walls are listening."

Calista looked around. No microphones in sight, but they could be hidden. She looked into her mother's dark brown eyes, her Welsh heritage her mother often told her, and noticed more grey hairs around her temple. She looked older. The sodium lights in the passageway picked out the fine lines around her eyes. Why hasn't she noticed this before? The excitement of the last month blinded her to the everyday things. She had not seen her father for two years and today she might.

She whispered back, "When, Mother?"

Mother checked her timepiece, an old fob watch from Calista's many-times-great grandfather. She closed the lid and rubbed her fingers over the smooth silver case. It's been promised to Calista when her Mother dies. Hugging her again she murmured, "Your father is hoping to get on the train at Mount Aorangi Station. The police are looking for him so we have to be very careful not to acknowledge him until we are safe in Queenstown. He will find us there."

Calista nodded. A swell of excitement filled her at the thought of seeing him again.

"Now, hush with your questions, we have to hurry." Mother took Calista's hand, her palm soft and smooth from spinning wool and together they ran along the passage, ever deeper into the dark coal-lined tunnel. Their footsteps echoed off the hard rock floor. They would probably be the last to arrive. They reached the turnstile at the station, breathless and hot, and handed their passes to a grumpy-looking guard. He scanned their tickets with his electronic wand, staring at Calista until she blushed before he let them through.

Many people mingled on the platform waiting for the train. She looked around. There were other girls there, accompanied by a parent, and a few boys. The boys were tall and kind of handsome and looked as if they spent hours keeping fit, which they probably did if they were breeders. There were no familiar faces.

Everyone was catching the Westport to Queenstown train, underground most of the way. Queenstown and the Remarkables range were under a synthetic dome and it was the only place anyone could go to get sunshine. Their bones would weaken without vitamin D. Those lucky enough to be classified as prime breeders, like her, could go for a month's holiday. At twelve years of age she needed supervision, so her mother could travel with her.

The mountain ranges were riddled with coal. It saved them from the Nuclear Dawn and water was plentiful from snowmelt and underground rivers. Water and coal powered the steam trains that carry the survivors of the 2150 nuclear war up and down the spine of the South Island, deep inside the Southern Alps.

At school, they learned about the Nuclear Dawn. There were lots of history lessons. All those religious fanatics finally got their hands on enough plutonium and nuclear waste to make a bomb or two…and explode them. Matched by the nuclear missiles from the bombed countries the whole earth seared. How lucky they were to live in New Zealand, as far away as possible from the destruction. The population here had enough warning to go underground into the shelters; with barely five years to construct the underground gardens and dig more living areas. Some didn't want to come in and some couldn't. They missed out in the ballot, and the history lessons tell that the remaining population outside will have all died from radiation.

By connecting all the mining tunnels that riddled the Southern

Alps, a vast underground railway system was made. Calista will get to ride a steam train for the first time.

Coal had become their saviour. 'God bless coal; God bless water and God bless steam engines.' It's a litany the children and tunnellers said every day. Coal heated the water to warm the gardens and the sleeping units. It fuelled the trains that are the only means of travel. Once, so they are told, people flew between countries. No one did that anymore. Only a few boats remained, and they sailed between islands and to Australia looking for survivors to increase the gene pool.

Mother said that sometimes underground living drove people crazy and she guessed her mother meant Daddy. He was one of the Carbonites. They worship coal because all things in life contain carbon, but coal has the most. While they waited for the train, Calista thought about her father but she turned away so Mother couldn't see the tears on her cheeks. As much as she loved him, she wished he'd just give up all this carbon worship and be her father again. He ran the water plant for their whole subterranean town… before he got religion.

The Carbonites don't want the coal in the mountains to be mined. They worship it as a sacred artifact, a part of God. In class they were taught that the Carbonites destroyed the heat exchanging plants and blew up the internal aqueduct, and accused the tunnellers of using the last pure carbon deposits available to man. If they were caught by the police they were digitally marked and thrown out of the Haven areas. This punishment is as good as a death sentence, but they sometimes survived outside for years. The teachers said if the Carbonites ever returned, the implants would trigger alarms at the portals, and once caught they'd be thrown out into the nuclear wasteland again. Eventually, the radiation will kill them.

The thought of her father suffering so much distressed her, and through tear-blurred eyes she saw their train arrive. A long fat cloud of steam trailed behind the shiny black engine. It puffed to a stop, its brakes hissing. A bright red number 586 gleamed on the centre front of the engine. It filled Calista with a feeling of kinship. It was a beautiful machine, its shiny steel body painted black and its brass pistons gleamed under the station's light. It looked like a living thing—a black dragon, hissing and huffing steam; something out of a storybook. She didn't know trains had numbers, just like her, except hers is tattooed between her shoulder blades, and only visible in a mirror. Because it's still healing, it itched her terribly. A man did it on her last visit to the clinic. She was relieved they didn't put it on her chest. It would be awful to look at it every day. Some of the girls thought having a number is something to be proud of.

They found their cabin and took seats against the window, facing each other. Mother put her bag on the floor between their feet. It had food and extra clothing. They'd get plenty at the health spa, but Mother hoped she could give some to Daddy if he made it. There was little to see through the windows, only the black tunnel walls, except when the train travelled through clear cocoons as it crossed rivers and the young glaciers. That was when she got her first look at the outside world, preparing her for the beauty of Queenstown. Mother had told her how breath-taking it was. Her parents went there for their honeymoon because Daddy had such a respected position. Lake Whakatipu is where the rich people played, under the domed sky. Not that many rich people were left. They died like everyone else. Mother said being alive is richness in itself.

It had been an early rising and a rush to get there. The rocking of the train and clickety-clack as it ran over the joints in the tracks made her eyelids heavy. Calista struggled to stay awake, to see the outside world when they passed through the cocoons, but her eyes refused to stay open.

She awakened later, and saw by her wristband that she'd slept for two hours and her heart sank knowing she's missed the first cocoon views. Her mother was reading opposite her and they exchanged smiles. Calista made her excuses and pushed past other passengers in their cabin, stepping over their legs and luggage. Those without carriage tickets lined the hallways, a warm mass of people, standing in a fug of unpleasant odour. Crying children looked grubby and tired; mothers made soothing noises and looked weary. She smothered the sharp stab of guilt that pierced her because as a prime breeder she had a seat and they didn't.

The need to find the relief facilities was urgent. A guard stopped her and checked her ticket. It was on the information chip in her upper arm where their settlement details were kept.

"First trip, young lady?" The guard in his silver uniform with black flashes on the sleeve made her heart beat faster. He reminded Calista of the doctors in the assessment clinic who probed and prodded, took blood samples, scanned her body and declared her 'fit to breed'. She'd have to return when her periods arrived and that thought made her stomach clench, but Mother said having children was a blessing and she shouldn't be afraid. She would be there to help her. But first she needed to build up her vitamin D intake.

"Yes, sir, I'm looking forward to my holiday."

"Do you have your family with you?"

"Just my mother." Her heart tripped a little as he scanned her arm with his light reader.

"Hmmm. Do you know where your father is?"

Mother warned her about trick questions from guards and doctors. "No, sir. I hardly remember what he looked like." This was a lie, so she concentrated on her breathing, keeping it slow and even, and hoped his machine wouldn't pick up the rise in her heartbeat. Of course, she knew what he looked like, but she needed to convince the guard of her disinterest.

"Have a good trip." When he turned away to question another passenger, she hurried on through the rocking carriages to find relief. Her heart was racing, her palms sweaty, and her nerve-ends raw. It was worse than how she felt on her first day at school.

After relieving herself, she crossed to the old crazed ceramic basins to wash her hands. The soot from the engine coated everything with a grey film. The disinfectant dispenser was empty. She shuddered and turned the tap handle with her elbow, rinsed and wiped her hands on her skirt. A check in the mirror showed her corn-row braids needed reworking. She had to wear her hair like this now. Stray hairs fell around her face and there were smudges on her cheeks. Her grey eyes were red-rimmed from sleeping, or else the coal dust was making them sore.

The smell of sulphur hung in the stale air. The cabin was warm and smelly, but she was reluctant to push her way back through the throng of passengers. She stood staring through the window and watched as the trails of white steam dashed past. Lit by the cabin lights they broke into wisps and disappeared. This carriage was at the front of the train, close to the engine. Except for the rocking and clacking, you wouldn't know the train was moving. The black tunnel walls passed like the inside of a chimney, dense and dark without a break in the monotony.

Back in the passage she weaved her way back through the mass of bodies. A voice said "Calista" and she turned her head instinctively, and then realized her mistake. It was her father's voice. Up ahead the guard was watching her. She needed to tell him where they were, but the guard was staring. She swung around, saw a child nearby... before she looked at her father; recognized his face, longed to collapse into his arms.

"I'll tell my mother on you if you pinch me again," Calista said to the child, trying to sound indignant. Then added, "She's in cabin sixteen; she'll fix you." With her back still to the guard she whispered, "Hello Father, I love you." He smiled and then melted into the people around her. With her face screwed in anger she rushed through the crowd toward the guard, hoping to have done enough to smother any suspicions he might have.

Back in the cabin, she reached over to find her e-reader in their bag and whispered to Mother that she'd seen Father. The minutes pass but he doesn't come. If only she'd been able to hug him. He looked gaunt and exhausted. He needed the food they had in the bag. Perhaps she could make another trip to the relief cabin? Would it look suspicious so soon after the first visit? Before she could decide, Mother excused herself and left the cabin, taking their bag with her. Calista hoped she saw Father on her way to the relief facilities.

Mother returned a good while later and without comment put the bag on the floor and picked up her knitting which she left on the seat. She was knitting baby booties. They don't know what sex her child will be but if she has one successfully then she will be expected to have more. Mother had spun a hank of very fine yarn from a small bag of merino fleece. Sheep were scarce. They don't breed well in captivity. These booties may have to do for all of Calista's children.

An hour later they arrived at Queenstown station. She was blinded by the daylight as they got off the train. No wonder they had to pack sunglasses. At the end of the platform, through the iron-railed fence she saw the sky—a beautiful blue. She hurried to the fence, dragging her mother with her. Mother laughed. "I remember my first glimpse," she said, running to keep up. They grasped the fence and peered through. The mountain range was reflected mirror image on the surface of the lake, so breath-taking Calista held her breath, and thought she imagined it. The snow on The Remarkables reflected the sun in a jagged band of blinding white against the sky, just like the postcards. She shut her eyes for a moment and took a deep breath, but when she opened them, the view was the same. It was not a mirage; it was a miracle.

They turned at the sound of a shout, and a scurry of movement on the platform parted the crowd. Her father was being marched toward them between two guards. Calista clenched her fists and stiffened her arms to prevent herself from reaching out to touch him as he passed. They disappeared through a side door. She looked at her mother. She was staring ahead, tears streaming down her face and Calista knew it was not the sunlight that hurt her mother's eyes.

Father was wearing a coat from our bag. She had found him after all.

Behind them the train began to move and she turned to watch. A slow hiss from its pistons followed by puffs of steam from its fat black funnel and the huge wheels began to turn, as slow as the second hand on the kitchen clock and then faster and faster. No. 586 gathered speed and left the station. Calista had read the train circled the lake to come back to this station before returning northward with a new load of passengers.

In a month they'd ride it again. She would have had her course of vitamin D and would face a future of insemination and motherhood. There was no choice. Breeders were precious. Lineage was important and, although her father was about to be cast in the nuclear waste, her mother's genes and his were a good mix. Calista was fit and healthy without any inherited diseases. The authorities would overlook her father's religious insanity for the sake of more healthy children. But she knew they would watch her in case she went the same way. Her father would never know his grandchildren. She may never see him again.

Calista cursed the Carbonites and their crazy fixation.

Chapter 2
(six years later)

"Calista."

She paused at the sound of her name. Only her father ever called her that and he had to be dead by now. Everyone else called her Callie.

A worker barged past clipping her shoulder. Several turned their head to stare as they sidestepped to avoid her. By stopping midstride she held up the flow, a breach of etiquette in the narrow rock passages.

She'd misheard. They'd had no contact from her father since he'd been taken off the train at Queenstown. Mother would have said so if she'd had any news; after this long on the outside the radiation must have killed him, surely? You'd think she'd have forgotten the sound of his voice, yet it sounded like him. She shook her head at her silly imagination and stepped forward to re-join the flow of workers.

The sodium light cast a yellow glow giving her fellow workers a sickly pallor. She must look the same. Thank goodness there were no mirrors in the tunnels in which to catch her reflection. The slight breeze of the air-conditioning ruffled the hairs on the top of her head. The monotonous hum of motors hidden behind the service doors reassured her that things were normal. Only the sour scent of sweat triggered a thread of alarm. Was there a wildcat fire in the coal seams somewhere deep in the mountain range, or had the engineers misjudged the temperature again? She imagined her plants in the hydroponic garden wilting with heat and gasping for water. She quickened her pace.

"Calista."

This time the voice sounded at her shoulder and she turned her head but didn't slow her steps.

The man who hurried beside her wore a hooded jacket. She glimpsed his beard but only when he raised his chin, turned his head and his gaze held hers did she allow hope to blossom into delight.

"Father?" She made to stop but he reached and gently eased her on, his hand against her back, his head close to hers.

"Not so loud, daughter. The walls are listening. Follow me."

He moved ahead with longer strides as if their encounter were nothing but a brief greeting, his pace leaving her lagging several steps behind. Her gaze fixed on her father's back and hooded head. To lose sight of him now would be dreadful.

Tension stiffened her body, and she swung her arms to ease it, rolling her shoulders and lowering them, knowing she had hunched them as if to hide. To an observer or a hidden camera, it would look as if she were doing the prescribed morning exercises while walking.

A torrent of questions poured into her mind. Within an arm's length her father strode in front of her with energy in his stride that spoke of good health; yet her delight was tempered with a fear that he might be apprehended. Her mouth went dry and she craved a drink. Despite the danger he may be leading her into she would follow him. She had so much to tell him but clenched her fists to stifle the urge to reach and touch him. With her mind filled with images of tunnel security guards pounding toward them she nearly missed her father's sidestep as he turned into a branch tunnel. She followed. His pace quickened and she jogged to keep up. Where was he going? She'd never ventured this far off the main concourse.

He paused at a service door and she stopped beside him, out of breath. He stooped and leaned close to the handle. The distinct scritch of metal on metal made her flinch. Would it be heard afar? When the door swung open, he pulled her into the dimly lit space. Only when the door closed and the latch clicked did he then wrap her in his arms, holding her so tight she finally fought to be released, to take several deep breaths. She feasted her gaze on his face, the same yet different from when she'd last seen him. He looked scruffy yet smelled clean; his scent flooding memories from her childhood memories that overwhelmed her questions for a brief moment.

"My darling daughter." He stroked her braided locks. "You are more beautiful now than I ever imagined."

She snuggled into his arms, wrapped him in an answering embrace and kissed him. His ribs were firm to her touch and his beard tickled her lips when she moved to kiss the tip of his nose.

"You're not dead." The words seemed silly as they fell out of her mouth. "How did you get here? How do you stay alive? Can you come and see Mother and my children?"

He held her at arm's length. "Children? Already? They don't waste any time, do they? How many do you have?"

"Two, Daddy." She reverted to calling him the name she'd used as a child. "They are so beautiful. Caleb is three. Vanily is one." A pebble lodged in her throat at the next thought. "I guess I will be inseminated again soon. As a prime breeder I'm expected to have a child every two years." She hunted for the positive. "But because of that Mother and I live well. We get good food, and the children are especially cosseted." She held his gaze. "They are our future."

Her father's mouth twisted, and she wished she hadn't echoed the oft-heard slogan. At this moment it sounded trite. He frowned. Her comment had irritated him.

"There's a future outside, too."

"But everyone dies when they go outside." Another fact she heard regularly through the sound system, interspersed between the piped music and lectures.

"Everyone in here will die too, eventually. It's nature's way. We can't have people living forever. That's unnatural." He stepped away and spread his arms. "And look, I'm still alive and I've spent most of the past ten years living on the outside."

With a step into his outstretched arms, she rested her head on his chest, inhaling the musky scent she remembered so well, before the Carbonite religion disturbed his thinking and his preaching caused him to be thrown out into the wilderness.

"How do you survive, Father? How did you get into the community?" She tugged on his arms, pulling him down onto a wooden seat that lined one rock wall, below the electronic switchboard above it. "Tell me. I can't believe you're still alive." In the dim light she ran her gaze over him, a closer examination, seeking any damage, looking for lesions or burnt skin. She'd seen photos of radiation burns. If he had any they must be under his clothes.

He sat beside her and clasped her soft hands in his calloused ones. The creases of his knuckles were blue-lined from coal dust; cuts and scars earned as a youngster when he'd helped with tunnel extensions. So many stories he'd shared that were part of her childhood.

She withdrew one hand and pulled her lunch from her coat pocket and offered it to him. "Mother made these sandwiches. She'll be so glad that you're here and can eat them."

He unwrapped the bread, carefully unfolding the wrapping paper as if it were a piece of precious silk fabric. He bit into the large wedge filled with cheese, greens and legumes and she watched in silence as he ate his hunger evident by the speed with which he devoured the food.

"You're as thoughtful as ever, Calista, always thinking of others." He wiped his mouth with the back of his hand. "That was delicious. Your mother always could make a good sandwich." He folded the sandwich paper and slid it into his pocket then smothered a small belch.

Her love for him made her chest ache—a pain similar to the love she felt for her children, but different. This love caused her heart to flutter with fear, her joy coloured by her apprehension for his safety—and her own.

"Talk to me, Father, please. I need to know things—and I'm late for work already."

"Where to start?" He ran his hands through his greying hair. Deep lines furrowed his tanned brow.

"Start with how you got in." She gestured with a sweep of her arm. "They say we are sealed in here to protect us from the radiation in the outside world. No radiation can get in—but if you did, then so can the radiation." Another thread of fear crawled up her spine. Could her children be at risk?

"They tell you lots of things that aren't true." He stroked her cheek. "You have to believe me, Calista. This is not my religion talking; this is your father telling you the truth."

Only after she nodded did he continue.

"We…the Carbonites and others…come and go as we like, through the air vents and water pipes. Also, the waste pipes give us access but they are not very pleasant." He screwed up his nose and she matched his smile, more from tension than his comical face. "We only use the waste pipes if the other outlets are being watched." He held up his hand as she made to speak. "Don't interrupt darling, please, I have so much to tell you." He cupped her face between his hands. His palms scratched her cheeks, but she didn't mind. "Enough of my emotions, I must get down to my reason for being here." His voice firmed and he adopted the tone he'd used when talking about his faith many years ago; serious, firm but with a touch of wheedle in it. He gave a wry smile. "See, nothing has changed. They tell you a lot of rubbish in here. Lies upon lies, mixed with myths to keep you happy. They make you frightened of the outside, so you won't think to question their edicts and rules." He stood and faced her. He seemed taller than she remembered. "Nearly ten years ago they threw me out for the first time and six years ago I saw you and your mother briefly on the train to Queenstown. Once more they threw me out and yet, here I am again, still alive." He lifted his palms and shrugged.

She had no answers, only questions. "But why hasn't the radiation from the Nuclear Dawn killed you? Are there many others living outside?"

"Yes. Many, thousands even…and yes there is radiation, but we think it's not as much as they predicted. It's everywhere. In the stock, the plants, the people and in the rain that falls to feed the rivers. It's most certainly in the snowmelt that waters your underground gardens."

No, surely her precious plants weren't kept alive with contaminated water? That meant they ate radiation in their vegetables. Her stomach clenched and she gasped. "It can't be. They say the water we use is pure. The underground rivers are pure. They say so."

"I see the Mics are still ruling." Scorn riddled his comment. He paced a few steps back and forth. As she looked up at him the light from the bulb on the far wall shone through the unruly hairs that capped his head creating a halo effect. Memories surfaced of his religious fervour. She must weigh what he said against what she knew. Fanatics could be dangerous. Who told her that? Instead, she asked, "Mics.? Who are they?" A security organization perhaps?

"Men In Charge. M. I. C.'s. They're still spreading doom and disaster, keeping their hands on the power, deciding who breeds and who doesn't. Who gets special treatment and who does all the dirty work. Have you ever seen any of them working at a menial job?"

13

"But they're busy running things." She knew this for sure. "They don't have time to tend animals or grow food. We have schools and teachers. They tell us about the world, as it is now and as it was before the Nuclear Dawn."

"And most of it will be propaganda and lies. Believe, me, Calista, there is hope outside. There's sunshine and rain, flowers and animals. We still have electronic communication with Australia and what is left of the World Wide Web. Humanity may have been mostly wiped out in Europe and the Northern Hemisphere but in the Southern Hemisphere mankind is surviving." He sat down beside her again. "People still get ill and radiation has damaged others but, like the land around the past nuclear power plant disasters, once man stepped away the animals and wildlife lived on and thrived for hundreds of years. It's the same here, outside."

"I just can't believe this." Everything he said was contrary to all she knew. Her brain refused to accept it, yet why would he lie? You don't lie to your children, unless to protect them. Was he tempting her with the outside to protect her? From who? The Men In Charge as he called them?

He stopped pacing and looked down at her. "Slowly we are building up communities in rural pockets, learning to plant and harvest to the altered seasons. Sometimes we get a drought, or floods wreck our crops but we carry on. In Quake City we survive despite the buildings have been razed yet again with more earthquakes. The concrete ruins shelter us and we travel by bicycle or on foot. We have sail boats." He grinned. "I've learned to sail. The old skills are thriving. We're in contact with other parts of the world because the Nuclear Dawn didn't kill machinery. Anything running on solar power is still going. We even have a limited power source from the hydro dams."

Disbelief caused her to shake her head. "Why don't we know these things?"

"Because, while you remain ignorant the Mics can manipulate your life." Her father leaned closer and patted the top of her head. "They've made you a breeder and control the life of your mother and children. Don't they?"

She nodded, remembering how she often felt controlled yet always consoled herself with the security her family enjoyed.

He paced again. Three strides one way, three paces back. "They tell you where to work, when to be inseminated and how many children you must have." He stopped and swung to face her. "Have you ever had sex? Fallen in love? Who is the father of your children? Do you know him?"

Swallowing a creeping climb of despair, suspecting he spoke the truth, she said, "I only know they both have the same father. Next time I will probably be inseminated with a different male's sperm."

"Charming." His mouth twisted. "And I bet the Mics are making sure their sperm is used." He pulled at his short beard and sighed.

She didn't know what to say.

He continued. "You should come outside with me. Then you won't have another child until you return and are ready to do so."

"But they might kill me when I return." The thought of leaving her children motherless, beaded perspiration on her forehead and she slipped off her polyvot cape. It whispered as it fell behind her onto the bench. The walls of the small service room threatened to close in on her.

"Another lie, Calista! Life is too precious to kill anyone. Even those of us who survive outside are never killed if we are caught in here. They put another electronic chip in our arms and pop us outside again. Look." He pulled up his sleeve, baring his tanned sinew-wrapped arm. She ran her fingertips over his upper arm but couldn't find the small chip they all wore...but she could trace the uneven lines of scars. He tilted her chin and smiled. "We cut them out. It hurts, but it means they can't trace our movements if we return."

"Do many return?" She groped through her mental fog of new information and searched for a familiar fact to cling to.

"More than you would think. We Carbonites have followers within this rock labyrinth. They slip us stolen medicine and any extra food they can spare; sometimes if we lose a crop, they give us seeds. In exchange we give them news of the outside world and what countries we have immigrants arriving from."

"Immigrants?" It didn't seem possible. Only those inside the tunnels and living under the dome in Queenstown were the surviving population. This is what she'd always understood. 'You have people coming to live here?"

"Yes, from other countries in the Southern Hemisphere. They sail here, mostly from the west. On the Web, Aotearoa is known to be the safest of the countries that survived the Nuclear Dawn."

He sat down beside her again and put his arm around her shoulders, calming the tremors coursing up her spine. "Come with me, Calista. Your mother will watch your babies. We can get messages to her from the outside. Your children are precious. No one will harm them. Sure, the Mics will be cross with you but when you return, they will be overjoyed to see you." His voice softened. "Someone clever and precious to the Mics needs to come outside, see the truth and return to spread the word. Then you can change things from the inside." He moved and clasped her hands in his. "I hate the idea of you spending your life underground."

The idea of going outside scared her. Years of conditioning triggered a wave of nausea at the very thought of it. Yet, here sat her father, bedraggled but as alive as anyone. The alarm buzzed on her timepiece, an old windup variety she'd traded for a hank of her mother's homespun yarn. "I should be at work. I'll have to think about it." She pulled from his grasp and ran her hands over her head, her braids hurting as she tugged on them, worrying about her children. The air in the small room lacked oxygen. They'd used it all up. The door needed to be opened. Panic tightened her throat. She swung her cape over her shoulders and when she stood her father followed and wrapped her in his embrace.

"Tonight, I will come to your quarters, if I haven't been caught by then. Talk to your mother, see what she thinks." He held her at arm's length. "We need a strong woman, a mother, someone who wants the best for humanity, not the best for themselves. We want to change your way of life but to do that we have to take a young leader and show them life outside first. You are my daughter and I know you have that strength. The Carbonite Council thinks you are the answer, the one who can do this."

His fervour unsettled her, and she removed his hands from her shoulders. His religion had caused enough damage. Could she live outside but not be swallowed by the Carbonites? First, she'd been chosen to breed; now she'd been chosen to lead. It wasn't fair. When would she get to make some choices in her life? Mother would know. She'd ask her what to do. "I need to go. I'm late already."

Her father opened the door and peered out. "It's clear. I'm sure you'll think of an excuse for being late at the gardens. Remember, you won't be punished if you leave. Everyone is precious. They're telling you lies to keep you here."

He eased her out the door yet kept one hand grasped to the bottom of her cape. She turned at the tug. A tear slid down his cheek and glistened in his dark beard, the scattering of grey hairs shone in the sodium light. She wanted to stay with him, to wipe away his tears but he waved her away. "I'll see you tonight. Give my love to your mother. Tell her I love her today as much as the day we married." In that moment she saw the remnants of the handsome man who'd carried her on his shoulders all those years ago and remembered the laughter in his eyes, the softness of his kisses and his bedtime stories.

"If I don't get there tonight someone else will come for your answer."

She turned away and ran down the passage, away from her father's arms into the humdrum of everyday life. Her footsteps echoed in the empty tunnels as she hurried to the hydroponic gardens. On reaching the door she paused to get her breath before she pushed it open enough to slide around, hoping to enter unnoticed.

"You're late," growled her supervisor and made a note on his clipboard.

"Sick child," she lied.

In the gardens the damp scent-laden air swirled around her like invisible treacle and the glare of the U.V. lights threatened to trigger a headache. As she tended, watered and harvested the plants she wavered in her decision. Could she spend her whole life having children?" Should she take a chance and see the outside? Would her mother cope while she was away? If she returned contaminated by radiation at least she wouldn't be expected to breed anymore...or would she? Their standard of living might decline. Others managed with less. They could too.

An overwhelming desire rose from deep inside her; a painful longing to be free. Could she visit the outside for a just short while? She imagined standing in the rain and experiencing the thrill of a storm. Perhaps she could sail in a boat or sit on a hilltop and watch the sun sink below the horizon. Holograms were all very fine, but wouldn't the real thing be better? Living deep within the Southern Alps was all she knew, familiar and comfortable. An existence apparently based on lies. Did she have the courage to visit the real

world? Her father wanted an answer by tonight.
   Would she breed or would she lead?

Chapter 3

The warm air and the smell of her mother's cooking greeted her when she opened the door to their living quarters. She shrugged off her cape and stepped out of her overalls, hanging them on the coat rack, ready for the morning (unless she wore them later, if her father came).

"You're late this evening," her mother said, entering the living area from the kitchen with Vanily perched on her hip, the toddler pink and scrubbed from a bath and dressed in her nightwear. Her mother's eyebrows rose. "Any particular reason?"

Callie muttered, "Just felt like finishing something," but at the same time beckoned her mother into the bathroom, where she flushed the toilet to cover their conversation. You never knew if there were microphones installed, so you had to assume they were. In a whisper she said, "I saw Father this morning. We had a long talk in a service cupboard." Even now she smiled at the memory. "He hopes to visit this evening, unless he is caught before then." Her mother's open mouth caused her to hurry on. "He wants me to go outside with him, Mother. To see the world…so I can come back inside and convince people to leave these tunnels." It all sounded very fanciful when she said it aloud. "What do you think?" So much depended on her mother's answer, and at that moment she realized she'd decided to go in spite of it. Expecting disappointment, she waited for her mother's answer.

"Your father always did have a convincing manner, which is one of the reasons I fell in love with him."

Not a blunt 'no' as yet. Her mother lowered the toddler to the floor and re-flushed the toilet. Vanily grizzled as she tottered around the small room and Caleb had begun to bang on the other side of the door. Enough noise to cover any conversation.

"Do you want to go?" Absolute honesty was required for this life-changing decision.

"Yes, I'd love to, but I'm worried how you will cope, left here with the two children."

"I'll be just fine. No one will blame me, and neither will the children suffer. I can continue my spinning and weaving, and perhaps you can bring me back some fleece. It's time you saw a sunrise from outside the dome and felt the wind on your face. When do you think your father will come?" Relief coursed through Calista, then the ease of her mother's acceptance made her ask, "You don't seem surprised."

"I'm not. I've been waiting for your father to come for you. It was always his plan."

"But you never said. Why didn't you tell me?"

"In case he didn't survive long enough to return for you." With that her mother picked up Vanily and opened the door. "Time for dinner," she said above the noise as Caleb begged for attention as well.

In the quiet of the evening with both children asleep, her mother knitted, and Calista read, checking the clock on the wall as the minutes passed. She feared he wouldn't come when a quiet knock and the slow turn of the door handle heralded her father's arrival.

"Aaron," her mother whispered and hurried to the door to wrap him in an embrace as he entered.

"Eleanor, my love," her father said so softly she didn't need to hear it. She could read his lips as he held her at arm's length. "My sweet, loyal wife."

She watched as her parents hugged, wiped tears from each other's cheeks and kissed again and again. A saved meal was placed in front of her father and he ate, his hunger barely disguised by the restraint he showed. All words were said in whispers.

"Will you come?" he asked when the plate was empty. She nodded and returned his grin of delight. "Will you manage?" he asked his wife, and she smiled her agreement. "Good, then we must hurry. Bring your cloak and overalls. They are priceless outside for their ability to withstand the elements and keep you warm. A small knapsack is all you can carry. We have tight spaces to navigate."

Yet, when it came to the moment of parting, she thought of pulling back, reneging on her agreement and staying. She kissed her children and inhaled their sweet scent; lightly touching their hair, wishing she'd cut a snipped off each small head to carry close to her heart.

"Dawdling won't make it any easier," her father said, "Come now…kiss them one last time because we must leave. You can come back anytime."

But could she? Her desire for knowledge beckoned like a flickering flame in a pile of thin twigs threatening to consume her. Perhaps once she'd been there, the longing would fade, and her curiosity would be satisfied. Her children were safe. She had to believe that they wouldn't be punished for her betrayal of all she'd heard and been told. She stiffened her back, hugged her mother and whispered 'Thank you' in her ear, then slipped out the door, following her father into the future.

Her father pulled her down behind a stock of pipes. "Workers coming," he whispered. She wondered if the men would hear her heartbeat. It pounded in her head, making her ears ache and her fear rose bitter in her throat.

The footsteps passed and faded until silence surrounded them once more like a blanket of security and her pulse slowed. After a short wait her father moved on, pausing at a tap and handing her a damp cloth. She took it wondering at its use and followed him through the narrow tunnel, shrinking her shoulders from the dripping walls. The dank smell from the wastewater seeped through the wet handkerchief she now held over her nose, the air now claggy in the confined space. She kept one hand grasped tight to her father's coat, her head down, following his footsteps, not wanting to look around in case she slipped on the wet rock. Then up steel ladders, along gantries and through locked doors to which he magically produced keys. Her mind wandered as her concentration slipped. Perhaps she'd make a mistake? Saying goodbye had been so hard, yet anticipation rippled through her, easing her sadness, urging her onward…down more ladders and along wooden-slatted walkways until they reached a porthole. He unlatched it, pushed the oval cover aside. He climbed through and stood then extended his hand to her. One high step more and she climbed over the sill into fresh smelling air.

She breathed in air so full of oxygen it made her gasp. The crispness chilled her throat like an iced drink. Her nose tingled and as her sight adjusted the outside world came into focus. Huge panels stood against the mountainside. She leaned back to look, amazed at their height. They reflected the moon, so much closer in the sky than she'd imagined.

"Solar panels for your electricity," Father said, anticipating the question hovering on her lips. The moonlight revealed a well-worn path down the hillside.

"No time to admire the view… Hurry."

Her father set off and she followed, stumbling, not used to the dirt surface where tiny pebbles rolled under her shoes. Small bushes tugged at her cape and scratched her legs. She imagined them welcoming her, saying 'Hello'. She slid and fell.

Father turned and hauled her up. "We'll stop soon. We must clear this hillside before dawn when the service shift arrives. It's better not to be seen."

An age later, or so it seemed, he put his hand behind to stop her and cautioned. "Careful, here is the edge."

She stood on the ledge, a rock shelf in front of a slab-like wall and clasped his hand to peer into the valley below. Her gaze lifted to the horizon marked by a group of lights nestled on a black velvet swathe. She pointed.

"Quake City, Calista. Our destination."

"It's so beautiful." The myriad of stars winked then blurred. She blinked to clear her eyes. "No one tells us this." She turned, taking a breath to get a grip on her emotions then held his gaze. "I'm so glad I came. I promise to learn all I can. Is this what you want of me Father? To lead—not to breed?"

He squeezed her palm in his and sighed. "You have to make that decision. I'd like to make up for the years I've missed spending with you, but you need to follow your heart. I'm hoping you will free the people from the yoke of the Mics." He looked up to the stars. "I may worship carbon as the building block of life, but I've learned we must also burn coal to live." He tugged her arm and moved back to sit down. "We'll rest a while."

Huddled together against the crisp night her father's arm tight around her, Calista knew she'd made the right choice. Just thinking about tomorrow filled her with anticipation before tiredness dragged her head against his chest and closed her eyes. She felt him lean back against the rock-face. A sense of contentment, new and satisfying, filled her heart and swept over her like a warm wave.

Her legs ached from the continuous slope of the path, her palms were grazed from her many falls and they stung from the cold air. She wanted to ask her father to stop so she could rest but pride kept her mouth closed. These feelings were part of her new life and she swallowed her self-pity. Outsiders did this all the time. Then the dark faded to grey, the stars disappeared, and a glow began on the horizon. Now she had to speak.

"Father, please can we stop? The sun is coming up. I want to watch?" A weary tremor caught her voice. She stopped and stood her ground, refused to take another step and sank onto a nearby rock beside the path. Her cloak rustled as it moved. It clung tighter, warmed her and seemed to whisper as it absorbed her exhaustion.

Father retraced his steps and joined her.

He held her hand while the crimson swathe rose and painted the underside of the clouds, then the gold crescent broke the horizon and the globe slowly climbed into view. Breathtaking, glorious, beautiful beyond belief and worth every moment of fear and doubt she'd ever felt. Nothing she'd experienced could rival this majestic event. When the sun had cleared the horizon, they stood up and walked on. The path levelled out as they'd reached the bottom of the mountain. Birds broke the night's silence, twittering in the bushes with one call repeating. She had heard this call at intervals during their descent, distance and mournful.

"What's that bird?"

"It's the call of a Morepork, a native owl. Listen to how it calls 'more pork' again and again."

She smiled as the words in the bird's call became clear. "We've been hearing it for ages."

"Yes, I've been heading toward it." He grinned. "It's our signal. If we follow the owl's call, we'll meet the welcoming party, waiting for my return." He mimicked the call and a fresh call sounded clear in reply. Father grasped her hand. "Come, Calista, come and meet some real people." He pulled her as he stumbled into a run along the path and onto the flat ground.

Too tired to keep up with his fast pace she let go of his hand. Her feet ached and she longed to rest. She studied her aching feet. She'd never walked for so long in her whole life. When she next looked up, he'd disappeared into the scrubby undergrowth ahead. From being in front of her, suddenly he wasn't. Panic grabbed her stomach until she heard his voice mingled with the shouting. She stopped on the edge of a stony scree looking down over debris and stones into what appeared to be a dried up river bed. A group of men surrounded her father, placing their hands on his head in turn then stepping back and bowing.

"Welcome back, Master Aaron."

"Safe return, Master Aaron."

"Your blessings, Master Aaron."

Her father returned their greetings in a formal manner before all the men hugged and clapped each other's back with hearty thumps. A small dog, white with black patches, jumped and whimpered at her father's feet. He held out his arms and the dog jumped into them, clambering higher to lick his face and ears. Her father laughed and buried his face into the dog's neck and rubbed its snout.

Then her father turned, caught her gaze and grinned. He pointed toward her.

"See, I bring my daughter Calista with me. She is our new hope. She is prepared to learn what we can teach her and take her knowledge back into the tunnels."

The men stared. Silence spread and stilled the chatter and a combined sigh seemed to escape the group. Not sure whether this signalled approval or disappointment she moved toward her father but lost her footing on the small stones. She slipped down the bank as the pebbles rolled under her feet. Positive she would land on her bottom she threw out her arms, only to find them caught and grasped by a young man.

"Thank you," she murmured, embarrassed to be so close to a male of her own age as he righted her and made sure she was steady on her feet.

"You're welcome," he replied. "My name is Mathew. You are Calista?"

She stood, glad of his help then brushed her overalls to clear away the twigs and grasses. She flicked her cloak off her shoulders and shook it so it settled against her back. "My friends call me Callie," she added. "Please call me that."

"I will and I shall try and earn your friendship." His dark hair looked as if it had been painted by the night, yet his eyes, deep and brown, caught the sunlight and seemed to twinkle. Perhaps they reflected the low morning light. Whatever the cause her heart fluttered; she swallowed yet couldn't find any words to continue a conversation. He touched her hand with his fingertips, curled them under hers and led her to the group who encircled her, and then her father and the men began to sing. The language and the song she didn't know but the emotion of the moment swept over her. No one could doubt their sincerity. At the end of the song, they each touched her head and bowed. Surely, she didn't deserve this mark of respect? Tears trickled down her cheeks and slid into her mouth, salty on her tongue. She smeared the dampness across her cheeks and sniffed, too tired to be embarrassed.

"Is it my hair, Father?" Her mother had freshly braided it the evening before. She tucked a few escaped wisps behind her ears.

"No, it is because you are my daughter. I am one of the Carbonite Council members. As such I am addressed as Master Aaron and have this band of loyal followers. We travel together spreading the word and helping the community, something like what the friars and monks of ancient times did." He put the small dog down. It ran around their feet, jumping, walking on its hind legs, begging to be held again. Aaron hugged her close, "But, yes, you are beautiful as well."

"And the song? What language is it?"

Aaron looked to the Southern Alps, rising behind them. "It's called 'The Land of our Fathers', a Welsh anthem sung by miners over hundreds of years." His gesture encompassed his band of followers. "We were all miners in the tunnels that you have left. We built them, burrowed them out of rock and joined together the coal mining passages." He held out his hands. "Like me they are marked with the blue of coal dust." He wiped a tear from his cheek.

"Come Master Aaron, come Mistress Calista. A meal is waiting," the tallest man called.

They turned and walked to where a fire burned beneath a large pot that hung from a trivet. Alongside three rabbit carcasses were threaded along an iron spike, held over the coals between two forked stakes. As she watched any man passing would give the spike a brief twist. The smell triggered her hunger. Perhaps a meal would ease her tiredness.

"The meal smells divine; I could eat a horse," Aaron said.

"But we only have rabbit," a man replied his mouth downturned. Everyone laughed. This seemed to be an old joke. "But thanks to Patch we have lots of rabbit and rabbit stew for all."

Her legs folded and she sank to the ground, overwhelmed by the new experiences since she'd left her home the night before.

"Here, youngster, this will see you right."

Someone placed a pottery bowl in her hand and pressed a spoon into her other palm. She blinked tired gritty eyes and unable to speak, nodded. She ate, savouring each mouthful. The tender meat with a strong flavour was accompanied by onions, herbs and tubers. Yams? Kumeras? Something she'd only read about. Root crops took up a lot of space and were rarely planted in the tunnel gardens.

"My compliments to the chef," she said looking around for ownership. The eldest of the group ducked his head in acknowledgment.

"I like to add carrots," he said, "But you can't find any on this plateau, not with all the rabbits about."

At the word 'rabbits' the dog jumped up, his ears pricked as he looked from her father to the other men and back again. "No, Patch, not just yet." Aaron patted the dog, easing its haunches down once more. "Later, Patch, when we move off."

Instead of giving her energy the food in her stomach made her sleepy and she had to put her bowl down before she dropped it. Her father came to her and led her a little way away from the others to where the riverbed had only sand, without rocks and pebbles.

"Lie down here, Calista. You and I will sleep for a few hours. Everyone will keep watch. You are safe."

Too tired to answer she lay on her side, tucked her backpack under her head as a pillow and pulled her cape over her head to cut out the sun. She felt it slither and spread over her legs. She'd heard that polyvot clothes could grow and shrink when necessary and the cloak obviously deemed this to be such a time. It would keep her from being chilled and would protect her from the sun. It was linked to her DNA and recognized her needs. Should anyone else try to use it, it would become rigid and hard as a plank, so she'd been told. She'd been given it after Caleb's birth as a reward for service. Only in the last twenty-four hours had she realized just what a precious gift it had been. She'd been told the cloak was almost indestructible, but could she match its strength in the journey they would share?

Chapter 4

Her mind jolted awake at the gentle shake of her shoulder. She lay still and peered through gritty eyes, her heart skipping until she realised where she was. Her father's mud- encrusted boots and dirt-splattered trouser bottoms filled her vision. A whiff of the tunnel's slime teased her nose and she sat up.

"Time to go, daughter." He brushed a few strands of hair off her face and tucked them behind her ear then picked up a blanket and joined the others who were moving about collecting things.

She stood and swung her cape over her shoulders. The fabric shimmied up her calves, twitching at her overalls as it settled to its original length around her thighs.

Everyone was busy. It was a wonder she hadn't woken sooner. Utensils disappeared into bags with a clatter and were then slung over shoulders and shrugged to a comfortable position. Two men passed around sacks, possibly filled with provisions. No one man looked overloaded. A thin tendril of smoke escaped the wet river sand to mark where the cooking fire had burned. The smell of the burnt wood lingered in the still air. All signs of their camp were being removed. The scene rolled out before her like a well-rehearsed play, each man acting his role with precise movements. No time wasted and nothing left for her to offer to help with.

The older bearded man passed her father a short knife, which he slipped into a holster on his ankle. A knife? What for? It looked lethal. Not something you would eat with, but definitely something you could kill with, animals perhaps? Wild deer, feral cats and dogs certainly, but what else? Then she remembered there were wild pigs. They would surely be more likely to run than attack. This only left humans as the threat. Perspiration dampened her palms and she wiped them on her overalls. Her heart hammered in her chest and her cloak shrugged around her in a comforting embrace. How stupid not to have thought of these dangers before she abandoned her children. At least they were safe, even if she wasn't. This new awareness of danger moved her toward the group of men. The need to hide among them, to protect her back from unknown threats dried her mouth. She cast about looking for a drink to slake her sudden thirst but before she could ask for water or query the need for knives her father returned to her side. He held out a pendant. "You need to put this on and tuck it into your shirt."

This was an order, not a request. The greenstone pendant dangled on a leather thong which was looped through a hole bored at the top. "It's beautiful," she said holding it at arm's length to see it properly. A pattern of lighter-toned lines ran through the deep green jade like fine veins and several silver filaments ran down each side. Under her fingertips the smooth surface of the pounamu slipped with the feel of a piece of rare velvet. A good four inches in length, the greenstone rectangle ended with a deep bevelled edge. She'd seen pictures of similar stones in the history archives, enough to know this was a treasure given to her for safe-keeping. A Taonga to be passed to future generations, should she be that lucky. She slipped the thong over her head.

"You can admire it later. Turn around. It needs to be shortened so it can't slip off."

He turned her around and shortened the thin leather strap until it rose higher on her chest and could not now be pulled clear of her head when he tested it.

"Now feel the back of it. There is a small, raised button. Can you find it?"

Her thumb caressed the smooth stone. "Yes, I can, it's just the slightest bump on the surface."

"That's an electronic safety button. If you press it the nearest Carbonite will come to your aid immediately."

A flash of concern made her wrinkle her brow.

"Don't worry my daughter. It's just a safety measure." He held her wrist. "Hope you never need to use it."

"Someone might want to steal it," she blurted, "I feel it's precious."

"It's bad luck to steal greenstone. Anyone seeing it will know it's a treasure but will also know that you have earned it." He rejoined the others as she absorbed this latest information, another hint of dangers that lay ahead. After undoing a button, she tucked the thong inside the neck of her shirt. The warm pounamu nestled between her breasts. The stone must be eons old and to her it signified hope and continued life, even if it doubled as a rescue remedy.

She'd forgotten to ask about the knife. Perhaps she didn't need one now that she had the pendant?

Energized by her brief sleep and with her new pendant tucked safely away she stood tall. A breeze snapped at her, blowing hair across her face, blurring her vision. From deep in her backpack, she pulled a long thin scarf and wrapped it around her head, tying it under her chin. Within a few days she would need to undo her braids and tie up her hair. That could be a good thing. Her braids presently marked her as being from the tunnels and to blend in she needed to look the same as other women and she had yet to meet one. Then she would know what to do with her hair. For now, she would have to follow her instincts and be herself. With renewed hope she hauled her backpack up and slipped her arms through the straps until it sat comfortably on her back. The others had stepped away forming a line, seeming to follow a track. Her father stood waiting for her and she hurried to join him.

They walked at a steady pace for several hours, stopping at small streams to fill drink bottles and wade across. Her boots, a mixture of polyvot and leather, kept her feet dry, but the top of her homespun socks became wet, so she stripped them off, tied her boots around her neck and wore her sandals instead.

After crossing the last stream, its shallow ice-cold water rippling over smooth stones, the wave tops sparkling in the sun, they climbed a low bank and over the next rise a small building came into view. A couple of shouts and the men in front broke into a trot, eager to reach it.

Her first shed; a novelty she walked around as soon as they arrived. Close up its weathered wooden sides reflected the sun in silver and grey toning, with only small flakes of brown paint left here and there on the northern side. The sides and the southern end had been blasted bare. The tin roof had a patina of rust thick around the ordered rows of nail heads. In places the roof buckled as if it had been sat-upon by heavy people. It would make a good viewing platform to view the surrounding plains. A ladder on one side confirmed this. Mathew climbed onto the roof and declared the vista clear of any other travellers for as far as he could see.

The tall man, who she thought was called Benjamin, produced a key and through the open door she saw a stack of bicycles, the first she'd ever seen, except for in pictures. These were wheeled out and the men began to toss coins, the winners choosing which one they wanted. Some had more paint on the frames than others. All had rusted handlebars with small patches of shiny chrome around the centre bolts when the bars met the uprights. All looked old. Two had baskets in the front, woven from hard reeds by the look of them and several had carriers above the back wheels. She ventured close to where Mathew stood with his prize.

"May I?" She reached to touch the metal frame, strong enough to carry a man, yet she could wrap her fingers around the supporting bars. The design unchanged in its basics for several centuries, the bicycle seemed a wondrous invention to her. How could they get it to stay upright and yet move forward?

"I can't ride a bike." Again, her lack of life skills in this great expanse made her feel useless.

"Not to worry. We can take turns doubling you. Another day, when we aren't in a hurry, you can have a lesson and see how you go. Eventually I'll find you a bike of your own so you can get around."

A bicycle of her own? Freedom to travel these vast expanses; to whizz along and perhaps see the ocean. The thought of such an opportunity caused a laugh to burst from her throat; her first laugh outside. Already the huge open spaces no longer frightened her. The sense of vulnerability caused by the lack of a tunnel wall for protection had gone—and she hadn't yet been outside for a whole day. Even in Queenstown everyone knew they were within the dome.

Here, on the Canterbury plains, the blue sky stayed above them, non-threatening, vast from horizon to horizon. She didn't need protection from it. It was only air after all, even if it was full of radiation. Life buzzed around her. Insects flew past, beetles scuttled over stones, spiders had built their webs on the lee-side of the shed and around her the group talked and joked. Even if she didn't understand the nuances of their speech, she heard the happiness in their voices. The effects of radiation can't be as bad as she'd been told.

Several of the bikes had a box above the rear wheel and what looked like a narrow solar panel mounted on a pole above the seat.

"What are they for?" Her voice was whipped away by the breeze as she pointed from where she sat sideways on the carrier, her legs out of the way of the wheel. She had to cling onto the saddle beneath her father to stop herself falling off.

"Those bikes are solar-powered, similar to the electric bikes before we lost ready access to recharge the e-bikes. They're great for going up hills, along the coast or over to Lyttleton. We're lucky to have these two. The others will take turns to rest their weary legs."

After a while she found her balance and the bike moved along without constant corrections by her father as he pedalled along the bumpy track. She hoped they'd stop occasionally to rest her buttocks. Being perched at the back of the bike on a narrow wooden platform, bouncing constantly over the ruts in the road would leave a few bruises by the end of the ride.

They followed narrow tracks that wandered across the plain with the tussock giving way to small bushes of manuka then scraggly grass grew on hillocks and in small gullies that had a trickle of a stream at the bottom. No doubt in the spring thaw these gullies would be filled for a brief time with snowmelt but today, in late summer, little water flowed through them.

The riders moved over the plain as a unit, sometimes in a string or bunched in a group where the trail disappeared into the clumps of grass. The leaders fell back, and others took their place. She looked over her shoulder to see that even the tail-end riders swapped about, but always she was in the middle, no matter who peddled the bike she sat on. As the riders took their turn with her, she learned their names and so by the time they stopped for a snack of dried rabbit and a drink a sense of belonging had crept over her. From Mathew the youngest to William the eldest, everyone made her welcome with smiles, the sharing of their history and a gentleness of nature she'd never experienced in any men she'd met within the tunnels. She suspected from the murmured conversations among them, doubling her was considered a privilege, not a labour.

The mountains shrank ever smaller in the distance their snow caps glistening like a white ribbon on the western horizon. The further away the ribbon drifted the deeper the cut in her heart sank. Like a raw wound it stung as she pictured her two children deep inside the range, in the dark, missing out on the feel of the breeze and the warmth of the sun. What if she didn't return to them? A shaft of panic rose up her throat, but she swallowed and buried it deep in her chest. The future beckoned. She had knowledge to acquire, life to experience and she determined to enjoy every minute of this adventure, before she returned to them.

Trees dotted the landscape, casting shadows beneath their branches. The group stopped to rest beneath the largest one, taking turns to drink from the water bottles. The coolness of the ground under the tree delighted her. She lay down and trickled the earth through her fingers. So much dirt everywhere; a world of earth to plant things in. The smell of decay from the leaf litter reminded her of compost in the tunnel gardens. An insect bit her leg and she slapped it dead, then the sorrow of killing a living thing threatened to bring tears. "Oh, I've killed it." The long night and busy day were taking their toll.

"Don't look so sad, Calista. It's only a sand-fly. We have more of them than we need, and you can swat as many as you like," Father said.

"That bite might itch," Mathew warned, coming to sit beside her. "If you scratch it, it may get infected. Better not to."

"They love new blood," Simon chuckled. He stood outside the cast of the shadow and when his beard jiggled the white streaks glinted in the sunlight. "They leave us oldies alone. Too tough to bite."

Father brought over a small bottle filled with a tincture of some sort. "Manuka oil, watered down. Spread this on your bare skin. It will keep them away."

More information to absorb; tiny flies that bite and a lotion to keep them at bay.

They remounted and headed off into the solid tree-line ahead. Now the trail undulated and twisted, down gullies, over streams and up winding tracks that required them all to get off and push the bikes. The walking was pleasant, cool in the shade and she stroked the tree trunks they passed, some with rough ridged bark, others smooth and pale with the bark hanging in curled strips as if the tree was peeling. Gum trees. She recognized them from her book at home.

The sounds of birds filtered through the conversation at ground level. Real birds this time, not recordings piped through speakers. She peered into the tree-tops, catching glimpses of colour flitting high. While doing this she tripped over an exposed tree root and had to keep her gaze on the track from then on, remember to stand still when she wanted to look up into the canopy. The bush had an air of magic about it and had the children been there they would have rushed about looking for fairies among the toadstools, again just like the picture-books at home. Some fiction had carried forward for centuries.

From the top of a hill, they admired a green plain below, divided by fine lines into large paddocks. William pointed. "Our destination for tonight," he said, "On the horizon."

She squinted and could just make out a small dot of a building. "What are the dividing lines in the fields?"

"Rock walls now. The old fences are mostly fallen over, the wire rusted away and irreplaceable. There're plenty of stones about. It takes men and time to build them, but they last longer."

They mounted once more and set off down a winding track through the trees. The lead cyclist raced ahead, disappearing from her view, his hair flying, his bike's wheels spinning and skidding as he braked on the downhill ride.

A shout from ahead, then more shouting as the riders disappeared around the corner. Simon stopped so suddenly she slipped off and stood, glad of the break. "Stay here," he said. Handing her the cycle to hold he ran ahead. Mathew came from behind to stand beside her.

"What's going on? If someone's injured, I might be able to help."

"I don't know, but we must stay here until we are beckoned," Mathew said. "Those are the rules."

But she wasn't a Carbonite, so their rules didn't apply. Putting the bike down she hurried ahead in case her nursing skills could be of use, with Mathew's shout of protest echoing in her ears.

Rounding a corner her heart contracted to see Kyle the lead cyclist struggling against the grip of a man on either side of him. His bike lay splayed on the ground, tangled in a thick rope which must have caught the wheels and knocked him off. The attackers' expressions changed from triumph to fear as Carbonites stood around them.

Surrounded by men with knives drawn, the two brigands looked around at their opposition and began to tremble.

Winston, the biggest of the group, stepped forward, his bulk making the captors look small. The nearest scruffy traveller flinched and tightened his grip on Kyle.

"Are you hungry?" Winston's tone held no anger, more of a mild enquiry.

The two men nodded. "Very," said one.

"We abhor violence so if you let our companion go, we will feed you. We have little but we can spare some."

With defeat bending their shoulders and lowering their heads, they released Kyle's arms. He unclenched his fists, turned and glared at the men then shrugged and stepped away to pick up his bike, brushing the dirt from the seat with gentle strokes, picking pebbles from between the spokes and bending to check the tires, as gentle as a new father with his child. Now she had tasted the freedom of cycling she could image the horror of having such a precious machine damaged, or worse stolen.

Father stepped forward. "We can take you with us to a farm that needs labourers. You will have accommodation and food—providing you're prepared to work." He passed them a piece of rabbit each. "No one will beat you to make you work harder. What you eat will depend on your labour freely given. Out here beyond the tunnels we do not allow such things."

Gnawing rapidly on the offerings, both men murmured their agreement. She wanted to ask if they were from the tunnels, but the moment passed as her father continued.

"You will have to run beside us. We are in a hurry to reach our destination by dusk. Agreed?" After an exchanged glance both men nodded.

In short order they were each tied to a bicycle by a length of their own rope and the group set off. The pace slowed to accommodate the weary trotting of the captured men, but soon the land flattened, and fields of grain ran along each side of the old road. Grass grew through the cracked bitumen surface. In places sand covered the road's surface and as they cycled through it the breeze lifted the dirt in small puffs which whirled away to settle elsewhere. It reminded her of a film about dust storms, each bicycle leaving its own small version in its wake.

She pointed to the fields of grain, recognizable as food crops from her gardening books. Her father, riding behind her, called, "Wheat, barley, oats and corn. All for milling into flour. The farm we are heading to has an old water wheel in a stream and they have resurrected the flour mill."

"I'd love to see that working," Calista said.

"You shall, if they have grain left from last season. The mice are kept down by several families of cats and the corn husks are stored high above the ground, with metal collars on the top of the posts to keep the vermin from climbing up and eating it."

"Is all this land farmed by the owner of the mill?"

"Not all, but most of it."

Her father's voice caught by the wind made his comments hard to catch. Did he say there were some smaller owners who supplied the mill and paid for their crop to be ground?

"The owner of the mill is a very wealthy man. He was lucky he had a stream and an old mill to rejuvenate." Now riding one of the solar-powered bikes, he sped up to be beside her. "It puts him in a position of authority and because of this we are respectful of his hospitality and donations."

"So, food is power?" Nothing new there, it was the same in the tunnels.

"Yes, food is the new wealth." The flat road made for easy peddling and the conversation continued. "He supports our cause with generous gifts of milled grain, which we in turn can bake into bread to feed the poor in the city."

"You have something to transport the flour with?"

"Yes, we have a large dray and two horses that we left here a week ago."

Simon spoke over his shoulder. Now that the road was easy, he'd taken his turn to double her. "I love horses," he said, "I've been breeding them for twenty years."

Father continued, "We have a bakery and ovens in the city and the power to run them from the Clutha and Clyde dams."

"And small forges for the horses' shoes?" Calista had noticed hoof prints in the sandy track beside the bitumen road.

"Yes, lots of the old ways have been relearned. Life is slower, but more satisfying."

"Let's stop for a while," Father called out and the group slowed and dismounted. Simon held the cycle steady as she slipped off, glad to ease her bottom and walk around, stretching her tired leg muscles. The group mingled and drank a little water each. Their captives were offered a drink and the rest of the rabbit. She looked around and saw above the grain fields, on a distant slope what had been a small house on the horizon had now morphed into a large mansion, two storied with a verandah around each level. It looked beautiful and huge.

"Is that where we're going?" She pointed.

"Yes," Simon said.

A light flickered on in one of the rooms. "There is electricity even out here?" Something else they weren't told of in the tunnels.

"I think it's generated by the same waterwheel that grinds the flour," Father added. The afternoon sun revealed a crosshatch of lines on his tanned face as he walked toward her. He looked particularly old at this moment and it surprised her. To think he'd made the long journey just to fetch her out of darkness and ignorance. Love swelled in her chest for the sacrifices he'd made. She stepped close and hugged him. "Thank you, Father, for this wonderful day."

"My pleasure," he whispered in her ear. "You're worth every minute of the years I've waited."

"My turn to double Callie," Mathew said, and folded his jerkin into a pad on the carrier of his bike.

The last hour of the ride became sheer bliss with padding under her tender buttocks. She really needed to learn to ride a bike. Surely the saddle had to be more comfortable than bouncing on a carrier.

Ahead of them, growing ever closer and larger on the landscape stood a house. A real one made of planks of wood and surrounded by open spaces. Another new experience. What next?

Chapter 5

Calista followed the others up the wooden, front steps and onto the verandah, trailing her fingers over the carved decorations on the newel posts. She stood among the group and waited while Father lifted a heavy knocker on the front door and banged it several times. She could hear the sound echo within the house then the light trip of footsteps approached, and the heavy door swung inward. A young girl, probably the same age as herself stood in the doorway, with a kerchief tied over her head, her brown hair falling over her shoulders and her dress dragging around her feet. She peered out at the gathered group.

"Yes?" Her gaze assessed them and then settled on Calista. A scowl flittered across her face and her smile dropped. 'The Squire is out the back of the farm. He won't be in until dinner time.

"We are the Carbonites. He is expecting us today and has offered us hospitality overnight," Father said.

The lass nodded. "Is this the breeder then, from in the tunnels?"

For the first time in her life Calista had the impression that being labelled a breeder might not be a good thing. The sooner she ripped out her braids the better. They shouted her classification. It would be more practical and might help her to blend into this new community, without the hostility she had unwittingly triggered in this young girl.

"This is my daughter, Calista," Father said. "She has travelled a long way in one day and would appreciate a chance to freshen before dinner, as would we all." Father's tone allowed for no misinterpretation and the girl ducked her head and muttered, "Come in. I will show you to your rooms."

"I know the way to my usual room," Father said, "It's my daughter who needs guidance."

The lass beckoned and started to climb a wide staircase that climbed one wall and curved along the back wall to meet the mezzanine floor. The balustrades wrapped around above them on three sides of the entrance hall and Calista turned slowly taking in the wonder of it all. What could be grander than this? A sharp titch of the tongue brought her back to reality. The young servant stood on the landing above, tapping her foot.

"Miss, I have other work to do. Please follow me." She tossed her long hair like a horse would flick its tail at an annoying fly, and then turned from Calista to climb the rest of the stairs. Weary and footsore Calista still had the energy to run up the stairs, catching up to whisper her thanks.

"What's your name?"

"It hardly matters, does it? Now you're here the master won't look at me."

"I don't understand." She truly didn't. "We are on our way to Quake City. I don't intend to stay here, and I don't know your master at all."

"You soon will." The girl opened the first door on the left along the passage. "This is your room. It has a bathroom attached, opens out onto the upper verandah and I was instructed to make the bed up for you. It's our best guest room," she said with a touch of pride.

Calista stepped into a new world. A gasp of delight escaped before she could stop it. "Oh, it's so beautiful. Thank you…"

"My name's Daphne," the girl said.

"What a pretty name," Calista said, and this drew a begrudging smile. "Did you pick the flowers?" A faint perfume wafted through the room from the vase of roses on a small table in the large bay window.

Daphne nodded. "Now I must go and help cook with the evening meal. Dinner will be served at six. You will hear the dinner gong even if you are asleep. I will bang it really hard." With that she rushed away, leaving Calista to shut the door.

She wandered around the room she'd been given for the night. A large bed with a thick fluffed up mattress took up most of one wall. She reached and fingered the strip of stiff, linen sheet turned over a pair of thin blankets. Across the foot of the bed lay what appeared to be a feather eiderdown. It rustled as she stroked it. She walked around the walls, placing her hands against the patterned paper, warm to her touch.

The bay window she saved for last, careful not to knock over the round table on which sat the large glass vase filled with white, cream and pink rosebuds. The net curtains, yellowed and frail, seemed to be on the brink of disintegration and she moved them aside with care to admire the view. They'd travelled a long way today. She could just see the mountains, a thin ribbon on the western horizon, almost invisible except for the sun glinting on the peaks. In the other direction lay their destination. No sign of it yet across the green plains. Perhaps she would see the city's lights tonight.

Through a smaller door was a small room lined with white tiled walls, with a bath and toilet. The taps gushed icy cold water and she ran a few inches into the bottom of the bath then slipped off her sandals, stepped out of her overalls and pulled off her shirt. Lastly, she removed her underwear and stood naked considering the depth of the water. Could she use more? She turned a tap with H on it and although it ran at a lesser rate after a few moments hot water joined the cold. When the bath felt tepid, she stepped in and sat down before she leaned back against the end of the bath, luxuriating in the caress of the water.

The desire to sleep closed her eyelids and made her sit up to use cloth and soap from beside the bath and wash herself quickly. A hard towel dried her and from her knapsack she took fresh underwear, lay out her only skirt and blouse to remove some of the creases, then slipped between the cool sheets. Bliss.

The dinner gong did indeed wake her. She pictured Daphne's small frame hammering a metal disc downstairs. The sound echoed up to the next floor. Perhaps Daphne wandered the house doing this? She dressed with haste then ran her fingers through her hair, pulling out her cornrow braids and stood in front of the dressing table mirror and brushed her hair until strands rose to chase the brush with each stroke.

At last, it felt as if the day's dust had been shaken out. Blonde ripples hung past her shoulders. She'd need to look for a suitable scarf when she got to the city. Tomorrow she would tie it in a single plait down her back but tonight it would have to hang free. She had two side combs which she tucked in, one above each ear and these held her hair off her face. Done. With an extra shake of her skirt, she slipped on her only pair of sandals and took a deep breath. No doubt when she reached the entrance lobby the smell of dinner would guide her to the dining room.

At the bottom of the staircase she paused, admiring the stained-glass windows high above the front door. She'd missed seeing them when they arrived, too busy admiring the inside of the house. A side-door opened, and Father hurried out.

"Good you're here. I was just coming to get you."

"I fell asleep."

"I thought you might have." He took her hand and led her through the door into a long room. It had six tall slim windows spaced along one wall through which she could see the verandah. The light poured in. Such a lot of light everywhere. Her mind was still getting used to the delight of it, and the glare. In the middle of the room a long table stood, above which hung a chandelier, its bulbs flickering as if driven by a pulse. Strange behaviour for lights.

"Welcome to my humble home, I'm Castor Seville," A portly man with a florid complexion greeted her, grasped her hand and pulled her away from her father even as she murmured her reply.

"Everyone calls me the Squire, but you can call me Castor," he whispered in her ear, then lead her to a nearby chair at the end of the table. "Aaron," he boomed, "You sit on my left, and you, young lady, can sit here on my right."

He pulled out the chair and waited for her to sit, then trailed his hand along her shoulder. His fingertips lingered on her upper arm for a moment before he stepped around to the head of the table and sat himself.

Father sat opposite her and paired down the table on each side were William and Benjamin, Simon and Winston, then Kyle and Mathew; paired in age order by the look of it.

"Service," Castor boomed, and Daphne hurried in carrying platters of food which she placed in front of each of them.

"Serve from the right, remove from the left, girl. How many times do I have to tell you?"

Calista's heart twisted as a blush rose up Daphne's neck and flooded the servant's face. How unnecessarily rude of the man?

"This smells delicious," Calista said, hoping to distract the Squire's attention. "What meat is it?"

"Our finest lamb roasted with our own vegetables. Only the best for a guest such as yourself." He waved his fork in the air to include the others, "And of course, the finest for my good friends the Carbonites, who do sterling work looking after those who are not as fortunate as everyone here."

The meat melted in her mouth, lamb being such a rarity in the tunnels. Only in Queenstown had she tasted its equal. The vegetables had piquancy, no doubt a result of the sunshine and rain—or the radiation. This random thought almost put her off the food, but hunger won, and she ate until her plate was clear. Daphne cleared the plates away and in the intervals before their dessert the men chatted across the table, including the Squire who had plenty of advice to offer on every subject from growing grain to the state of Quake City's eccentric power supply.

She started as a stockinged foot rubbed up her calf, lifting the hem of her dress and she tucked her legs away under her chair. Although he looked down the table and talked to the others, she had no doubt it was Castor's doing. Again, his foot sought her leg as he leaned back in his chair but this time she stood.

"Father, excuse me, could you guide me to the nearest toilet?"

As Father stood Daphne arrived with plates of freshly cut fruit.

"Take Miss Calista to the bathroom," Castor said, pointing to the door into the hall, and Calista followed Daphne out of the room. She hoped a few moments away would stop the silly game Castor Seville was playing because she really wanted to return and eat her dessert.

Her short absence didn't deter the man.

"Allow me," Castor said and left his seat to get the jug of custard from the far end of the table and bring it to her. While pouring the custard over her dessert he brushed her arm once more and inhaled deeply as he leaned close to her. Did she smell? She looked to her father for help but, engrossed in a discussion with William about how the lamb had been cooked, he didn't notice. Perhaps she was imagining things because from then on, the Squire ignored her, and she enjoyed the small glass of homemade cider that followed their meal. The notion of slipping into the large comfortable bed became irresistible and she stifled a yawn. Time to leave.

She stood. "Excuse me, Squire. Thank you so much for the delicious meal. Truly the best I've ever tasted but if you will excuse me, it's been a long day and I'd like to retire to the lovely room you have given me, to rest."

The Squire stood and all the men did also. "Of course, it's been a long journey from the tunnels." He beamed, the light from the chandelier now lighting his sparse hair like half a halo around his head. "Can I escort you up the stairs?"

The absolute last thing she wanted. "Thank you, but I can find my way and you have guests to entertain." She turned, nodded to her fellow travellers, caught her father's gaze and raised her eyebrows briefly. Did he know what was going on? Then she hurried out of the room, up the stairs and into her room. Only when the door clicked shut behind her did she let out a breath of relief. Never had she met such a man. But then, what experience had she had with men? None at all. Perhaps all men behave like this? No, the Carbonites had been kindness itself. Surely Father had noticed Castor's unnecessary attentions. Then again perhaps he had been the perfect host. A rest would clear her head.

She began to take off her clothes when she heard a knock and the door opened. Castor Seville entered and in an act of modesty she held her blouse to her neck. She'd like to have said 'get out of my room' but it was his house after all. He shut the door with a backward kick, and it banged when it met the door-jamb, then the latch clicked like an exclamation. Her pulse quickened.

"Sorry to disturb you, Mistress Calista." His grin belied his words. He wasn't a bit sorry. His gaze slid over her from head to toes then up again. She remembered the doctors doing this and it made her skin crawl.

"I wondered if I could interest you in staying here for a few days. I think we could both benefit from getting to know each other better."

"I think my father has plans for me and I believe we are to leave early in the morning." Not wishing to cause offence, she added, "But thank you for your hospitality and your offer, I will have to decline."

He stepped closer and stood in front of her, his fingers feathered up her bare arms, lingering on her shoulders. A shiver ran through her.

"You are cold? Let me put your blouse around your shoulders." He pulled it from her grip and placed it around her back, his head lowering as he dropped a kiss on her cheek.

Fear coursed through her and her knees threatened to give way.

"I hear you already have two children? So, you are fertile as well as beautiful?" A tremor shook him and now she knew where this was heading. Here was a man who wanted children. Daphne's original comments came back to her. Were the women outside sterile from the effects of radiation? His gaze lingered on her pendant. She wrapped it in her hand and pressed her trembling thumb on the back of the stone, hoping her father's promise would come true.

"I do have two beautiful children," she said and stepped back a pace. "My mother is looking after them for now."

He stepped into her personal space once more and gripped her upper arms, his fingernails digging in her bare flesh.

"I intend to return to them as soon as I have received the education my father has planned for me." Her thumb beat a desperate tattoo on the back of the pendant.

"There are more exciting things to learn about than the stuffy old theories of the Carbonites." He wrapped a finger around a lock of her hair and slid his hand down her hair to trail his hand behind her ear. His touch slipped onto her neck. "There's real life to live; more pleasurable than insemination."

Her heart raced and her thumb pressed again and again as she stepped back trying to evade his relentless approach. Where were the Carbonites?

"Come, Mistress Calista. Don't be frightened. I can feel you trembling. It matches my own desire. You have accepted my hospitality; surely you are prepared to compensate me in return."

She'd read of rape. Was this how it began?

A loud knock rattled the woodwork and the door pushed back. Over Seville's shoulder she drank in the sight of her father stepping into view. Never had she been so glad to see anyone.

Seville dropped his hand to his side, stood taller. "A little too cool for a walk but it promises to be fine by morning. Perhaps we could take a stroll around the garden then?" he said pretending to be talking about the weather.

Relief robbed her of an answer.

"Ah daughter, I wondered how you were settling in. Everything all right?" Father strode to join them, turning to Seville with a wide smile. "So good of you to put us up, Castor, and as generous as ever with your tithe. We have the cart loaded ready to leave in the morning."

During this exchange Calista slipped her arms into the sleeves of her blouse and buttoned it up. She picked up her cape making ready to leave the room. A walk, anywhere, was preferable to Castor Seville's company.

Another knock and Mathew stood in the doorway his eyebrows raised, head cocked.

"Look, here's Mathew," she said. "I'd totally forgotten he'd promised to take me out and teach me how to ride a bicycle."

Before her father or Castor Seville could comment she hurried past them to the door. "My riding lesson, remember?" she muttered as she swept past Mathew onto the landing. She grasped the smooth banister for support as she hurried down; the steps seemed never-ending until she rounded the bottom curve, crossed the hallway and paused at the doorway. Only then did she look back to check if Mathew had followed her. At least she was away from Castor's touch.

On the lawn below the front steps, she stumbled to the trunk of a large oak and rested her forehead against the tree. Grasping the rough surface for support, she took deep breaths and willed her heartbeat to slow. She inhaled the woody smell, so new so delicious. The bark seemed to whisper to her, probably insects scurrying about inside. Relief weakened her knees and she had to regain her balance. The pendant worked. Two Carbonites had come to its call.

Mathew approached, his footsteps getting louder across the gravel drive. She released the tree and turned; his cheerful grin belied the seriousness of the past few minutes.

"Thank you, Mathew; I really did need to be rescued."

"I'm grinning for the benefit of any watchers"' he said then stepped back and raised his voice a little. "Now we need to find you a bicycle." He pointed, "They're in the stables, around the back of the house."

He bent and picked up a few acorns and slipped them into his pocket, before taking her hand in his.

"Father mentioned the mill, can we go that way?" She heard the tremor in her voice. Still her heart raced, and she took several deep breaths.

"Perhaps not this evening. First, you'll have to do a few circuits of the back yard or out in the paddock on the cycle, to find your balance and gain a bit of confidence."

"I'll do anything, just don't leave my side," she whispered.

They walked along the side of the house in the shade. "Are women barren outside?" she asked, heat rose to her face but her determination to understand this world overcame her embarrassment having to discuss such a female condition with a young man.

"Yes, some can be. Many aren't, but often conception can take a long time. Sadly, men in power expect to have first choice." So, he had noticed, even if others hadn't.

She shuddered. All this beauty and grandeur hid a darker seamier side of life outside the tunnels. She would need to balance the good against the bad, but first she had to learn to balance on a bicycle so if she were threatened again, she could at least escape at speed rather than at a run.

They found the bikes leaning against the outside of the barn.

"Pick one," Mathew said pointing at them. "They are all the same."

They looked rather ridiculous. How could she possibly ride something so thin? Two wheels in line, a seat and handlebars to hang on to. The handlebars steered the contraption. She knew that much from watching and pedals you pushed with your feet.

"I'll hold it steady while you get on. I've done this heaps of times. All I need to do is run along beside you, holding you up until you get your balance."

She screwed her face in disbelief. "It can't be that simple?"

"It is. Come on, we'll use this one, without the solar panel which is extra weight even if it does help you move along. You'll have to earn the right to ride one of those." His smile belied his statement and with a pounding heart she stood on one pedal, hoisted herself onto the seat and leaned a little forward to grasp the handlebars.

At a run he guided her across the yard and into a nearby paddock. "Now, we've plenty of room for you to wobble in."

The movement was wonderful. She bounced along until Mathew seemed happy with the ground in front of them. "It's flat from here on. Off we go. I'll run beside you and hold you steady, but you have to pedal too."

She did. It was harder than she imagined. The men had made

it look so easy. Determination gripped her and she pedalled as strongly as she could, feet revolving, legs rising and falling opposite each other. She concentrated on the ground in front, watching for bumps and her hands ached from gripping the handlebars so tight.

"Relax," said Mathew, his words coming in gasps as he ran beside her. "I've got you by the saddle," he added as he dropped back from running at her shoulder. She had it. She could feel the flow of the machine, the breeze in her hair, the achievement of making the bike move forward. "It's wonderful," she said. No answer. She turned her head for his reply and her heart leapt. Mathew stood way back in the paddock. She had been riding on her own—and with that she wobbled and fell off.

Laughter bubbled up her throat and she grinned as Mathew ran up. "I did it. Bit shaky, but I did it."

"It just takes practice. Do you want to ride back, then we'll go and see the horses?"

"Yes, please to both. Will you hold the bike again?"

"Only until you are steady. I won't let you fall." His hand brushed hers and his breath was warm on her cheek as she mounted the seat. For some reason his touch sent a twinge through her, a feeling she'd never had before. Attraction to the opposite sex? Was this how it affected you?

"Ready?"

She nodded. She didn't trust her voice at that moment. And so they returned to the gate. A wobbly start, a fast middle and again a fall to stop.

"Next time I must teach you how to dismount," Mathew laughed as he bent to grasp her wrist and pulled her to her feet. She caught a whiff of his male scent. He looked hot from running. She brushed the grass from her good gown. Not the best of clothes to learn to ride a bike in, but what fun.

"Now, the horses," he said and while he pushed the bike with one hand, he held her hand in his other. A sense of joyous security swamped her, and she stifled a yawn. Either tiredness or excitement was making her short of air.

Chapter 6

Aaron excused himself after listening to Castor's hour-long rant about how, because of his prestige and position of wealth, he should be allowed to breed and his insistence that Calista be allowed to stay with him for a few weeks to acclimatize to life outside the tunnels. Did the man think he was stupid? Not once while listening did he nod or agree. He'd refused to commit himself to an opinion until Castor had finally run out of arguments and had begun to repeat himself.

As if he'd risk his daughter's wellbeing with such an arrogant man. If the Carbonite's were not beholden to him for wheat and seasonal fruit he wouldn't come here again, but unfortunately Castor had a point. He did have power and possessions that he'd generously shared with them, up to now. This would probably cease once he found Aaron and his followers had left, because leave they would, as soon as dawn broke. Aaron's jaw ached from withholding his thoughts, and his fingernails had driven into his palms as he restrained himself from punching the man. Castor's advances on his daughter had only been stopped by Calista's quick thinking and her pressing the pendant around her neck.

A shudder rang through him as he hurried down the staircase and began the search for his daughter. Mathew would have taken her somewhere to safety. He just had to find out where they were.

He found them in the barn and as he paused to regain his breath, he took in the sight of his sleeping daughter. She lay across the hay bales, her head resting on what he recognized as Mathew's folded jacket. Her cloak was moulded snuggly around her acting as a blanket. The last twenty-four hours had caught up with her.

He nodded to Mathew who sat nearby, vigilant. A pang of guilt twisted his gut. He'd pushed her so hard since they'd left the tunnels, not thinking of how unfit she would be compared to his travelling lifestyle. Except for a brief sleep she'd kept up without complaint. His love for her made his eyes fill and he wiped the tears on his sleeve. Showing emotion never worried him and he turned to Mathew, full of gratitude.

"I owe you, son."

"You owe me nothing, Aaron. It's a privilege to travel with you."

"She's worn out," Aaron said, "and I pushed her too hard."

"I think excitement has kept her going." Mathew looked at the sleeping woman and Aaron noted the tenderness that swept his face. "We came here for the bicycles and she managed to ride one, with a little help, along the paddock and back again. I must show her how to dismount next time." He smiled at the memory. "Not that she hurt herself. The grass is long and soft in that field. And then she saw the horses, Aaron. If only you could have seen her face. We fed them a carrot each. She stroked their heads, giggled as their soft velvety lips stroked her palm and you could hear her inhaling their smell. Her joy was a delight to watch. What a restricted life she's had."

Aaron nodded. "I've neglected her badly in the past. I have to make it up to her now."

"She couldn't believe how the hay smelt and lay down for just a moment." He shook his head, "That's all it took, a moment, and she was asleep. I put my jacket under her head and she didn't wake."

Aaron sat down beside the boy and put his arm around his thin shoulders. "Thank you, Mathew. Thank you for taking her away so quickly and for staying here on guard." He took a breath, couching his words with care. "We need to leave at dawn, loaded with the goods Castor has given us. He may not be so generous in the future when he realizes he is not getting what he desires."

"A brood mare," the young man muttered.

"Quite. He has a couple of young girls already, but of course he is aware that Calista is fertile. I should have had her take her cornrows out earlier. Still, the damage is done, and I won't allow his intentions to interfere with our purpose in life. We will have to take the consequences and find other sources of food if need be."

"Do you want me to stay here or go and find the others so we can get the carts loaded and ready to leave at sun-up."

"Would you? I'd like to stay here with her so if she wakes, she knows I am here. Also, should Castor find her he won't dare make a move in front of me. He might be powerful, but he has a reputation to maintain and having me against him won't do his façade of bountiful provider any good the next time he comes to town searching for adulation and satisfaction."

"It's a bit like 'hide your daughters' every time he arrives, isn't it? Only this time it's your daughter."

"Sadly, it is."

Aaron watched as Mathew rose and walked away into the night, with a waning moon to guide him from the barn to the staff quarters. The youngest of their band, he was one of the most faithful of the small group. An orphan, he'd approached Aaron two years ago and asked to join. Despite their journeys and the long hours working to help others, nothing had made him look for other company. He had grown to be like the son Aaron had never had, and now it seemed he had two children to watch out for. Castor would recognize him as a rival for Calista's favours.

She dragged her gaze from the magnificent sunrise to the rump of the horse in front of them. Calista leaned against her father's shoulder and put her arm around his waist. The clip-clop of the horses' hooves became a soothing encore to her ears, and she inhaled the crisp air flavoured with wafts of ripe plums, dried grasses and something she thought might be the smell of rain on warm earth. A shower had passed quickly over them as they moved through the gates and out onto the track heading for Quake City, to be there by evening according to her father.

After her fright last night, she had woken this morning to the sound of the cart being loaded and her first glimpse in the dawn light was of her father, sitting close by, stilling the quiver of fear that woke along with her memory.

The sway of the cart rocked her as a hole in the road caught the wheel and she chuckled with delight. What a wonderful way to travel. The breeze caused by their passing under the trees stirred her hair, now hanging free, except for a small scarf over her head and tied under her hair at the base of her neck. It kept her hair out of her eyes and hid some of the tight waves caused by the constant corn-rows she'd been required to wear in the tunnels.

"My hair is all crimped from the corn-rows," she'd complained as she'd picked the bits of hay out of it before tying the scarf in place.

"Not for much longer," her father had said. "Let's hope the first wash will remove them finally. They put your life at risk, because the corn-rows shout you are a mother." Being a mother sounded much nicer than being a breeder, but after almost five years of plaiting she doubted one wash would take the tight waves out. If need be, she would cut her hair right off, but she kept that thought to herself for the moment.

"Father, I've been wondering. What do the Carbonite's do? Are you a religious group?"

"Not exactly, but we are like the monks of old I guess." Aaron flicked the reins and the horses sped up now that the road in front was a smooth track.

"Why are you persecuted and thrown out of the tunnels each time you are caught? I find it strange that you are not harmed, but simply tossed out into the elements."

"That's the punishment. The Mics think the radiation will kill us, saving them the trouble."

"And it doesn't? We are told we are safe only if we stay within the tunnels."

Aaron snorted. "Where to start? Let me think."

The countryside rolled past; flat land, some in pasture with cattle and sheep. She'd never seen so many sheep in one place. Various green crops that looked like wheat or barley, with dry heads and due to be harvested covered distant rolling hills. Was this still Castor's land? She shuddered at the memory of his large hands on her flesh.

"Cold?" asked Aaron.

"No, just a sudden tremble. I have my cloak to warm me. It's all so new—and exciting." She touched his knee. "Can you tell me now about the Carbonites?"

"We are like a band of monks. We help people in need…with food and medicine when we can find it or make it. We gather food from the source and deliver it into Quake City to feed others. Life is even more sacred since the nuclear dawn. Even the Mics won't kill if they can help it. Yes, the radiation makes some people ill, yet there is no escaping it. It's in the air, in the snow, in the water, the air we breathe and the food we eat. It's in everything—so we have to learn to live with it and carry on."

"But it's not in the tunnels." As she spoke, she felt him tense beside her and draw in his breath.

"Calista, you have been brainwashed. Every drop of water you consume, or feed to your precious hydroponically grown plants, has radiation in it. It all comes from the snow on the Alps. I should know. Once, I was in charge of the water systems throughout the tunnels and the testing of the water. One of the reasons they threw me out was because I spoke of the contamination in the tunnels and begged people to join me and live a freer life outside, even with the radiation."

So that's why he'd disappeared from her life. It would take longer than a few moments to absorb the great lie that kept the population in the tunnels.

"And the other reason."

He laughed with real humour, and grinned at her. "Because I decided to help people within the walls. To hold small gatherings to counter their broadcast nonsense. I encouraged people to think for themselves and the Mics didn't like it—so they tossed me out."

"Alone?" The thought of him alone in the high mountains, in the snow and ice, made her eyes prickle, or perhaps it was the dust kicked up from the horses' hooves. She rubbed her face.

"They rounded up a small band of us, so we had a nucleus to start with."

"Are they all still with you?"

"Except for two. They died. They were old men when we left, and life was hard to start with."

"But why call yourselves the Carbonites? It sounds like a religion to me."

"A name seemed important and there's carbon in every living thing. Trees take in the air, remove the carbon and breathe out oxygen. If we worship anything, I guess we worship the trees for cleaning the air. Tree-huggers is apt, but it's not a serious name. We needed something that sounded grand."

"So, you became the Carbonites."

"Yes, we all liked it. It has a nice ring to it."

"I like it too."

She waited, knowing he couldn't be hurried. She remembered conversations with him as a child. Sometimes she would think he'd finished and then he'd begin again.

"Also, the coal that's used to drive the steam trains in the tunnels and power the electric plants is the finest coal in the world. It's made from dead forests compressed millions of years ago. The original carbon sinks of this world when it was being created. Did they tell you this in school?"

She shook her head. "No."

"I didn't think they would. Once all the coal is gone, they'll have to come out, so I guess you could say we worship the coal as well. It would be better shared than coveted by them. I rebelled against them mining it so greedily—and said so—loudly."

The cart slowed as the horses paused and considered the ford in front of them. Aaron clicked his tongue and flapped the reins on their rumps. After a moment first one then the other, stepped into the shallow water and the cart rocked its way across the stream, the wheels slipping on the stony riverbed. Patch, who'd been balanced on the sacks of flour, yipped and slipped off his perch.

Once safely across Aaron continued. "This is why I wanted you to come with me. I need you to return eventually and convince the people to leave the darkness and come into the light. Even filtered sunshine through nuclear-dusted skies, is better than being in the dark all the time."

She knew she'd have to return. She couldn't leave her children forever, but just at the moment she had too many things to enjoy and discover. She pushed the images of her children from her mind and smothered the scary prospect of returning to be inseminated. Not a joyful conception, which she presumed normal conception, must be.

"Plus, there's another thing. Everywhere we go, we plant trees. Native seed is hard to come by. Sometimes we get seeds from travellers from the West Coast, but Castor has the large oak in his front garden, and others around the farm. They're hardy, vigorous with large leaves. Each time we visit we fill our pockets and bags with acorns and plant trees whenever we rest along our travels. They're not native, but they are at least trees of some sort."

The image of Mathew picking up an acorn flashed into her mind.

"See," said Aaron and he pointed to a small grove of young trees.

"We stopped there four years ago. Now there is a small stand of young trees, nearly tall enough to give shade and already breathing out oxygen."

For the rest of the morning, she kept an eye out for sapling oaks. Each one she saw filled her with pride for being her father's daughter. Anticipation at seeing Quake City tightened her chest. Her breath shortened and she had to consciously relax. Only her second day of freedom and her brain ached, overfull with new images and information.

After three hours of a steady pace, they crossed a long bridge over what her father called a braided river. She could see the silver strands of water that reflected the morning light as they wove their way through and around the banks of stones. She squinted upstream through half-closed eyelids and could see the image of the streams being plaited as they met and diverged repeatedly. A pretty name for a life-giving waterway.

"We'll rest here." Simon called, "Time to rest the horses." The small train of cyclists and two wagons turned left and rolled along a rutted track to stop in the shade of a line of poplars.

While the men unhitched the two horses from their wagon shafts, she wandered over to William who was gathering sticks and setting a fire among a circle of stones that had obviously once sat contentedly in the riverbed and now looked scorched and split. A well-used fireplace.

"Can I help?"

"No, thank you, girlie. Stretch your legs. Go and walk in the river. Nothing like fresh water on your toes. It's nice and shallow at the moment."

"It gets deeper?" She shaded her eyes against the glare and studied the threads of silver trickling past them.

"Aye, in the spring with the snowmelt and in times of heavy rain in the ranges, it will flood and almost crest the bridge; sometimes a day or two after the rains have finished. You have to keep an eye out." He looked to the ranges. "But you'll be fine, there's been no rain in the hills in the last few days." He crouched and blew on the dry grass that smouldered under the pile of sticks.

Fascinated, she watched as a small flame flickered, caught and ran along a fine stick, where it was joined by another and within moments the pile of wood ignited into a cheery blaze. William balanced a sturdy stick between two poles.

"Here lassy, fill this with water please." He handed her a battered billy, smoked rimed on the outside. "Nothing like a fresh pot of tea."

She hurried to the water's edge, looking for a hollow in the stream deep enough to gather the water into the pot resisting the temptation to remove her boots and paddle. Not today, not just now.

William hung the pot on the crossbar, and she stood, her gaze fixed on the beauty of this simple method of making tea. A movement caught her attention and she turned to watch the horses. Simon led them up the bank. Water dripped from their large round lips and their tongues searched and caught the drips. They pulled toward the grass and Simon carefully tucked their leads into their chest harnesses and let them go. The horses hurried off, grabbing mouthfuls of long grass, ripping it with their teeth and hurrying to next enticing clump until after a few minutes they slowed and began to graze, taking their time, raising their heads to look around, then returning to the grass beneath their hooves.

"Won't they run away?" she called to Simon.

"Haven't done yet." He smiled and pushed back his cap to scratch his head.

"Why not?"

"I guess we're their herd. Where else will they get a warm shelter at night and hard feed to chomp on. Even get groomed and sometimes new shoes." He nodded. "I think they're happy to help us."

"Plus, you love them," she added. It was obvious to see and he nodded slowly again.

"Yes, there's that as well."

"Food's up," Benjamin called, his tall frame bent over as he placed their meal on the cloth he'd spread on the ground. She joined the others as they sat around the picnic, filling buns with bits of cold meat, greens and a few delicious finely sliced tomatoes for trimming. "Compliments of Mr Seville's cook," Benjamin commented between mouthfuls.

"We are truly grateful for your continued friendship with the good lady," Winston said, his long legs spread straight out, his bulk looking uncomfortable so close to the ground and his hunger evident in the amount of filling in his bun. The general amusement and gentle teasing of Benjamin told Calista this was a long-standing friendship, prized by the others for the rewards it produced.

"Just don't go proposing marriage," William quipped as he handed around mugs of tea. "We can't afford to lose you."

Everyone lay back and dozed after the meal, but a persistent fly annoyed her, until she sat up and looked around for the horses. They were nearby and so was Mathew, looking to the south from where they'd come. She shifted her gaze and saw Winston, over by the bridge, standing on the rail, looking north and then toward the coast. Two Carbonites, awake and alert. Were they on guard? So, not everybody rested after a meal. She'd not heard any instructions given. It must have been pre-arranged. The erect spines and alert gazes of the two spoke of some hidden danger she didn't know about. There was so much to learn. Her heart contracted and she suppressed a shiver then decided it would be better to enjoy the day rather than frighten herself silly with imagined terrors.

The flat placid land stretched all around them. It looked restful and enticing; an expanse to wander across, a land growing things to eat and trees casting shade to enjoy. What possible dangers could it contain? Even the dog sat alert on top of the wagon. Her gaze drifted again to both men, nothing had changed. They were still alert, their heads turning slowly, surveying the horizon. Vigilant — but on guard against what?

Chapter 7

Dusk softened the sharp edges of the cityscape as they approached, and Calista swallowed a lump of apprehension. She breathed deeply and observed, keeping an open mind about the new vista fast approaching on the skyline.

An hour later they were among the structures she'd only seen in books. But these buildings stood, hunched or crouched on the ground, depending on their strength against the earthquakes that continued to hit the bruised city.

Nothing pristine or clean. None appeared untouched. Many had broken windows, like eyes punched out; leaning walls that looked as if they would fall at the next quake, and roofs that poked into the air, like arms held up, signalling to be rescued.

Yet among the destruction here and there she saw a firm shape, box-like, solid, with lights flickering behind curtains, obviously populated with survivors. She imagined families grouped together, children wrapped in warmth, with food and stories being shared. She dragged her mind from the image of children. Too painful to think about at this moment. Before she could return to the tunnels she had an education in real life to experience, according to her father.

Darkness crept around them until she couldn't see the road ahead, and only the occasional lit window peeped through the inky fog, as the air cooled and mist drifted around them. But the horses didn't slow. With sure-footed pacing they pulled their loads, the wagon wheels rattling over the uneven paving like muffled gunshots when the rims hit holes in the broken tarred surface.

The keenness of the horses to reach their home base infused

her with a sense of excitement. At last, she was in Quake City, her father's home. A place he'd spent the last years in and where his work began. He'd promised her a warm bed and security and she longed to be able to sleep in the knowledge she was safe. Last night she'd been exhausted, tonight she was running on adrenaline. Her spine complained from the day's ride and she longed to jump down and run alongside the wagon just to stretch her legs.

All her inner thoughts vanished as the horses slowed, turned and trotted through high, solid-wood gates into a courtyard. Behind her she heard the gates close and saw a solid bar dropped between two wooden lugs. There were shouts of welcome around them. Strangers gathered around with willing hands and their bounty was soon being unloaded and carried into the two-storey building. Lights came on in the upper story and she heard female voices greeting the returning travellers. Other women to talk to—what a relief. So many questions she had that could be answered by them.

A light touch on her foot brought her gaze down to see Mathew standing beside the wagon, one hand raised the other holding a lantern aloft. "I'll help you down, Calista."

"Of course—sorry. I'm so busy looking around."

He held her hand as she stepped down and didn't let go as he led her in through a doorway and into a large room, obviously the kitchen, where cupboards were being stuffed with produce. The bags of flour from the second wagon were being carried into a storeroom on the shoulders of the Carbonites she knew, plus others she hadn't yet met. Mathew's grasp comforted her in the strange surroundings. So much space! A huge oven on the far wall caught her attention and she pointed.

Mathew smiled and whispered, "Wait until you smell Mrs Sutton's bread. She'll be baking in the morning, I bet."

From out of the chaos of crisscrossing helpers, a large woman made her way toward them, weaving around the workers. Her smile, wide on red cheeks, made Calista feel as if she was the most important person in the world.

"My dear girl, let me welcome you to our home; your home too." Her arms wrapped Calista in a hug that pulled her in to rest against the large soft pillow of the woman's breasts. Perfume, possibly lavender, tickled her nose and unbidden her eyes filled as the woman released her and stepped back.

"Mrs Sutton, may I present Aaron's daughter, Calista. Calista this is Mrs Sutton." Mathew placed her hand into Mrs Sutton's and only then did he release his grasp. "I'm officially handing her into your care, Ma'am."

"Thank you, Mathew. And I receive her with delight."

"I'm here too," Calista said. "Do I get a say?"

"Only if you want a drink or something to eat," Mrs Sutton's smile took the edge off her statement, "Because, if not, my responsibility is to show you where your room is and make sure you have everything you need. Aaron has charged me with this duty and there is little I wouldn't do for that man, more especially his daughter." She ran her hand down Calista's arm. "We have been waiting for your arrival and are so glad you decided to join us."

"I'm delighted to be here and thank you. I'm sure you will be able to teach me a great deal." This formal reply seemed to amuse Mrs Sutton. Her grin crinkled her cheeks and her hazel eyes sparkled with hidden amusement. "Oh, I'm just a cook, darling, with a bit of housekeeping thrown in. I'm looking forward to learning about life in the tunnels from you."

Calista pushed the rush of memories back into their box.

"But not tonight. I see I have made you frown. My apologies." She turned and over her shoulder called "Follow me, little one. The men will have already taken your bag to your room."

They climbed a wide wooden staircase, the treads worn smooth and dipped in the centre from the tread of a thousand feet. It creaked here and there. No one could creep up these stairs unheard.

At the landing, the passage wrapped around in a mezzanine floor. It seemed really high to her, but then so had Castor's upper story. No doubt she would get used to it. Along one side were four doorways, matching the opposing four and Mrs Sutton led her to the far end. The door opened into a room, obviously on a corner as there were two windows, one in each wall. What a luxury. Although only the golden light from the lanterns below showed through the glass, somehow she just knew that the sun would stream into one of the windows in the morning.

Joy filled her as she took in the large bed, the dresser with a mirror attached and several occasional chairs. With a flourish Mrs Sutton opened a narrow door to reveal a toilet and hand basin, and then even more surprising another door revealed a cupboard and on the floor her knapsack rested.

"You can hang your clothes in this wardrobe."

"I only have one dress. It won't take up much room. Mostly I live in these overalls." She ran her hands down her dusty trousers. "But I can certainly hang my cloak up."

She lifted it off her shoulders and it rustled as if to complain as she hung it on a hanger in the cupboard and closed the door. She could hear it rustling still while Mrs Sutton showed her where the light switches were.

"Do you have electricity all the time?" Calista looked around in the dim light that the centre light-fitting's three bulbs spread, barely chasing the gloom into the corners.

"Most of the time, but we try not to use too much. Supply is erratic. Often in the summer we only use lanterns." She moved across the room and pulled aside a curtain by the corner window. "This is where the alarm switch is. If you press it a light will come on outside and everyone will see it. Also, a bell will ring downstairs."

"But I have my pendant."

"Can't ever have too much security, dear." Her smile softened her remark. "And you might lose your pendant."

"Oh, I wouldn't, Mrs Sutton. Never."

"Just call me Mary, darling. Mary is all everyone else calls me. Except for young Mathew, who loves to be formal every now and again." She swept her arm around, "It's all yours, little one. Now, I'm off downstairs to supervise. Come down when you are ready. There is only one door into the courtyard, so you are safe and so are we all. If you'd fancy a hot scone, I'll be putting some in the oven very shortly."

And with that she bustled out of the room. Her footsteps faded, except for the occasional creak from the treads as she went down the stairs.

After bouncing on the large bed and almost being swallowed by the soft mattress, Calista washed her face and combed her hair, wetting it on the surface and pulling the waves down as hard as she could. Still, it crinkled. Tomorrow she'd give it a thorough wash. Her only dress she removed from the knapsack and hung in the cupboard. Her cloak stopped quivering and stilled, resting close to her gown. She stroked it and whispered, "I'm safe here. I'll be back soon." Sometimes she thought the cloak had a personality like a pet.

She peered out the window that overlooked the courtyard below. All was quiet. Opposite and across the yard, the tall doors that led into the barn were open, along with a small door above them that must open into an attic of sorts. For storage perhaps?

She could just make out the long wagon poles on the front of the wagons, now leaning on the floor, the wagons on an angle. Where were the horses? To the right, at the end of the courtyard a high wooden fence blocked access, joining the house and the barn. The horses must be stabled near where the wagons rested. How she loved those magnificent animals. The urge to stroke them, inhale their smell and feel their restrained energy under her palms swept through her.

She would go and see them. Perhaps she'd be allowed to groom them; her way of thanking them for their strength and the work they'd done through the day, carrying her from Castor's house to her new safe home.

She pulled on her hand-spun jersey, thinking of her mother and hoping she was coping with the children and the Mics, who would not be pleased with her absence; then hurried down the stairs and into the kitchen. Sure enough, a pile of warm scones graced the centre of the large wooden table. A tub of butter, such a luxury, stood beside the food and around the table her fellow travellers were sitting and chatting. Winston moved along to make room for her, but she shook her head.

"I want to see the horses. May I?"

"Of course, Miss Calista. Mathew is feeding them now."

"I'll take him some scones then," she said, and buttered a few, popped them on a platter. "They did such a good job today. I want to thank them." This sounded a bit silly, even to her. "The horses, I mean. They are such magnificent things. I've never seen horses before."

"More horses than cars these days," murmured William, from the bench where he stood helping Mary preparing vegetables.

Her conscience pricked. "Can I give you a hand?" she offered, pausing at the door. "I can come straight back."

"Nonsense," said Mary. "Off you go." And William grunted his approval, so she left, her heart light and her steps quickening as she crossed the courtyard to the stable.

As she guessed, to the right of the wagons were the stalls for the horses, each behind rails. In the first pen the mare they called Bess stood, her head down in a bucket of feed, the munch and grind of her jaws sounding as if she was enjoying her meal. In the next the gelding, Buster, also had his head in a bucket of feed and beside him Mathew stood, brushing Buster's coat in long sweeps along his back and over his haunches. Even in the lantern light the fine dust could be seen drifting upward at the end of each stroke. It must feel good to be groomed.

"I've brought you warm scones, Mathew."

He stopped and turned to face her. He really was a handsome fellow. Her heart did a jig and she wondered again at her attraction to him. He was probably several years older than her, and much taller, but it was his kindness and quiet manner that charmed her the most.

"Thank you, Miss Calista. I'll be a moment. I'll wash my hands and join you."

She nibbled on a piece of scone as she waited. The butter had melted slightly, the dough crumbled and dissolved in her mouth, the sweet chunky bits included in the dough could be dried plums or dried grapes. She didn't know which, but whatever they were, these scones were truly the most wonderful things she'd ever eaten in a long while; a comment she shared with Mathew when he sat beside her on a long wooden form.

In a companionable silence, they shared the food. As she licked her finger and swept it around the platter to catch up the last of the crumbs she asked. "May I help you groom the horses? I'd like to do something in return for their work today."

"Of course. I'll show you how, because you have to brush them the way the hair grows and you have to be firm too, to get the dust and burs out. While you do that, I'll check their feet and cut away any bot-fly eggs that may be stuck to their fetlocks."

"Bot flies?"

"Pesky things that give them worms. They rub their mouths on their front fetlocks and swallow the eggs, which grow into worms. It makes them scrawny and they have to share their food with the worms."

She shuddered. "Awful."

He shrugged. "It's life. We do drench them occasionally with manuka tea and that helps keep them healthy. Sometimes we spray their fetlocks with water that we've boiled eucalyptus leaves in, to keep the flies away. It's okay in winter—no flies about then." He stood and put his hand out to help her stand.

Again, his grasp warmed her palm, and a tingle disturbed her insides. Was this attraction?

Even as Mathew showed her how to hold the brush and the way the hair grew toward the tail; his every touch of her hand made her wonder again at her feelings for him.

They worked in silence until Mathew was satisfied his charges were fully checked over. Calista heeded his warnings and didn't walk behind each horse but ducked under their necks instead to cross to the other flank to groom them. He murmured all the names for the body parts until eventually she said, "Enough. My brain is full. I'll learn more next time I groom them."

He laughed. "They'll be fine for the night now. I'll just check their water and then we can go in."

She leaned over the rails and watched him talk to and stroke Bess and Buster.

"You talk to them like family."

"They are our family. Without them we would be hard done by to carry goods around." His gaze softened as he looked at them.

"And you love them."

"I do. They're very precious." He stood taller and held her gaze, "Like you. You're precious as well."

She shook her head. "No, I'm just someone with so much to learn." She smiled, his gaze so strong it disconcerted her. "I'm not sure what my father wants of me, but I'm trying to absorb all these new experiences. I'm shocked to find how many lies I've been reared on."

Mathew took a step, reached for her hands and pulled her close. "You are doing just fine so far. I think Aaron wants you to one day liberate those people trapped in the tunnels, but in the meantime, we are all to look after you." His voice lowered and he leaned in. "You mustn't ignore your importance. You are extremely precious, especially to me," and he kissed her cheek.

Surprise made her pull back. She'd never been kissed by a man before, other than her father. She rubbed her cheek. "Sorry, Mathew. That was a big surprise."

He tossed his head back and laughed, joy on his face. "So, I'm the first boy to kiss you?"

"You are." The tide of a blush rose up her neck and her cheeks warmed. "Not that it wasn't nice."

"Plenty more of those where that came from," he teased and took her hand. "Come on, time to go inside or they'll be sending someone out to check on us."

Her first kiss. Already the mother of two children and she'd never before been kissed by a man she was attracted to. The irony of it hit home. Damn the Mics and their control of her life. Anger flared like a hot rod in her chest and strengthened her decision to be her own person from now on. Any doubt she'd harboured about leaving the tunnels vanished. As much as she loved her children, their father was unknown. He had no right to them, now or in the future. She would have to return to the mountains eventually—to rescue them and her mother.

Her mind switched to her father. He'd driven the wagon into the courtyard, been beside her as she looked at the gate being locked, and then she'd gone into the house with Mathew. She hadn't seen him since. No explanation—just an absence that puzzled her. Could he be resting somewhere in the house? He'd delivered her to safety and he probably had other things to attend to. Yet it hurt that if he'd left, he hadn't taken the time to say goodbye—because his absence had seemed like a gap in the scenery for the past few hours. Something she'd been aware of on the periphery of her vision, a missing piece of her existence.

Just as she got used to him being there, he disappeared again. Where was he?

Chapter 8

It was four days before she laid eyes on her father again. Her wonderings aloud and her questions were slid over and bypassed by anyone she queried. No one could, or would, say where he'd gone or how long he'd be away. Perhaps they didn't know either. Had he brought her all this way to just leave her here? Matthew left and returned, muttering about duties to do and things to fix. The Carbonites never seemed to rest and neither did she, because always there was a task to finish. And when that was done, another job was lined up for her.

The days were filled with domestic activities within the stockade. Never had she seen so much food to be dried or turned into jam or pickles. Every day they made bread, rising early in the morning to mix the batches using the three yeasts they cultivated the evening before; normal bread yeast, then sourdough to be fed, plus potatoes to be grated, sugared and left to ferment as the starter for the Rewena bread. Popular amongst the Māori population, the Rewena bread had a nutty flavour and Mary added to the flavour even more with sunflower seeds and ground millet and quinoa.

By mid-morning, the divine smell of freshly baked loaves attracted customers, who brought with them goods to barter for the bread. Mary always kept back enough loaves to feed the Carbonites and their followers, but every day they ran out of bread long before the queue finished. The grubby faces of the children clutching their goods to barter seemed at odds with the delight when they received the warm loaves into their arms and scampered off with their prize. Always in groups, mind, never alone.

"Safety in numbers," Mary said. "Hard to rob a bunch of children who can toss a loaf of bread faster than you can tackle them."

"Does anyone else in the city bake bread?" Calista had flour dusted up to her elbows as she kneaded the morning's loaves, dropping them into the greased tins lined up on the counter like so many open mouths.

"A few other places do, but it's a matter of supply of flour. Castor Seville has a mill, as well as growing the wheat, and we are lucky he donates us extra above what we buy. We will have to limit our production soon because what you brought back this time has to last until next summer's harvest. Some bakeries have to grind their own grain before they can use it."

"The wagons were loaded with sacks of flour when we arrived. It seemed so much at the time but when I see the long line of customers, I can understand how it might not last."

"It has to. This lot," Mary pointed to the tins being filled, "will go to the hospital today. Once a week we take our turn to bake their bread. I've closed the barter window. It's hard to say no, but we can only hope that some food is better than no food for those that come."

On the bench beside the window lay a selection of vegetables, eggs, butter in pots and even a side of home cured bacon. A treat for the next morning, Mary had promised, as she'd slapped away the prying hands of the kitchen help, all having a peep at the luxury tied in its muslin bundle.

"All that for breakfast?" Calista couldn't believe it.

"No, only some of it. The rest will go into the cool safe—the one with the lock on," Mary said, her smile belying the implication behind her statement. Some food had to be kept under lock and key. At that moment a coo-ee echoed through the open back door and Calista recognized the voice.

"Father?" She wiped her hands on her apron and hurried to hug him.

"Did you miss me?" His eyes sparkled and he kissed her cheek. He was clean-shaven and looked younger.

"Only a little." An understatement. She couldn't suppress her joy at seeing him again. "You didn't say goodbye."

He shrugged. "Things to do, people to see." He grasped her shoulders and held her gaze. "I knew you were in safe hands." He looked across the room. "Didn't I, Mary?"

"Aye," She nodded and continued to knead, her hands a blur as she pushed, rolled, turned and folded the dough. "We've kept her busy, Aaron, and it turns out she's a great little cook."

"Smells like it. Is there a slice of fresh bread for me?" Aaron took her hand and walked to the bench where the bartered goods lay. "Are we getting enough?"

"Not equal value, but I can't turn people away. As long as they bring something, I give them a loaf, or two, depending on their goods." She pointed. "Sometimes we get a treasure. See the bacon?"

"I do. How many loaves did that cost?"

Mary swept her arm across her forehead, wiping the stray hair from her face. "It's a returned favour for the support we provided in the spring. The family is now established on a small block of land and this is their thank you. Their one pregnant sow has established their bacon business."

He raised it to his nose and inhaled. "Smells wonderful. A slice for lunch perhaps?"

Mary chuckled, "No, not even for you. If you're here for breakfast, you can have a slice."

"Will you be here, Father?"

"Should be, but first, today you are coming with me to the hospital. Then, there's a market day at Ferrymead. We can go on to that, so you can see how the population of this city is thriving." He raised his eyebrows. "Does that sound like a nice day out?"

Her heart jumped. It sounded exciting. "Can you spare me, Mary?"

"Just as soon as we get this batch into the ovens, little one. Then we can have a nice cup of tea and a rest while it cooks." She beckoned. "Come on, Aaron, join in. The sooner it's done, the sooner you can go."

Calista returned to the mound of dough, cutting off a piece and kneading until it rolled on the floured bench but didn't stick to the surface. She watched her father. His hands were as quick as Mary's. He'd done this before, many times by the look of it.

With the bread cooking in the three large ovens, they sat around the large table, sipping hot tea while Mary and Aaron talked of opportunities for the Carbonites to help organizations and things they had collected or found that they could barter with, to support their work.

At times it seemed to Calista that Mary and her father were speaking in code, so strange were some of the phrases and names used. But then again, she had so much to learn in this new world. Each morning she marvelled at the sun rising over the Port Hills like a miracle after the dark of the tunnels. Each afternoon it disappeared below the far ranges. Her mountains—lined like a blazing white ribbon on the western horizon, distant, snow-capped and calling to her. Each time she glanced westward, she imagined her children's voices asking her mother where she was.

By the time the bread was cooked and cooled enough to be handled, two hours had passed. The wagon, with Bess between the shafts, was ready in the yard. Today Winston and Benjamin were coming. Both tall, yet Benjamin looked as thin as Winston was large. They had their cycles ready, not the solar charged ones but the conventional cycles she had briefly ridden a few days ago. She hadn't had time to try again, and looking around the courtyard she doubted there was sufficient space for her to get up enough speed to stay upright on either cycle. Perhaps she'd have another go today.

With the smell of the warm bread wafting past them they set off at a steady trot out through the double gates and onto the road.

"Is all this bread for the hospital?" There were forty loaves behind them, sitting on racks and covered with a wide cotton sheet, anchored down with bricks at the corners.

"Almost. We will keep a few back to take to the market day, in case we see something we need." Aaron flicked the reins on Bess' rump. They'd slowed at a crossroads and had turned right, heading northward now.

"Is it far to the hospital?"

"About forty-five minutes, by horse, but we need to hurry to make the market by midday." Her father blessed her with a grin. "We might miss out on some bargains if we're too late."

She wondered what were bargains and what wasn't. Everything seems precious and rare to her. She couldn't think of one thing that would be surplus, except perhaps plums at the moment. "We could have brought some jars of jam," she said, "to barter with."

"Don't worry, all that jam you've made will vanish over winter. Just you wait and see."

Would she last the winter without returning to the tunnels? A thread of disquiet stirred within her. Once winter set in, she couldn't imagine being able to return to the tunnels until spring. Rivers would rise, rain would fall in great amounts and it would snow, so she'd been told. Travel was restricted.

No coal driven central heating here, like they had in the tunnels where the seasons were mostly hidden from view. There was coal, her father had told her. Lots of it from the mountains. The Mics couldn't control all the mining, but transporting it took time, which in turn made it a precious commodity. Winter was supposedly a time to sit in front of the fire, keep warm and reserve your strength for the next year, Mary had said. She doubted the Carbonites would rest during winter. Rest didn't seem to be in their vocabulary.

The drop-off at the hospital took barely fifteen minutes. Again, willing helpers rushed out to unload, and she could see the sense in her father's insistence that a portion of the bread be kept separate and in a box. In a flurry of out-stretched arms the loaves were whisked inside to shouts of joy from the kitchen. The smell of soup was tempting, and Aaron accepted the offer of a bowl each, declining the offer of a slice of fresh bread with it. As much as her mouth watered at the thought, she agreed with her father's comment, that they had some at home and this bread was for the ill and ailing.

Bess turned east, as if she knew the way, and they followed a long straight road which her father promised would lead them to Ferrymead and the market. The scenery became repetitive. Long stretches of shattered houses, some with signs of habitation, and others totally abandoned with weeds hugging the walls and vines climbing over the broken structures. Here the ground had spat out piles of sand, in places half-covering buildings. Liquefaction, she was told when she pointed. Some buildings had been partially demolished, the bricks and timber could be seen being used to rebuild other houses that had withstood the quakes, 'so far', Winston had added. An ominous statement. She hadn't experienced an earthquake and wasn't sure she wanted to.

The desolation eased as the road rose to higher ground. The houses here were mainly wooden, windows intact, chimneys smoking and an absence of weeds in the guttering. Yards with rows of vegetables, hen coops, even some chickens scratching in the open. Cows, sheep, pigs, a goat here and there and children, especially the children, caught her attention as they played, climbed and squealed their delight.

She tapped her father's shoulder and pointed. "The children have so much room to play in. Despite their poor surroundings they sounded happy."

"They are. They know nothing else. They have family, love and hopefully enough to eat," her father said.

"Education?"

"Some." He twisted his smile. "Survival is more important than education at present. We hope to spread education as the population becomes healthier." After a silence he added. "Children can't learn on empty stomachs. It was proven centuries ago. So, we feed them, and then we teach them something sensible. Survival skills, like how to light a fire, how to catch a rabbit and skin it, how to cook a meal. Practical things."

"Of course," she said. Dismay that reading and writing could be so far down the scale of survival skills saddened her. He must have seen her expression.

"Books will come later, we hope."

So, her reading skills would not be that useful. She didn't know how to catch and skin a rabbit either. She'd have to get someone to teach her, or perhaps she could sit in on a lesson one day soon. But not today, because ahead she could see banners flying from flagpoles, bunting strung high between each end of a high tent and the sound of a fiddle being played. The closer they got the louder the noise. So many people, walking, milling around, crossing in front of them and tables lined each side of the road as Bess slowed and picked her way through the crowd until they reached a wide space, surrounded by stalls. She'd never seen so many people together, not since she'd been to Queenstown when she was eleven, just after she'd been branded. She shuddered and pushed that thought back in its box.

This was the market. What a wonderful event! The air seemed to be electric and full of energy. The sun bounced off trinkets and shiny teapots. Glass baubles dangled on thin threads and swung in the breeze. Conversations were shouted and laughter rang through the air like a bugle call to happiness. She thought her head would explode from the visual overload.

"You might find a stall with clothes, Calista. You could do with another dress or some more overalls. Keep your eye out for something."

The horse seemed unfazed by the noise. She walked with a slow grace through the crowd, stopping for seconds at a time until a path forward cleared before she took another step or two.

"Will we stop? Can I get down?" She'd seen some dresses hanging by a nearby tent. She pointed. "Look over there."

"In a minute," her father said, but she didn't listen.

The thrill of the possibility of choosing a dress consumed her. She leaned down, opened the box, grabbed a loaf of bread and jumped down from the wagon. She pushed her way through the crowd, murmuring 'excuse me' constantly until she reached the tent.

She ran her hand over the dresses, fingering the cloth, amazed at the colours and patterns and wondered how she could try them on. All the time, the bread remained firmly tucked under her arm. How many dresses would one loaf would buy? One or two? The noise around her changed, lowered its tone, and then fell away. Silence. The air became menacing and she looked around. She was encircled by women. They stood very close. One hand reached for the bread. She shook her head. She swivelled and felt a tug from behind. She moved the bread to her front, holding it tightly with both hands, the dresses forgotten.

"My goods are better," hissed the one closest.

"No, come and look at mine," wheedled another.

"I'll swap you three dresses for that bread," called one from behind her.

Her heart leapt into her mouth. What had she done? Then beside her stood Winston; tall, protective, strong and gruff. The crowd retreated several steps. The grasping hands returned to their owners' pockets.

Relief swept her and her heart dropped back into place. Instead, a sense of stupidity overwhelmed her.

"I'm sorry, Winston."

He shook his head slowly from side to side. "Never mind, Miss Calista. You weren't to know." He nodded to the crowd. "Step back. Give the lady some room." He reached for the bread. "I'll hold that for you." He gently turned her back to the dresses. "Take your time. I'm sure this will get you two dresses."

Calista looked to the stall holder, who bobbed her head in agreement. She patted her head making sure her scarf was firmly in place, hiding the residue waves in her hair. Perhaps she had wavy hair anyway? Maybe the waves weren't as a result of years of cornrows? Her attention returned to the dresses and after some deliberation she chose two from the half dozen that appealed.

"Can I have these two please?"

She held them out and Winston passed them to the lady behind the table, whose gaze hardly wandered from the load of bread Winston held high. Soft words were exchanged, too low for Calista to catch, but in a flash the bread and dresses were exchanged. Winston guided her through the thinned crowd, back to the wagon where Benjamin stood on the wagon alongside her father. She thought of the remaining bread in the box and how she'd put it and her father's good work at risk with her reckless dash to buy a dress.

"I'm sorry, Father."

He reached for her hand and pulled her up into the seat beside him. "Not a worry, Calista, but next time just listen a bit better. These people," he waved in a circle, "are sometimes very hungry. Other times they are full of food and hope and wouldn't have worried you." He slapped the reins and Bess stepped forward. "Crowds can be very unpredictable. Remember that."

She had the sense of being chastised, yet no one had said a cross word, but she sat silently as they progressed through the market, stopping at various stalls. Always there would be discussion and the exchange of bread for goods was transacted discreetly, sometimes at the wagon itself, or the loaf wrapped in a cloth. Fortunately, the aroma of freshly baked bread had long dissipated. Instead, she fingered the cloth of her new dresses, admiring them again and again and longing to get home to the stockade to try them on. She could alter them if need be, either shorten or take them in, because she'd bought them thinking they may be a little large in places. With the wagon loaded with bags of potatoes, fresh greens and even a wagon wheel Kyle had spotted alongside a lean-to, Aaron turned the horse around.

"Time to head home," he said, and back they went along the same road, now half as crowded where stalls were being dismantled and loaded onto drays.

"Daddy." A child's high-pitched voice rang out and Calista turned to see a small girl, possibly three, with blond curls and blue eyes. It was like looking into a mirror several years ago.

"Daddy," the little girl called out again, but a woman grabbed her and pulled her away, turning her back on them, the child looking back over her shoulder, pointing and protesting. A small boy, older and taller, with dark hair like the woman's, stood staring at the receding wagon. Calista held his gaze, liking his smile and when he waved, she lifted her hand and waved back. He grinned wider, turned and skipped off to join the woman, who without a backward glance grasped his hand too and pulled both children with her into the crowd.

"Who was that?" she asked.

"No idea," said Aaron. "Just some random, confused child."

There hadn't been any sign of confusion as far as Calista could tell, just a small girl who thought she'd seen her father. No doubt the child's father looked a lot like Aaron…or Winston…or Kyle.

Chapter 9

Knowing by the path of the sun that they'd travelled in a semi-circle and that the journey home would be at least an hour away, she relaxed and enjoyed the sway of the wagon and the rhythm of the horse's gait. But a short way from the market on yet another route homeward a cyclist approached at speed. It was Kyle, his ponytail of hair flapping from side to side, the solar-driven cycle coming to a stop in front of them. He simply stood there, blocking the horse and not saying a word until her father handed her the reins, dismounted and walked up to speak with him. A mumble of voices with Kyle pointing in the direction of home and more conversation. The two men parted, and Kyle turned around and rode out of sight once more.

"Change of plans," her father said. "Kyle says there's a roadblock ahead, possibly a skirmish of rival gangs. We have to take a detour."

"Gangs? What would they be fighting over?"

"All sorts of things. Coal, food, fuel, women—anything." He sounded cross. "They might even want Bess, so we are going another way."

They turned around and after a mile took another road toward the east, taking a parallel path to the road from the market. "We'll take a detour and go up the Summit Road a way. Bess can do the hill easily without a load. The view is really worth it."

The afternoon sun was heading toward the mountains. In two hours, it would be dusk.

"Will we get home before dark?"

After a long silence, just as she was about to ask again, Aaron said, "We might have to stay the night at a tavern on Tunnel Road. We'll see how we go."

The wagon clipped along at a fair speed, Bess at a fast trot with Benjamin and Winston pedalling hard on each side to keep up. Ahead the Port Hills reared, ever closer until they reached the base of a narrow road that climbed, winding its way skyward.

"We're going up that?" She couldn't believe it.

"We are. It's only for foot traffic and horses. Bess will be fine."

They climbed for an hour, a steady plod of Bess' hooves, and at one point Calista made to get down and walk but her father's hand restrained her. "No," he commanded. "You ride up here."

No room for argument in his tone, she wondered what news Kyle had brought that had upset him.

Finally, on a wide corner they pulled into a viewing area, a circle track with a wooden table and bench seats tucked against the hillside, a waist-high rock wall on the outer edge of the curve and she went over to it and looked at the magnificent view north. The long white beaches of Brighton, the breakers of the surf disappearing into the distance and further north Kaikoura, where whales played, her father said.

Yes, it was a wonderful view—but was it worth the huge detour and Bess' effort to get them here? No, she didn't think so. While Winston and Benjamin removed Bess from the shafts and poured water into a bucket for her, Calista did as her father wished. She admired the view, made the necessary noises of appreciation and asked questions about the vista spread below.

"One day soon I'll take you to the sea," he promised. "We can sail a boat; you can paddle your feet in the Pacific Ocean and wriggle your toes at low tide and find shellfish in the sand." The hill behind them reared even higher, covered in scrub and trees that leaned northward as if their tops were constantly trimmed to the matching sloping angle each wore.

"Why are they like that? Does someone trim them?"

Aaron chuckled, "Only the wind. It gets fiercely windy up here at times."

As if it had heard them the air stirred and a breeze began.

"Southerly coming," Winston called.

"Aye, time to go," Aaron said and for the first time in the day she stood alone as he went to help Winston and Benjamin re-harness Bess into the shafts. At least the horse had had a feed of oats as well as the water. Calista leaned on the wall, her hands wrapped over the scraps of lichen that clung to the rocks and the wind, hitting her back, picked up her hair and blew it round into her face. She shaded her eyes against the glare of the ocean.

Whales to the north. What a sight that would be, but as to this view? She remembered her view from the mountain when they left. The moonlit landscape and then later the land below them as the sun rose. Yes, this was a grand view also, but was it worth the hurried scurry to the base of the Port Hills, the haul up the road just to see it. No, it wasn't, but she didn't say so. The poor horse. Yet neither Winston nor Benjamin made the slightest protest of the silliness of all that effort—for a view.

There were so many things she didn't understand. There must be nuances she wasn't picking up. Body language she was missing altogether.

"Calista, time to go."

She turned from the view. Well, she'd seen it. Been the dutiful daughter, if a bit foolish once today. Perhaps now they could go home? A longing to be near Mary, swept over her, filling her with an emptiness. She wanted to be among familiar things, her room, the warm kitchen, and the security of the stockade.

There was too much space up here on the hill.

Surely, couldn't they have skirted around the threat of gangs and found their way home? Taken a detour, rather than climb the road to the lookout. A niggle of doubt about her father's sanity blossomed. Had the Mics been right? Was he crazy after all?

No, he was a good man, working hard to help people. Everyone is allowed to be a little odd and if scenery was his thing, then it was a harmless enough craziness.

Calista woke to the sound of the birds, their early morning chirps increasing in volume and length as more awoke to join in the chorus. How she loved the sound.

It had taken an age the night before to find lodgings in a tavern that would also house Bess and the wagon. Several would have suited but didn't satisfy her father. The horse and wagon had to be stabled out of sight he'd insisted—and the wagon with its goods could definitely not be left outside. She was beginning to learn that it did not pay to argue with him. It was a waste of breath, which was probably why Benjamin and Winston mutely followed his lead. Their smiles when this tavern had met his requirements matched the relief she felt in her heart. Then he'd insisted they needed two rooms and that he would share her room and Benjamin and Winston the other. She truly didn't care a jot as long as she could put her head down and sleep somewhere, anywhere would have done. The men sorted Bess and the wagon, and they had shared a meal in the far corner of the dining area where the light was so bad, she could hardly see her food. It didn't matter, food was food, and as soon as she could she'd escaped upstairs to wash and slip between the cool linen sheets. Bliss, even if she did have to sleep in her underwear and didn't have anything fresh for the morning.

The sliver of daylight crept around the window blind and streaked the wall beside her. If she got up, she might catch the sunrise. With great stealth so as not to wake her father she slipped on her blouse, then her overalls and holding her shoes she slowly turned the door handle, wincing as it clicked. Her father didn't stir. Even in the poor light he looked quite exhausted, the lines on his cheeks making deep crevasses, made even worse by the shadows as dawn did its best to light the small space. But she'd woken Patch. The dog, curled on the foot of the bed, raised his head and looked at her. His expression seemed disapproving.

Once in the passage with the door softly closed behind her, she stopped to get her bearings. At the end of the long passage, a floor-to-ceiling window lit the narrow space and as her eyes adjusted, she noticed with a start that a few feet away Benjamin sat in a chair. His head rested against the wall, his eyes were closed, and a slight burbling snore escaped with every breath. Even stranger, he had a gun resting across his knees. Was he acting as a guard to their room? She began to creep past him, but didn't see his long legs in the gloom and caught her foot on the toe of his boot, bumping it against the chair leg.

He snorted, sat up, raised the gun and levelled it at her.

"Benjamin, it's me, Calista," she whispered, barely able to get a breath out of her constricted throat. His eyes widened and he lowered the gun.

"Sorry, Miss Calista." He rubbed his face with one hand and pointed the gun to the floor then rose and leaned in close. "Please don't tell Aaron I was asleep. I'll get into all sorts of trouble."

"But what are you doing here? Guarding our door?"

He nodded and beckoned her as he moved away down the passage. "Where are you going?" It's barely light."

"I want to see the sunrise, if I can. The birds woke me."

He shook his head slowly from side to side. "I'll have to come with you."

"Why? I'm only going out on the road to see if I have a view to the east."

"No, you can't go alone. Not allowed." He held out his hand and she ignored it.

"Says who?" This was ridiculous. She wasn't a child, to be watched every minute. She was a fully grown woman and a mother as well. She swallowed the anger and waited for his answer as she bent and slipped on her shoes.

"Your father says," he mumbled, "but you are not supposed to know. Please don't tell him I told you." He led her further down the passage to the top of the stairs.

She took a deep breath and thought for a moment. "I can see you are only obeying instructions, but it would really help me to understand if I knew why I need protection—and from whom or what," she added hoping to get the full story and not a brush off.

His brow wrinkled and his mouth moved around as he thought. Would he tell her? "I promise not to tell anyone that I know. Truly I won't. But it would really help me understand." She held his gaze. "There are so many new things for me to learn and knowing I'm in danger just frightens me, especially when I don't know why." She turned her back to him and set off down the stairs. If he really had to protect her then he'd follow. He did.

At the bottom of the stairs, she hurried along the hall and out through the front door to the main gate, looking up and down the road, hoping to see the sun rising between the ruins across the road. The Port Hills cast their shadow almost to the tavern but even as she watched, the shadow crept back in a steady withdrawal, sliding away over buildings and patches of grass. Any moment now the sun would peep over the hills. The birdsong bounced off her ears as each variety tried to out-sing the rest in their welcome to the new day.

"It's Castor," Benjamin said. He stood beside her, looking around them, the gun still dangling from his fingers. She hoped he knew what to do with it. Did it even have a bullet in it? She remembered her father saying bullets were extremely hard to come by.

"Castor Seville?"

He nodded. "He arrived at the stockade yesterday, demanding to see you. Wanting to talk to Aaron. He frightened Mary and said he wouldn't leave until you came back."

The scene with Kyle arriving, delivering a message and leaving immediately, flashed before her. "So that's the message Kyle brought? Not about a roadblock at all? Or gangs fighting."

"Mary sent him to stop us returning home. She reckoned Castor will go off somewhere today, looking for a woman or a girl."

"But he'd really prefer me?"

"Seems like it." Benjamin shuffled his feet, head down for a moment, before he returned to scanning the deserted street.

"Thank you, Benjamin. I really appreciate your honesty. I won't tell Father that you fell asleep on the job." She smiled to soften her next statement, "But you owe me. I might need the favour returned in the future. One day I have to go back to my children, and I might need your help."

"I'm not happy about that, Miss Calista. I hope you don't need me to keep any secrets." He smiled, a blush creeping up his neck. "You can see I'm not very good with secrets."

She laughed and he returned her grin. "But you are a lovely fellow, so let's just watch the sun come over the Port Hills then we can go for a walk. You can hold my hand if you like and people will think we are together. Do you think that will work?"

"I'd like that, Miss Calista."

"Oh, please stop calling me that. Just call me Callie. I insist. I'm not a bit like a Miss Anybody. I'm just a girl from the tunnels trying to fathom out this new scary world."

They stood together on the street, watching the sun creep higher in the sky as the night retreated back over the mountain ranges on the horizon behind them. The birds settled, the day began, and they strolled along the street like old friends. People appeared through broken doorways and from around corners. At last, they turned back, melded with the trickle of humanity and walked to the tavern where breakfast had begun to be served.

This is where they were when Aaron found them. She waved across the room and called out as he passed the doorway, Patch at his heels. He turned abruptly and she watched worry slip from his face as he saw her. His smile wiped away the creases and he looked more like the father she remembered.

"Come and join us," she called. "It's delicious. Benjamin is keeping me company," as if it was the most natural thing in the world to be eating breakfast with Benjamin while her father slept.

Aaron pulled up a chair to the table and helped himself to the toast and coddled eggs.

"The bread's not as good as ours." Calista said, offering him a plate of buns. He shook his head and pointed to the toast he already had. "Are we heading home after breakfast?"

She waved to Winston, who had apparently been outside, possibly looking in on Bess and the wagon or looking for her and Benjamin.

"I'm not sure." Aaron buttered another piece of toast before he added. "I'll see if I can find a working telephone. There might be one here in the office. I'll ring Mary and see if there is anything she needs us to get while we are here. Then we can make a decision."

"That sounds like a good idea," Calista said. "And ask her if Kyle has heard if those gangs have moved on."

She watched as her father looked puzzled at her suggestion, then he remembered his explanation of yesterday's detour. It was like reading a book, now that she knew what to look for. "Yes, of course. I'll do that too."

She nudged Benjamin's ankle under the table but refused to catch his gaze as he turned to her in surprise. She felt safer for knowing what was going on even if she had to pretend ignorance.

"You look happy this morning, daughter. Did you sleep well?"

"I did and I watched the sunrise, with Benjamin. It was stunning. I could watch it every day—and I probably will." He frowned. She really shouldn't tease her father. He didn't deserve it…but two can play the game of secrets.

Chapter 10

She could hear voices down in the kitchen. She looked out of her bedroom window and saw Bess and the wagon had returned. Her father had driven away yesterday after they arrived back at the stockade. She'd been busy showing Mary her new dresses and suddenly he wasn't there anymore. Again, she had felt abandoned. He never said goodbye, just disappeared from her surroundings and she now knew better than to ask where he was. All answers were vague, and a different subject was immediately introduced. She'd got the hint—don't ask.

Instead of running down the stairs, she walked with slow soft steps, close against the banister to avoid making the steps creak. She wanted to hear what was being said and despite her mother's oft-said warning that no one ever heard good of themselves by eavesdropping, she crept to the kitchen door and listened.

"So, what are your plans?" she heard Mary ask.

"I thought I'd get Mathew to take her north. They could go to Kaikoura, see the whales, do a bit of fishing."

"On the bicycles? They won't be able to take goods to trade or carry much with them."

"A tent and a primus. Just basic things. Mathew can carry those. Minimum clothes in backpacks, and I'll give Mathew some money in case they need to stay somewhere."

"But she can barely ride a bike." Mary sounded indignant.

"She'll soon learn. It'll get her away from here and out of his reach. Plus, we can look him in the eye and honestly say we don't know exactly where she is." She knew who her father meant. Castor Seville.

"That's a bit deceitful, isn't it?"

She imagined her father nodding before he answered. "It is. But I'm protecting my daughter and I don't care how many lies I tell."

"Mm, you're getting a bit of practice at that already."

"Don't you start, Mary, I have enough of that at home."

Calista wondered where home was if it wasn't here? Did he have another place to stay? Was that why he continued to disappear?

"Besides," her father continued, "the neighbours told Winston yesterday that a man has been hanging around, asking questions about us and asking if they'd seen a young woman arrive. I don't like it. Someone else might be looking for her."

"Like who?" she heard Mary ask, then footsteps approached the door and she hurried down the passage and didn't catch her father's reply. The door stayed closed and the footsteps receded. Mary must have fetched some crockery from the dresser next to the door. The conversation resumed, quieter than before and she had to return to the door and press her ear against the wood to hear.

"Aren't you tempting fate sending the two youngsters off together? Anything might happen. They're both so young. Remember when you were that age, Aaron."

"I do, very well." After a small silence he added, "I don't care. The lass has given birth to two children conceived by artificial insemination and still doesn't know diddly-squat about life. He's a good lad. He's like a son to me—and I know he'll look after her. If there are complications, I will cope with them when they happen. Until then, I'm going to keep her out of Seville's way."

His voice rose and frightened her father may be about to open the door and find her listening, she turned and hurried up the edge of the stairs and paused at the top. Her heart thudded and she took several deep breaths to calm herself. A trip to Kaikoura to see the whales sounded like a great adventure. Plus, she too trusted Mathew. He'd look after her. He'd proved that once already and she always felt safe with him.

The staircase squeaked and cracked as she bounced quickly down the centre of the treads, announcing her descent loud and clear. She opened the door to the kitchen and put on a surprised expression. It didn't take much effort because she really was delighted to see her father.

"Father, you're back," she said, "from wherever it is you disappear off to." She forced a wide smile to take the edge off her comment. "What are your plans for today? Is there anything I can help with? More bread, Mary?" She pointed to the stacked bread tins. "Or can we take Bess on a bartering trip again?" She stepped forward and gave her father a hug, knowing how much he worried about her safety, and then crossed the kitchen to the Aga stove to make a hot drink from the kettle that sat on the hot hob at all times.

"Come and sit down, Calista," her father said. "I'd like to put a proposition to you."

With her drink made she joined Mary and Aaron at the table and waited. Whatever he said she would have to pretend it was all news, despite knowing what was coming.

"How would you like to see the whales at Kaikoura? It's a great time of year to see them. They are coming up the coast from Antarctica, heading to the tropics." He fiddled with his cup, turning it in circles several times before he held her gaze. "I thought I'd get Mathew to take you. He's a good lad, knows the area and could arrange for you to go out on a fishing boat for the day. Would you like that?"

"It sounds like a wonderful idea. But how would we get there?"

"You could cycle. I can't afford to part with Bess and the wagon, and you might be away a week to ten days. It will take several days riding to get there."

She looked at Mary. "Can you do without me?" She now knew the workload in the kitchen.

Mary nodded and smiled. "Only just, but I think you should go. I've seen them often. They are the most magnificent creatures well worth the effort to get there."

"I'd love to go, Father. I might fall off the bike a few times, but I'm sure I'll get the hang of it by the time we get there." She reached for a biscuit, asking as casually as she could manage, "Where will we stay at night?"

"We have a tent you could use. The weather forecast is for good weather, so now is the time to go."

"What does Mathew think?" Had anyone even asked him?

"I'm sure he'll be delighted. Anything to get out of carting coal. The poor lad looked like a chimney sweep when he arrived home last evening," Mary said with a chuckle. "And Buster looked worn out from hauling that weight from the mine. The horse could do with a few days rest as well."

"Only for one day, then Kyle will have to continue fetching the coal. We have to get as much as we can before the rain and cold stops us."

So that's where Mathew had been. Getting coal from the Alps. She wondered whereabouts along the mountain range the coal mines were. She would ask Mathew when next she had a chance.

"When would we leave?"

Her father pursed his lips, his eyebrows drew closer to each other as he thought. "Probably not tomorrow morning. Mathew will need a couple of day's rest and time to get organised. I guess the morning after that will do, unless something happens that needs you both to leave earlier."

Like Castor Seville reappearing, knocking on the gate of the stockade and asking to see her. It wasn't said, but she now knew the real reason for their journey north. She would stay within the house, helping Mary, learning homemaking skills and not provoke any panic by going out the gate, until she and Mathew left.

That evening she retired early after the evening meal, saying she was tired, but really, she wanted to think. She needed to sort out the minimum clothes to take and she had found a cache of books in one of the storage cupboards, so she was devouring them, learning opposite history to what she'd been taught at school. She opened the wardrobe and her cloak rustled. "Yes, I will certainly be taking you," she said, stroking the cloth. It shivered and stilled. She wondered what magic it had woven into it and where it had originated. It didn't show any wear and hadn't deteriorated in the four years she'd owned it. She wondered if someone else had owned it before. It had a homely feel to it.

One of the Mics had presented it to her when Caleb had been born…"in recognition of birthing a healthy child," he'd said. Too embarrassed to ask if every mother got one, she'd shyly accepted it, awed by the presence of one of the Tunnel's Executive. She'd stifled the urge to curtsy. Her mother would have probably stopped her if she even began to drop one knee, and she smile at the memory. Mother could be quite stroppy if backed into a corner. Her two children would be well looked after in her absence. But, one day in the future she would need to return and get them, because despite the poverty and hunger, the children she saw were happy, with room to run around. Basic small pushbikes and tricycles, even scooters, were ridden anywhere where there was an unbroken slab of concrete or bitumen without cracks and grass growing through. The risk of disease was greater outside, along with the effects of radiation, but as Father pointed out, there was radiation in the tunnels too, in the water they drank and the air they breathed, plus sodium lighting and darkness everywhere. She shuddered at the memory.

It had taken a brief month and already she loved the light of this world; the sunrises, the sunsets, the sound of birds and insects — and the smells. So many new smells, some good — some dreadful. Of all the new smells she best loved that of the horses. Their distinctive odour spoke to her of strength and loyalty, and she walked to the bedroom window to peer into the gloom of the evening. Yes, the lantern shone in the stable. Mathew would be talking to Buster and Bess, probably grooming them and telling them his hopes and dreams. Perhaps during their journey to Kaikoura, she would be able to draw him out and learn more about his plans for the future. Would he always be a Carbonite, or did he have hidden desires to do something else?

"We've lost a breeder." Wallace Howe opened the meeting of the Tunnel Executive with this statement, although it wasn't the first item on the agenda.

His two co-executives sitting at the small round table with him looked up from reading the monthly reports in front of them. The sodium lighting gave all three a sickly complexion, made even worse by a total lack of sunlight. Their skin had a gloss from the various natural oils they used to compensate for the lack of vitamin D. and Wallace knew he looked as unattractive as the other two. Coupled with the oily gloss were the wrinkles now appearing on their faces and necks. He'd clung to his position of power because of the favours he privately dispensed to supporters and presumed the others did the same. The annual allocation of train tickets each received, for trips to Wanaka and Queenstown to enjoy life under the dome, often extracted a promise of lifetime support. So far no one had stood against them at the tri-annual executive elections. Nine years in office already and he hoped he might have the job for life. Just occasionally, Wallace's conscience pricked, but mostly he smothered it and convinced himself of the good they were doing in protecting the tunnel residents along all the various living stations within the Alps system.

"Who and how?" Peter Pengally's query halted his thoughts. "It's not as if she could get lost in the tunnel system. What happened?"

"And when did it come to your notice?" Aric Sanson pushed his agenda to one side and frowned over the top of his much-repaired spectacles, the bridge across his nose sporting new blue tape.

Must have sat on them again. Something he was prone to doing as his sight failed. Wallace swallowed, took a breath and laid the case before them.

"It came to my notice three weeks ago." He avoided meeting the gaze of his fellow directors. "Calista Waterman didn't turn up at work and at first it was thought she was unwell, but after a few days the head gardener contacted her mother, who made vague excuses, so it was some days later I was finally notified."

"And you didn't think to tell us?" Aric's tone was caustic. "Your breeder, the mother of your two children has gone missing."

"I hoped she would return, especially when I checked the computer records and found she had left the tunnel complex by an air vent in the middle of the night."

"But how did she find a way out? Someone must have showed her. The exits are not common knowledge." Pengally sniffed. His constant sinuses were an unfortunate sound effect the others had learned to live with.

"Her father, at a guess."

"God, that man's a nuisance. We're constantly throwing him out. You would think he'd be dead by now, living out in the radiation for all these past years. Must be at least ten years by now since we first expelled him. Are you sure it was him?" Aric righted his glasses which had become lopsided.

"No, but I can't see Eleanor allowing her daughter to leave with anyone else," Wallace said. The other two men nodded.

"Can you refresh us with his background, and do we know where she might be? We can't have breeders running off. The last thing we need is for it to become a trend. We invest a lot of time and money in them." Pengally slapped the table with the flat of his hand.

Wallace lifted a file from under his agenda and opened it. "Here's a quick précis. He arrived in the country as a refugee, supposedly from Australia, one of the last shiploads to arrive in Westport. His given name was Aaron Wojciechowski—Polish and totally unpronounceable, let alone try to spell it. He worked in the tunnels as a miner for many years then transferred to managing the water system. He had a natural bent for fixing machinery. Might have had mechanical training in his youth, but he never volunteered that information. Anyway, we called him Waterman from then on, an easier option than his Polish surname. He met and married Eleanor, one of our inborn tunnel residents, about twenty years ago and after several years she gave birth to Calista."

"No wonder you're concerned. At least she didn't take the children. Perhaps they will draw her back?" Aric said.

Wallace kept his voice level, stifling his personal fears. "Yes, that's a strong possibility. I'm hoping she will return of her own accord, but the loss of any breeder is concerning."

Pengally snorted. "An understatement. I presume you've already set a search in motion."

"I have. She is due to be inseminated in the next few months. She needs to return."

"Not to carry another of your children, Wallace. You've already got her first two. Anymore would be sheer greed. What about letting one of the young men become a father? We can't have too many of the same genes in the gene pool." Aric smirked.

His comment reached its mark and Wallace retaliated. "Look who's talking. You have three that I know of. How many others are there? You've been on the Executive longer than any of us. I bet you've pulled a few strings in your time."

Aric opened his mouth to reply.

"Enough," Pengally snapped. "Let's stick to the subject. What steps have you taken to retrieve her, Wallace?"

"I sent out two scouts, one north and one south. The southern searcher returned after a week. There'd been no sightings that way, but northward we picked up her trail at Castor's property. One of the workers talked of meeting up with a band of men and one young girl, before they began work for Castor. Everyone else on the property was tight-lipped but general conversations revealed the Carbonites had recently collected flour and some of the autumn harvest of plums, apples and pears."

He picked up the report and refreshed his memory.

"It seems the Carbonites, of which we know Aaron Waterman is a leader, has a property within Quake City. It's fortified with only one entrance. It has high gates and is surrounded by high fencing. Locals speak of sighting a young girl on several occasions, but she is always accompanied by several men and never on foot. To retrieve her we will have to wait our opportunity and literally grab her and run. Several of the Carbonites are strong-looking men."

"Would there be local support for our attempt?" Aric asked.

Now it was Wallace's turn to scoff. "Really? Are you crazy? Do you think we can get anybody in Quake city to help us when these people are the main charity organization?"

"Sarcasm doesn't become you, Wallace." Aric quipped. "So, what's your plan?"

"I have dispensed two men, trusted and loyal, with rewards promised for her safe return. They have already left and should be in Quake city by now. They will watch and wait and when the opportunity arises, they will act."

"Without violence, I hope." Pengally muttered." We don't want damaged goods."

"Of course. She's not a criminal. She is a treasured part of this community and we need her back."

"And if she returns and turns out to be her father's daughter, fomenting rebellion—what then?" Pengally blew his nose loudly and stuffed the cloth back into his pants pocket.

Wallace shrugged. "We will jump that hurdle when we come it. May never happen."

"True. First, we have to find her. Damn the man. Should have killed him years ago." Peter Pengally pulled his agenda close. "However, you seem to have it under control. Keep us informed of progress."

"There will be no talk of killing while I'm on the Executive." Wallace said. "We have few enough survivors of the Nuclear Dawn as it is. Life is too precious to extinguish—even one annoying man."

"Then you'd better make sure you stay on the Exec and get re-elected," Pengally said, "because he seriously tempts me. Now, let's get down to real business."

Nothing more was said about Calista's absence. Wallace tried to think of her being on a brief holiday, though why she would want to venture into an atmosphere with increased radiation he couldn't imagine. Not that the tunnels' residents knew they were drinking and breathing radiated water and air. As long as they felt secure and safe the residents seem prepared to put up with many other disadvantages. The rise in rickets, skin complaints and depression from lack of sunshine were of concern. They couldn't send the whole population to holiday annually under the Dome. The sickest got preference—after the breeders of course.

The lights flickered and for seconds the men sat in the dark before they were bathed in an orange glow again. He hated the lighting system, but in his case going out into the sunshine would only make his life much worse. Not that he had told anyone of his skin's allergy to sunlight. The doctor had agreed to omit it from his health records. It took a train ticket to Queenstown to fix that. Even the doctor was open to bribes. He might sire his third child after all. The doctor was also in charge of insemination. Luckily, all sperm looked the same. He smiled to himself.

"Found something amusing on the agenda?" Aric asked.

"No. Just a private thought," Wallace answered and turned his thoughts to the everyday problems of looking after the thousand souls who lived within the tunnel complex and under the Dome.

Chapter 11

"Up you go," Winston said, as he lifted Calista up onto the wagon. She was barely awake. The lantern cast a soft glow as Mathew held it aloft. She turned and watched him check the tray of the wagon where the two bikes lay, along with full panniers carrying basic supplies and a backpack each with their clothing inside. He tucked the corners of the blankets under the cycle wheels, effectively hiding the wagon's contents, and then handed the lantern to Benjamin before he climbed up beside her. Bess stood, a picture of patience in the wagon's shafts. She also looked as if she'd rather be asleep in her stall.

Benjamin held the lantern as he made a final check of the horse's harness and in the faint light Calista saw the mare's hooves were each wrapped in sacking.

"Why are Bess' feet wrapped?" she asked and tucked the edges of her cloak across her knees, keeping out the morning chill. Autumn was whispering in the dark and she was glad of her overalls and her warm socks in her boots. No doubt she'd have to change later if the day warmed up.

Winston leaned in to whisper in her ear, "Don't want to wake everyone in the house, or the neighbours, as we leave. Horses' hooves can sound very loud in the dawn air."

Asking why they were leaving before dawn seemed yet another question no one would give her a straight answer to, but she was glad that they were being driven to the outskirts of the city before she and Mathew began their adventure. She had been told that much. After yesterday her legs were sore. If she hadn't been so exhausted last night, she probably would have had trouble sleeping because of the pain in her thighs. At least she now knew how to ride a bike.

The day before, along with William and Simon, she had ridden a bike into the city to Hadleigh Park. The route they took twisted around back streets and through alleyways, to avoid potholes and cracked tarmac, according to William who knew the area well. Plus, the most recent earthquake had apparently severely damaged the main road into the city. Not a good route to take a learner rider on, Simon had also informed her.

It had taken them an hour to reach the community gardens and in exchange for three hours weeding and cultivating they had cycled home by yet another winding route, with bags of vegetables: carrots, several pumpkins—with more promised, not to mention courgettes and the tail end of the cucumber and capsicum harvest. She'd loved the gardens. Real soil for the vegetables to thrive in and Mary's smile of delight had been rewarding enough for their joint effort. A promise of some potatoes if a Carbonite took a wagon to the gardens within the next few days had Winston offering to collect them on his way home this morning.

But her legs! Not that her bottom fared much better and in front of her was a journey of more sore muscles, softened by her excitement at seeing new places.

The city's streets were a maze, but she guessed if you headed in the general direction you would eventually see the huge ancient trees of Hadleigh Park on the horizon and once there the centre of the city with its twice-broken cathedral was within walking distance. If they went that way this morning, she would probably miss seeing it in the dark. One day she would visit the ancient ruin, which stood as a salute to all religions, that, like the Cathedral, were shaken and broken down—but never completely disappeared.

The sound of the bar being lifted from across the wooden gates, brought her back to the present, accompanied by the grunts of Kyle and Simon as they pushed them open.

With a soft click of Winston's tongue and a gentle flick of the reins on Bess' rump, the horse stepped out and the wagon's shafts rose a little and moved forward. The journey had begun. She stifled another yawn and forced her eyes wide. She mustn't miss a thing.

Their beginning was almost silent, except for the occasional creak from the wagon's wheels. Bess paced slowly along the broken road with muffled plods, past dark windows, and the black shapes of buildings. No moon lit their way, but the horse seemed to know where she was going.

"An hour to sunrise," Winston murmured in her ear. "We can stop and watch if you like. I know you love sunrises."

"I do," she whispered and wondered why they were keeping their voices low. Surely speaking wouldn't disturb the neighbours' sleep. Like so many things in this world every day presented new puzzles to solve, but today she was determined to enjoy the moment and leave the planning to someone else. Even Mathew beside her appeared to be dozing. She hoped he'd be more talkative once their trip began in earnest.

Three hours later she and Mathew stood beside their cycles and watched the wagon's outline grow smaller in the distance and then disappear completely over the horizon. Bess and Winston were heading homeward. She felt abandoned and apprehension tightened her stomach. Now they were truly alone, the road in both directions bare of traffic, foot or horse.

"Shall we?" Mathew pushed his cycle forward, ran several steps and then mounted, not waiting for her reply. It was follow, or be left behind. He remained quiet and she hoped his lack of conversation didn't mean he was sulking or moody. She hated people who did that and often thought they must gain a perverse delight in punishing others with their silence.

Determined to enjoy the day, regardless of what was causing Mathew's silence, she mounted her bike and pedalled hard to catch up to him. Riding two abreast they kept up a steady pace for as long as the road was flat. Once they hit the first of the hills Mathew finally spoke.

"It would be better if you turn on the electrics to help you with the climb. Remember I showed you the gears earlier?"

"I thought I should save the power for later, when my legs are tired."

"No need. It's a sunny day, the solar panel will be recharging the battery as we go. It was reading full this morning so doesn't have any extra storage space."

She did as told and slipped the lever into the first position. It certainly helped and she was able to cycle up the incline without any effort, although she felt guilty when she passed Mathew and saw the perspiration on his face and neck.

"Should I stop and keep level with you?" she called as she inched past.

"No, ride to the crest and then stop and wait for me. I'm fine. I just haven't ridden much lately. Too much carting coal and driving a wagon. I'm out of practice."

He didn't look at all out of practice, but he certainly looked tired.

"Do we have to ride far today? Could we stop early afternoon and rest? Somewhere with a view perhaps?

He grunted his reply. When he arrived at the crest and stopped beside her, she tackled her concern head-on.

"Mathew, you are very quiet. Neither you nor Winston have hardly spoken to me today. I'm feeling as if I'm a nuisance and this trip is a burden you don't need. If you are going to be this silent for the whole trip then I'm going to turn back now. I don't have to do this trip and you especially don't have to come with me. We can turn around and go home and just say it was a bad idea."

"We can't go back," he said, looking away from her to the road ahead.

"Of course we can. We just coast down the hill, bolt across the flat and into the city. You must know the way home to the stockade."

"I do. But we still can't go back."

Stifling the urge to stamp her feet in frustration, she took a deep breath. "Then tell me why we can't go back and why you are so miserable. Otherwise, unless you forcibly restrain me, I'm going to turn around and go home. I can't bear the thought of spending days with you in this mood. It's not my idea of a holiday."

The morning had heated into a warm midday. Her cloak and boots were packed in the panniers but even her feet in sandals were beginning to hurt. On his sweat-sheened face she watched indecision fight with concern, but she didn't speak, simply stood silently waiting for his explanation. It had better be good because she had no intention of moving another inch forward unless his explanation satisfied her.

'We can't go back," he finally blurted. "Except I could, but you can't. It's too dangerous."

"It's not that dangerous. I'm sure I could find my way to the stockade eventually." He sighed, as if she were a child who refused to understand. She knew from raising her children, how he felt, but she wasn't going to help him. "Tell me why it's dangerous, otherwise, this minute, I'm getting on this cursed bike and setting off back to Quake City."

"It's Caspar."

"Oh no… not that again."

He turned and held her gaze. "What do you mean 'again'"? His frown drew his eyebrows together until they nearly met.

"I know all about him coming to the stockade and wanting me. I know that's why we spent the night away, after Kyle cycled and told my father he was there. I know that Father wants me out of the way in case he comes back." This time she did stamp her foot. "Honestly, do you all think I'm stupid?"

His gaze dropped and she carried on. "I'm quite capable of telling Caspar to his face that I have no intention of being his breeder, not his or anyone else's." She put her bike down and stepped closer. "I am not a child, Mathew. I'm nearly eighteen. I've been forcibly inseminated, given birth to two children. I've even been tattooed with a breeder number. How do you think that makes me feel? Like an animal—and I'm not an animal. I'm never again going to let anyone push me around. I'm going to live my life how I want to. Not how you, Father or the Mics want me to." Now tears welled and trickled down her cheeks. She didn't care. The floodgates had opened, her emotions burst into the open. Damn all men.

She heard his bike hit the road and felt him close. His hand brushed her arm and she turned, leaned against his chest and his arms encircled her while she wept. When her sobs ebbed to a few shuddering breaths, she apologised and wiped her face with a handkerchief he offered.

"It's not just Caspar Seville," he said. "Others are now asking about you. The neighbours have told us they are being questioned. Aaron thinks the Mics have sent men to find you, to take you back."

Fear rippled through her and she shuddered. "I didn't know that," she murmured. How ungrateful she must appear. All these people worrying about her safety. "Is this why you are sulking?"

Now it seemed it was his turn to get angry. He released her and stepped away. She wished his arms were still around her. It had been a wonderful feeling.

"Me? Sulk? I've never sulked in my life. I'm worried sick about how we are going to get to Kaikourua without being caught up with by either Caspar, his agents, or the damn men the Mics have sent." He looked down the hill they'd just climbed, then along the road ahead. "I'm only twenty-four. How am I supposed to protect you? Just me, alone?"

"But you're not alone. I'm here too. That makes two of us to plot and scheme. I don't want the Mics to take me back to the tunnels either. Now I'm free, I may never go back."

She said it without thinking and realised in a moment of clarity the decision she'd already unconsciously made. Saying it gave her the conviction to take any action necessary. She doubted if she could ever face those sodium light tunnels, ever again. Until that moment she had been avoiding the obvious. She didn't want to go back—ever.

"Let's stop here, have something to eat and talk about what we can do to stay safe and still get to Kaikourua." She reached for his hand and pulled him to the verge and pushed him down. "Sit there. I'm going to sort some food for lunch, and a drink—and we'll do this together."

Too bad if he didn't like being bossed about by a woman, for once she was going to be in charge. She thought while she spread out the meal and while they ate she considered and discarded several ideas, then settled on the best two, for the present anyway.

"At the next big town we reach…"

"Cheviot," he said.

"At Cheviot, I intend to get my hair cut really short. Done properly, because I could hack it off now in clumps but it would be obvious that I'd done that."

He nodded. "Good idea."

"It's too long and despite many washes, I can't get the waves out, so perhaps it has a natural kink. I've always had long hair since I can remember. This will change my looks, plus if I can find some peroxide I might make it even lighter."

He raised his eyebrows but didn't disagree. She hurried on. This was the tricky bit. "I think we should travel as man and wife. Our pursuers won't be looking for a married couple. It's a good disguise. Do you mind?" She held her breath.

"You do realise we will have to sleep together anywhere we stay," he said, a blush creeping up his neck.

"I do." She laughed, "In fact, we can start practising tonight, in case we are disturbed by other travellers. It will strengthen our story and we have to learn to be comfortable with each other." She held his gaze. "I've never slept with a man before. Have you?"

"Neither a man—or a woman," he said. "I'd prefer to sleep with a woman," he added, a twinkle in his eye and they both giggled.

"Well, that's settled. It's not much, but it's a start. We will have to improvise as we go along." With that she collected the remains of their meal, packed the food into her pannier and stood waiting for him to lead the way to find somewhere to spend the night, somewhere off the road, sheltered from the wind and where they should be safe.

At least in Aotearoa there were no bears, snakes or deadly animals. Only a few wild pigs roamed the forests, but as long as they put their food high in a tree it shouldn't attract them. Kyle had told her the wild pigs were hard to find, harder to catch and were more frightened of people than the people were of them. They were a delicacy if they could be caught and you really needed a team of dogs to find them.

"We should also keep an eye behind us for others on the road. Those approaching should be safe, but anyone approaching from behind could be from the tunnels. We might have to leave the road and hide until they pass," Mathew said.

"We can do that," she agreed, riding beside him as they coasted down a gentle slope. "Plus, if we see a family coming it might be a good idea to join them. What do you think?"

After a short silence, he said, "Depends on the family's make-up. How many and whether there are a lot of men. We don't want to be out-numbered by men. Any one of them could also be looking for us. Aaron suspects there is a reward offered for information."

Her heart sank. Just when she thought she'd solved one problem another appeared. Now she had to be suspicious of everyone.

Chapter 12

"What on earth are you doing out there?"

"Just checking that the water won't run into our sleeping area if it rains." Mathew could be heard rustling around in the dusk, which under the tree canopy seemed to be almost dark. Calista peered into the gloom.

"Mathew? Are you coming to bed?" She looked at the canvas cover that hung above her. If it did rain it would fill up with water in the middle and collapse with the weight. This young man didn't seem very practical when it came to camping. Perhaps she'd read more books on camping than he had.

When he didn't answer, she slid out of her sleeping bag, 'down-filled' her father had assured her, and felt around for the long stick she'd found earlier. She'd suggested he drape the canvas over the pole, between two trees, but two such trees weren't obliging in this bit of bush and all stood too far apart. Instead, they had picked the tall bracken ferns and heaped them on the forest floor. At least they were springy and better than the hard ground to sleep on. She propped the stick into the thick mulch and wedged the flat end up into the middle of the canvas. It should hold unless one of them knocked it in the night—if he ever came to bed.

She smiled to herself and wriggled back into her sleeping bag and waited and waited. Finally, he crept onto their bed of ferns and she heard him slide into his sleeping bag beside her.

"What were you doing for so long?"

"I was waiting for you to go to sleep."

"Why?" A long silence followed. She was just about to ask again when he answered.

"I wasn't sure what to do." His voice was soft and if it hadn't been dark she was sure she would have been able to see him blush. At times like this she wanted to hug him. He was a gentle soul and the best friend she'd ever had.

"Honestly, Mathew. If we are to disguise ourselves as a married couple the least we should be able to do it act in a relaxed manner with each other." She didn't know men could be this difficult. "You could move over closer to me. Perhaps snuggle into my back because it's getting colder by the minute." More silence. She tried again, "Then I can get my cape to stretch over the two of us if you are closer. At least I will try to convince it to cover you as well. That's something I haven't tried before but it should work if I think very hard about it."

The bracken crunched and crackled as he moved closer until she could feel him barely spooned into her back. "That's better. Now let me think."

She lay her hands on her cape, which lay draped over her sleeping bag and asked it nicely, albeit silently if it would stretch to cover both of them. For moments nothing happened, then under her fingertips she felt movement and the cape rustled and stretched as she had asked. Truly, it was a wonderful thing and she silently thanked it.

"There," she said, "now if it rains we will at least be kept dry. And I propped the middle of the canopy up so the water runs every-which-way, off us."

"That was a good idea," he conceded. "Have you been camping before?"

"No, but there were books about it in the tunnels and I read a lot when I was bored." It sounded a bit uppity, so she added. "I didn't have to work hard and struggle to survive like you did. There are probably lots of practical things you know about that I don't."

The dark became an envelope of indigo that wrapped them tight. Visibility disappeared. The nightlife of the bush stirred and a morepork called nearby, to be answered moments later by another, like a delayed echo. Their calls and replies continued for some time and just as she was drifting off to sleep Mathew said, "I only learned to read recently. There are lots of words I don't yet know."

"Then I can teach you—if you'd like me to," she offered.

"Thank you, I'd like that." He slid his arm over her side, his hand rested on her ribs and he hugged her against his chest, his breath warmed her neck. It made her feel secure and protected. She hoped he had a few warrior skills if they ever needed them. It seemed he had a stick in his sleeping bag.

They stopped, dismounted and looked along the main street of Cheviot. Once a town of five thousand it now looked lucky to house five hundred souls, but obviously had become a staging post for many travellers. A scattering of shops lined both sides of the road with hoardings for food, a general store, crafts, and several large municipal buildings made of solid concrete. All appeared to have escaped any permanent damage from earthquakes or had been cleverly repaired. There were also signs hanging outside several buildings, advertising accommodation available. Which one to choose?

"Did Father recommend any particular place?" Calista wiped her forehead with a grimy handkerchief. She'd be glad of a shower, preferably warm. Washing in the cold running streams, as they found them, had been the only ablution available and her skin was beginning to itch. She slid a finger up under her headscarf and scratched above her ear.

"Yes, Aaron said to look out for The Plain's Hotel, not that it's a pub any longer, but he said they had clean accommodation. It's a two-storeyed building."

"So are many of them," she said, with a sweep of her arm.

"Then we'll just have to find it, won't we?" His voice sounded ragged and she guessed he was as tired as she was. Hadn't he been moving coal before he arrived at the stockade? They'd left just over a day later and had just cycled about a hundred and fifty miles. Not to mention sleeping on hard ground each night. Camping was definitely over-rated.

"Right…let's do that." She smiled, hoping to cheer him up but he squinted into the late afternoon sun, checking the road behind them.

"Nothing following us, so far today."

She reached and grasped his wrist. "Thank you for all your care and worry over the past few days, Mathew. And the way you've looked out for both of us, especially when talking to travellers going toward Christchurch. I think you maintained our cover story with flair and enthusiasm." That made him smile.

"It was fun, in a way, pretending to be married."

"And we're not finished yet," she added. "Tonight we will have to share a proper bed."

Leaving him with that thought, she mounted her cycle and pedalled slowly on, scanning both sides of the street, and looking for the hotel her father had recommended. Did he know the proprietor? Had he stayed there? Probably, as he seemed to be constantly leaving the stockade and coming back. Most of his movements were not discussed, at least not in front of her.

The secrecy puzzled her but she shook the thought away as she noticed a worn sign swinging gently in the breeze, with the name barely visible, outside a large wooden sided, two-storeyed house. She stopped and peered up. Yes, this must be it. The sign read 'T e P ains Hotel', the 'h' and 'l' were worn away. But Te stood for 'the' in Māori, so it seemed appropriate. With a 'thumbs up' to Mathew, now straggling towards her at a slow pedal, she opened the small wooden gate and pushed her bike up an uneven path made of old bricks.

It had been a long slog of two nights and three days before they came down out of the hills and onto the plain this morning. To sleep in a real bed would be heavenly.

The house's exterior had once been cream, she guessed. Age, weather and a nation-wide scarcity of paint had turned it into a grey building with patches of cream here and there like large freckles scattered the weatherboards. After leaning the bike against a nearby fence post she climbed the steps to the front porch and grasping the vertical metal handle pushed open the heavy wooden door, so old that a plaque with 'letters' engraved on it, was screwed above the slot in the centre.

She expected a shabby interior but was surprised to find all the wooden surfaces gleaming under the light spread by a seven-bulb chandelier which hung in the centre of the lobby. A pleasant mix of lavender and beeswax pervaded the air with a hint of meat roasting somewhere in the depths of the building. It smelt like she imagined a home should and for a moment tears pressed the back of her eyes as she thought of Mary and the stockade. A sanctuary from the madness of the world. She swallowed to hold the emotion back and stepped to a counter displaying the sign 'office.' With a firm bounce, she tapped the bell on the counter. The ring echoed. She could almost see the sound racing up the staircase to the top floor and imagined it could be heard at the back of the house too.

A voice called "Coming!" from somewhere distant and as she waited Mathew stepped up beside her. She didn't know his surname. They were Mr and Mrs 'Who' she wondered. Grateful to have him near she reached for and clasped his hand.

At that moment, a woman appeared at the counter with a dusting of flour on her nose and stray threads of hair across her face, which she swept and tucked behind her ears, then smiled in welcome.

"Good afternoon, can I help you?"

Time to let Mathew do the talking.

"We'd like a room please, Mr and Mrs Althorp for a night."

"Or more," Calista butted in, then bit her lip. The desire to stay put for a while had overwhelmed her. Was his name really Althorp or had he just made that up?

"Yes, or longer perhaps," Mathew added. The lady looked at a large ledger and, in the silence, Mathew continued. "We're on our honeymoon and have no set plans, so might stay a few days…if you have the space."

Calista guessed he felt as frazzled as she did.

"You were recommended by Aaron Waterman," he added and she noted the quick glance the lady gave them, coupled with a nod.

"Of course I can fit you in, for as long as it suits," she said. "I'm Mrs Beets, Betty to most people, including Aaron, and you are most welcome." She turned the ledger around. "Just sign here, please. It's five dollars per night, bed and breakfast. Dinner is an extra dollar per day, all paid in advance, daily or as it suits."

"We'll have dinner included, please. It smells divine." Calista smiled to soften her interruption. To hell with the expense. Her father had given her money and she intended to use it. Wasn't that what money was for, to use? Never having had any before it was a bit of a novelty.

"Could we pay after we have settled in and talked more about how long we're staying?" Mathew queried and she realised that like her he probably had money hidden on his person. "Plus, we will need to lock up our cycles. Is there a shed?"

"There is. It hasn't gone away since Mr Waterman was here. I'll get your key and show you to your room and find a spare key for the shed."

They followed Mrs Beets up the narrow staircase, which had once had a carpet runner but was now bare boards in the centre. Green paint bordered the side of each tread where the carpet hadn't reached. Three doors along the passage, on the left, Mrs Beets stopped and opened a door to allow them to enter. The room was large with a double bed in the middle. A floral quilt covered it, with large pillows at the top. The linen was white and crisp to her touch and she stroked the counterpane. So lovely. On each side of the bed stood a chair and from the window she could see the roofs of a scattering of houses. She raised the blind to see the view and saw endless green fields that finally reached the bush-clad hills. "No sea view," she commented and realised Mathew and Mrs Beets had been having a quiet conversation on the side.

"Wrong way," Mathew said, closing the door after Mrs Beets. "You need to look east. The window is facing west." He busied himself emptying his bag and putting a few toiletries in the tiny bathroom and toilet while she bounced on the edge of the bed, excited and invigorated. Her tiredness had evaporated like rain on a hot day.

"I'm going to find a hairdresser and get my hair cut. There must be one somewhere. I'll ask Mrs Beets if I can't find one. What are you going to do? Do you want to come with me?" She hoped not but had to ask.

"No, I'm going to lock up the bikes, take a shower and have a rest. Then I'll talk to Mrs Beets. See if there is anything I can do for her. Things she needs fixing perhaps. Your father said she might be happy to exchange repairs for board and lodgings."

A pang of guilt tugged. She'd been so wrapped up in her own wants she hadn't paused to think what might be required to pay for their lodgings.

"Do you have any money?"

He nodded. "Aaron gave me some but it won't go far."

"He gave me a little as well, so we'd better keep the door locked at all times or keep it with us. I have a money belt." She patted her waist. She looked around the room. "This is quite lovely, isn't it?" He grunted. She couldn't bear to waste a minute in idle conversation. "Sorry, but I really have to find somewhere to get my hair cut. It's hot and heavy and once it's off I can get rid of this scarf." She paused at the door, "Thank you again. You are a lovely man." Without thinking she stepped forward, kissed him on the cheek and then hurried out and down the stairs, across the lobby and out into the sunshine.

The main street didn't look that long. She'd walked both sides and surely would find somewhere to get her hair cut. First, she had to take in the sights and sounds of Cheviot…absorb the atmosphere, enjoy the breeze and the freedom of this small town. After their days of travel she finally felt she'd arrived where she was meant to be and for once—she was alone.

To hell with the whales in Kaikoura. They could wait. Cheviot seemed like a great place to be at this very moment.

After a satisfying afternoon and a delicious evening meal, she admired her new hairstyle in the bathroom mirror. Hardly room to move, but she turned and twisted trying to see the back. It felt as if her hair had curled there too. She'd found a hairdresser in a small alcove at the back of the general store, along with an old-fashioned barber's chair and a wide mirror in which to watch him work.

He'd been reluctant to cut her long tresses until she went to grab his scissors and chop it off herself. Then he knew she was serious. To begin with he'd braided it from the base of her neck, and tied it tight with a ribbon before he cut it in one piece and laid the plaited braid on the windowsill beside them. Then he'd spent ages trimming and cutting, 'shaping' he said until he was satisfied. She couldn't believe how lovely it was. Perhaps because the weight had been removed, her hair now curled around her face and as far as she could see along each side. She hoped it would last. Gone was the straight hair she'd had as a child and of course her hair had been braided since she'd been tattooed, ready for breeding six years ago, nearly seven. It hadn't had a chance to hang naturally since.

An added bonus had been when the barber had asked if he could keep her hair, for his sister, who made cloth dolls and sold them. Happy for it to be of use to someone, she agreed. Then, he refused to take any money for his services, saying her hair had more than paid him—and his sister would be rewarding him for ages with home-cooked biscuits. All-in-all a wonderful experience—and now she had to go to bed. It would be the first time she'd shared a bed with a man, and she hoped he knew what to do because she certainly didn't. It can't be that difficult to learn. If anyone had to be her teacher, she was glad it was going to be Mathew. He was truly the kindest person she'd ever met and sometimes when she looked at him her stomach flipped. That must be attraction, surely?

She stood calming her nerves with several deep breaths then stepped lightly into the bedroom and twirled at the end of the bed.

"Like my new hairdo?"

He leaned back against the large pillow but his shoulders were hunched and his smile seemed forced. "It's lovely. You're very beautiful, Callie. It really suits you. I didn't know you had wavy hair."

"Neither did I." She climbed into bed and sat next to him. The tension was palpable. She could almost reach into the air and snap it with her fingers. She'd thought about this situation and had decided she would take the lead because tonight she intended to learn about sex. At least she was now sweat-free and clean after a lovely long shower, and not dusty damp from cycling all day.

"Shall I put out the light?" It might be less embarrassing in the dark.

"Yes…please."

So she scrambled to the end of the bed and pulled the cord that hung down from the ceiling. The large single light bulb switched off and the room plunged into darkness. She kneeled there for a few moments waiting for her eyes to adjust and felt the bed move as Mathew lay down. Gradually, the moonlight filled the room and she could see the faint outline of the furniture. Unable to resist, she stepped to the window. The moon was huge and orange, an unbelievable sight.

"Have you seen the moon tonight?" She turned with her query.

"I have. It's a harvest moon. We get them every autumn."

"Well, it's a first for me." It wasn't going to be the only first tonight, either.

She climbed back into bed. Mathew lay on his back, almost rigid beside her as she eased under the sheet and further down the bed.

She lay still, remembering their first night camping, when he'd spooned into her back as requested so her cloak could cover them and she'd asked if he had a stick in his sleeping bag. He'd snorted and rolled away, only to come back much later when she demanded he keep her warm. During the following day, thinking about the previous night, she realised he'd had an erection and she'd embarrassed him by being so naïve and stupid. After that, she had been careful not to put him in that position again, except at this moment, in the moonlight, she could see the blankets propped into a small tent between his thighs. Well here goes nothing—she would broach the subject that was probably on both their minds.

"I see you've brought a stick to bed again."

"Don't be a tease. You know it's not a stick," and he rolled onto his side facing her. She rolled toward him and answered softly. "I know that now, but I didn't on the first night. I'm sorry if I embarrassed you then. Although I've been inseminated and given birth to two children, I've never had lessons on how a man's body works, only how mine functioned." She reached and stroked his jaw-line. "I've been tattooed and inseminated, but I've never made love to a man—and I'd like to." She heard his intake of breath.

"Are you teasing me, Callie?"

"Certainly not." She tried to sound indignant. "I'm quite serious. I'd like to know what making love is all about and I'd really like you to teach me."

After a few moments, just when she thought he was about to refuse, he pulled her close. His lips covered hers in a soft kiss that became more passionate quite quickly. His tongue slipped between her lips as if to taste her. She broke their kiss.

"Do you know what to do?" It seemed a logical question.

"I do."

"When…" but his finger rested across her lips and stopped her question

"Don't talk. Just relax and try to enjoy the feeling," he said as he lifted the nightgown Mary had insisted she pack, and stroked her side. She shivered with delight as he cupped her breast, then caressed her back. Yes, this was great. Certainly different from being washed and dried by your mother. Much more exciting.

His fingers searched where her flesh divided, quick strokes that matched his heavy breathing. She wondered at the desire that rose within her. An emptiness that needed filling and the exciting sensation that crawled up her spine, as his probing continued. She sought his mouth and met his lips, her heart filling as they kissed long and deep. They broke apart as he rose on one elbow, kissed her nose and moved over her. She raked his back with her fingernails, the urge to meld with him overwhelming, mind filling, a desperate need to satisfy.

Then he began to tremble and said, "sorry, can't wait." His knees moved her thighs apart and he slid into her. They didn't seem to fit. Totally uncomfortable she pushed him away. Desire told her it couldn't be right.

"Wait a moment. Something's not right," and she reached blindly to the side, grabbed his pillow and dragged it beneath her. Common sense whispered this should work, and it did. When he entered her again, slowly, with care, they fitted together perfectly. A good design after all. A glorious warmness consumed her and her brain stopped analysing. Her body took command. She moved with him, surprised at the increase in tempo. This was fun—then just as a tingle began to stir in her heat, after one last thrust, he stopped. Propped above her chest, his expression was one of pure adoration and joy. At least he'd enjoyed it, even if she now wondered if that's all there was to it.

"Are you finished?" There had to be more to sex than this. Where was the climax? Had she missed it?

"I'm sorry. I couldn't wait. I've been dreaming of making love to you ever since I first saw you coming down the hillside with your father." He eased onto her, his head on her shoulder his breath warming her neck. "It'll be better for you next time, I promise."

"I hope so," she murmured, wondering just how experienced he was, but instinctively knew she shouldn't ask. "Can we do it again soon?"

He chuckled. "I've unleashed a dragon—but you will have to wait. I'm really tired." He rolled off her, pulling her with him so that they lay face to face. "Let's sleep now, and see what the morning brings. I'm usually quite keen in the morning. It will be better, Callie, truly,"

And it was, much better, but she intended to keep practising.

Chapter 13

Wallace Howe studied the agenda in front of him and concentrated on taking quiet slow breaths to lower his rising blood pressure. These meetings could be a waste of time.

Beside him, Peter Pengally tapped his pen on the table, the sound interrupted by an occasional sniff. Sometimes Wallace wanted to hand him a handkerchief but he knew Pengally didn't even know he was doing it and bringing attention to this habit would only embarrass both of them.

They'd thrashed their way through the finances, always a touchy subject. Never enough money earned to compensate for the expenses. How do you house hundreds of people without overspending? They had to buy in coal now, as well as sugar and starch products. Their workforce was ageing and the young men did not want to become miners. Truly, if it wasn't for being sheltered from most of the radiation-soaked atmosphere they might as well all move out of the tunnels.

He kept this opinion to himself knowing that expressing those kinds of thoughts would only elicit suggestions that he could do just that, and thus vacate his seat on the committee. He enjoyed the sense of power being part of the ruling Council gave him, not to mention the perks, like two weeks in Queenstown annually at the full Council meeting. It was one of his perks that was next on the agenda: a chance to have his sperm used for breeding and his prize breeder Calista Waterman, was still at large.

"Right then, let's get on." Aric Sanson, pushed his lopsided spectacles up his nose and pulled his agenda closer. "Calista Waterman... Wally, what's the situation with her?"

He hated being called Wally, but after a deep breath, he put as positive a spin on his report as possible, to what was basically all bad news. "Our scouts report that they have lingered around the Carbonite's stockade in Quake City for the past few weeks but have not seen her. Talking to the neighbours and even children that have been to the bread window, she is not visible in the kitchen either, which she was previously. It appears…" he paused wishing he didn't have to admit this, "that she has gone somewhere else."

Aric's sharp intake of breath signalled his displeasure.

"However, our scouts chummed up with one of the Carbonites, a fellow named Benjamin, he's a cook and sometimes works in the community gardens. Through chatting to him while working alongside, this Benjamin fellow let slip that she's gone north to see the whales."

"Perfectly charming," sarcasm dripped from Aric's comment. "Gone to see the whales. How utterly lovely for her. Meanwhile, she is supposed to be back here to be inseminated." His voice rose. "We do not cosset breeders so they can run away and look for whales. Do we?" He glared at Wallace.

Not a question that needed an answer, so Wallace ignored it and said, "I think it's true because our scout told me the man then tried to backtrack and said he didn't really know her at all, and perhaps she'd gone south instead. I think we can assume the first comment was right and the Carbonite then wished he'd never said it." He paused and as Aric opened his mouth to speak, added, "So I instructed our men to travel north and follow her trail. If they are able to locate her, they will capture her and forcibly bring her back. We can't have this sort of absconding behaviour becoming known. In fact, we can't tolerate it at all."

Peter Pengally nodded. "Quite agree. We are losing men at Arthur's Pass station. Every week one more disappears from the working parties who load the coal into the wagons. Winter is on its way. We need that coal to warm the tunnels and send on to Queenstown. We need men to load it. Our own mines need more workers which at present we can't attract. A labour shortage is looming imminently."

The short silence was broken by Aric's query. "Can we use her children as a form of blackmail? Could we get a message to her or that damn father of hers, that the kids are sick, or her mother is ill?

Spread a rumour. Would that work? I believe maternal instinct is strong in young mothers."

"Better to have her return voluntarily, than drag her back," Wallace added, "But it might work. I'll send a message to that effect to our scouts, for when they catch up with her. Don't want them openly telling people they are from the tunnels. Some of the locals don't like us very much."

"That's an understatement—jealous bastards," Aric Sanson polished his glasses, sighed and pushed them back into place,

"I don't want a lot of money spent on this," Pengally said, now tapping his pen on his teeth. "Anything over budget will be met by Wallace Howe." He looked at Wallace, who nodded.

"We have greater priorities than Aaron Waterman's damn daughter, breeder or not. If we have to drag her back, won't she only flee again?" He sniffed. "Also, as Chairman of this committee, I want it recorded that there will be no violence used in the return of this breeder. Aric, make a note of that as well."

Aric scribbled in the minute book, finishing the notes with a firm full stop, and another push to place his glasses in the correct spot on his nose. He grinned at Wallace with a smirk of satisfaction.

Wallace clenched his fists under the table, resisting the urge to punch him. He wanted to point out that a bit of push and shove might be necessary to get his breeder back. "I'll pass that message on to the scouts," he said, "but we have to get her back, somehow."

He didn't like the idea of his children growing up without a mother. Who knew what damage might be caused to their personalities, and personalities were really important in such confined areas as the tunnels. Their existing 'shrink' was overworked as it was. Even he sometimes wondered if he wasn't going a little crazy.

Perhaps it was the radiation? How much longer could they keep their people in ignorance of the radiation they were consuming in the daily allocation of water? He made a few notes on the side of his agenda and consoled himself that things were much better here in the tunnels than the conditions outside. All the more reason to get his breeder home safe and hopefully undamaged by the diseases that thrived on the outside, where medicines to cure most illnesses were now a distant memory.

Calista woke and reached to the side, but the bed was empty. Mathew was off out somewhere, no doubt doing jobs for Mrs Beets. He said she had given him a long list. After a wash and a quick brush of her mop of curls, she dressed and went to the kitchen where the smell of bread cooking made her mouth water.

"Can I help with anything Mrs Beets? Mary, at the stockade, taught me how to make bread. I could give you a hand if you liked." She looked around but the kitchen seemed to have been tidied and any signs of baking had been cleaned away. The smell held the promise of the delight ahead.

"First off, you can call me Betty, and then can get me some eggs from the back of the henhouse. I'll make you scrambled eggs for breakfast. Would you like that?" Betty's raised eyebrows disappeared under the tangled fringe that hung over her forehead while the rest of her hair stayed tied back with a band. Perhaps she was trying to grow the fringe out. In the meantime, it hung almost into her eyes.

"I'll go and look," Calista said and hurried outside, then across the back yard to where a small wooden shed stood at the end of an enclosure of rusty wire netting. A mob of scrubby looking chickens scratched, many of them rushing to the wire upon seeing her. She searched around the back of the shed but couldn't find even one egg on the ground. Were they too small to find? She returned to the kitchen. "I can't find any," she said. "I've looked everywhere on the ground."

Betty tutted, wiped her hands on her apron and smiled kindly. "You are from the tunnels aren't you?"

Calista nodded, not sure if she should be ashamed or proud. "But please don't tell people. We're in disguise."

"I thought so. Aaron's daughter, I guess. I can see the family likeness." With that she patted Calista on the shoulder. "Follow me. It's time you learned about chickens and eggs." For some reason Betty thought this very funny. When they reached the henhouse Betty lifted a lid on the top of a box-like affair at the back of the shed. "There," she said.

Along the straw base of the box in several hollows nestled eggs. In one partition a hen sat, objecting with clucks as Mrs Beets searched under her and removed three eggs.

"Doesn't she mind?" Calista asked, wondering why the hen hadn't pecked Betty's hand.

"They seem to go into a dream state when they are about to lay. Sometimes they get broody and are a real pest," Betty said. She turned and handed the eggs to Calista. They were warm to hold and perfect in shape. Truly a wonder to behold. "These are not fertile," Betty said and pointed to another run further over. "That lot are breeding hens and several are sitting on clutches. The rooster is a noisy fellow. You probably hear him in the morning." Calista nodded. "But in the winter we'll eat him. I have other young ones coming on and I've been promised a Shaver rooster to use. They are good layers, the Shavers." With that, it seemed the lesson was over and with the rest of the eggs held in her apron Betty set off back into the house with Calista in tow.

"Cut some fresh onion up fine for the top of your eggs. Raw onions are good for your health," she said as she bustled about, breaking eggs and whipping them with a little milk.

Calista cut an onion from bottom of the plait that hung beside the wood stove. They smelt fresher than any onion she's ever seen. As if it were a jewel she removed each layer of skin, not wanting to waste a shred, and sliced off an end.

"You'll be Aaron's eldest daughter then?" Betty Beets commented, her back to Calista as she stirred the pan.

"I'm his only daughter," Calista corrected her and then wondered at the silence that followed. Had she offended her?

The smell of toasted bread and the freshly scrambled eggs made her reach for a plate and place it on the table, ready for the food. Betty turned, a warm smile greeted Calista and she forgot about the strange comment as she sprinkled the raw onion on top of the golden pile.

"Now, you eat that up and I'll make us a nice cup of tea."

As Calista ate her breakfast, Betty made the tea and sat down opposite her, poured them both a cup and sipped hers, a slight frown passing across her forehead. Once Calista had cleaned her plate and picked up her tea, Betty reached across the table and patted her arm.

"Your father is really proud of you, you know. He's talked of you often when he's stayed, and I remember him saying he wanted to get you out of the tunnels and into the real world, so you could have a life." Betty took a deep breath. "And nobody has told you, have they?"

Calista wanted to ask 'Told me what?" but Betty hurried on. "About three years ago, he was here and we celebrated with a home-made wine because he was excited. He'd just had another little girl, a sister for his son. He doesn't tell lies your father. He's a Carbonite. They tell the truth—but sometimes you have to ask the right question to get a truthful answer."

Calista's mind was reeling. Her father had a son and a daughter? Therefore, he had another wife somewhere. The image of the little girl at Ferrymead flashed in front of her. The feeling of recognition, of having seen her somewhere before. Of course, she looked familiar. The child must have been her sister. Now she had curls like the little girl—and the small boy who raised his hand in a sort of acknowledgement? He knew. Even the boy knew she was his sister. Tears pushed at the back of her eyes and she rubbed them. What had her father said? 'Just some confused child', if she remembered correctly. He ignored his own flesh and blood, the child who called out 'Daddy' because he didn't want Calista to know. Was he ashamed? She thought of her mother, so loyal and alone. It wasn't fair.

"There, I've made you cry. I'm so sorry, but you should know."

"It's just the onions," Calista whispered, knowing full well that was a lie.

"Men have needs, my dear. And it's a cruel world for a woman alone and very dangerous. I'm sure you father's second wife is a lovely lady. He seems very happy."

A knife twisted in her chest, her heart ached. How dare he be happy with another woman. What about her mother, Eleanor, his first wife? She sniffed back her tears and let the anger that rose have free rein. A red mist passed in front of her vision, then dissipated. It was better to feel angry than weepy sad.

"It's the way of the world now," Betty continued. "There aren't enough men to go round. Many were killed by the radiation and trying to fix the things that the EMP destroyed, when those Northern Koreans exploded that nuclear device above South Australia. Then men drowned trying to cross Cook Strait between the islands. More drowned trying to fix the water supplies and broken dams. Now the coal mines take them too, with explosions and rock-falls. It's a harsh world for a man, and there are many widows about who need protection—and love."

How could she be so ignorant? All the silences now made sense. The nights her father disappeared, the way he slipped off and nobody said anything about it. She drank her tea, silent, thinking, letting the anger rise and fall until she had it under control. Questions raced around her mind but she chose just one, for knowledge.

"What's EMP?"

"It stands for Electromagnetic Pulse," said Betty. "It's what happened in a split second when the nuclear bomb exploded in the atmosphere over South Australia. It knocked out every single electronic device and electronic equipment in Australia and New Zealand. No idea how far it went actually." Betty warmed to her subject as if glad to get away from the personal revelations. "Took them ages to get a basic telephone system up and running again. Radio waves are good and were not affected, so we use that for important messages around the country. Even the electricity was out until they resorted back to the old way of sending it along the lines, without those electronic switchboards. It's still not reliable, but we're glad of the bit we get, on and off." She held up the teapot. "Are you alright? Would you like another cup?" She reached and clasped Calista's hand in hers. Warm hands, strong and comforting that held on tight, conveying concern.

Calista blinked rapidly. "Thank you, Betty, for telling me about my father. I just wish someone had sooner…like Father himself." She almost spat that out. "I feel as if I've been blind and stupid."

She stood, carried her plate to the bench and took a deep breath. Enough wallowing in self-pity. Time to move on. The ignorant girl child had gone, she didn't need to be pandered to any longer.

"Thank you for the delicious breakfast, and thank you so much for being honest with me. You're right. I never did ask the right questions, but in the future, I will. Plus, I'll have a few things to say to Mathew, when I can find him. I bet he knows."

"He's off up the road to get timber to fix some dry-rot on the side of the house. He won't be back till midday at least. He's a good lad that…and I presume he's not really your husband."

She felt a blush rising, but honesty seemed to be the theme of the day. "Not legally, but he is in the biblical sense."

Betty nodded. "Ah well, there's a lot of that going on as well."

Calista paused on her way to the door. Anything to change the subject. "Can you explain to me where the library is? Is there one in town? I'd like to borrow some books. Mathew has recently learnt to read and I said I'd help him."

"It's a big building in the main street. Further down, the first concrete one, two-storeyed, looks very official. The local village committee meet on the top floor and there are some meeting rooms there for sewing groups and men's clubs but the whole bottom floor is the library." She sipped her tea and added, "You'll recognise it from the bars on the windows."

"Was it a prison once?"

A deep rumbling chuckle escaped. "Oh deary me, you do have a lot to learn. No, honey, it has bars on the windows to stop people breaking in and pinching the books to burn them for fuel."

Calista gasped. The horror of it, burning books to keep warm. They were rare and precious things. Many had been lost in the fires and initial confusion after the Nuclear Dawn, so she'd been taught. Things must have been really bad. "Do they still do that?

"Not unless they want to get shot. There's a shortage of bullets, but the town committee has a few put aside and isn't afraid to use them if the occasion arises."

She must have looked horrified because Betty stood and gathered her into her arms.

"Don't worry you won't get shot for an overdue book and remember always, your father loves you dearly and is very proud of you. Anything he's done has always been in your interest. Don't be angry, Calista. Anger only eats love away, and we all need love."

It sounded like good advice, but she'd have to think about it for a while. At present she wanted to punch her father in the chest, beat him on the back and scream at him for keeping her ignorant. Hadn't he said he wanted her to learn about life?

But then he'd never said that he would be her teacher, and she was certainly learning all about the outside world today.

Chapter 14

The library was indeed where Betty had said it would be. Calista paused at the top of the three stone steps and calmed herself with a few deep breaths. She hated conflict of any sort and the thought of discussing her findings with Mathew caused a sick feeling in her stomach. He must know about her father's second family. Of course he did. She would stew on the facts for a couple of days, calm down and become rational before she brought the subject up.

Meanwhile, in the next few moments, she would enter a world of books, probably more than she'd ever seen in her life before…she hoped. A thrill of anticipation, just knowing all the information was there waiting for her to absorb it, pushed aside her disappointment at her father's duplicity.

She stepped over the doorstep onto the wooden floor and walked towards the reception desk, crossing a wide sunbeam shining in through floor to ceiling windows, the dust-motes dancing around her; a truly magical sight that caused her to pause and look around. The high ceiling looked to be supported by books, with rows of bookshelves on every wall and many more stacked on shelves in-between. A scattering of desks filled the few empty spaces and people sat at them, reading. Old, young, even very small, all studying pages. A mother sat on a pile of cushions, her voice lilting as she read to a group of small children grouped in front of her, sitting cross-legged and still.

At the main desk she asked if she could borrow a book or two, adding that she was staying at The Plains Hotel and Betty had said she would vouch for her.

"Fill this form in please," was the request, which she did as best she could. She wondered for a moment whether to put Calista Waterman or Calista Althorp, then decided to stick with the truth and wrote her real name.

She wandered the children's section and chose three books of varying levels, not sure just how much reading Mathew had done, then, no longer able to ignore the pull of undiscovered knowledge, she drifted to the reference section. What a selection! She found some books on natural remedies and one on the building of the hydro-electric dams on the Clutha. Because there were large notices everywhere stating 'reference books cannot be removed from this building', she sat at a nearby table, placed Mathew's books beside her and began to read about the construction of the dams.

Although the nuclear EMP had damaged the electronic workings of these dams they had been partially repaired, sufficient to allow some electricity to be routed around the country. The pictures of the construction process, using huge machinery, were fascinating. The lack of diesel and petroleum products, now unobtainable, meant all such machinery lay rusting when and where it ran out of fuel. Sometimes cannibalised for parts, the metal wrecks looked like rusting carcases. She'd seen some around the city. She tried to imagine what it would be like to drive such monsters. Possibly like riding a steam train, but quieter. Not as personal as riding a cart behind Bess and probably not as smelly either.

Across the table, a young woman read what had to be a medical book from the coloured plates Calista could see of the human body and various organs. Even upside-down some of the pictures looked ghastly, with gruesome injuries and skin defects. The woman was scribbling extensive notes in a large exercise book alongside.

Eventually, Calista couldn't hold back her curiosity any longer. The longing to speak to another woman, one who looked about her age and who wasn't a mother figure, overwhelmed her and she blurted out, "Do you enjoy reading about medical things?" She hoped to open up a conversation.

The woman stopped writing and looked up. Her face, thin and angular, appeared stern until she smiled. In that moment, Calista felt she was the only person in the world and had this woman's sole attention. What a wonderful gift to have and the woman looked so much younger when she smiled. Faint lines creased around her eyes. She twisted her long dark hair between her fingers, then stopped as if considering her answer. After a pause, long enough to cause Calista to wonder if she'd offended her, the woman began to speak.

"I never stop learning," she said. "Every book I read teaches me something new, and this library…"—she spread her arms wide in delight—"has more medical books than our library at the Otago University."

"Do you go to University? What do you study?" Her questions raced out. "I've never spoken to a university student before…is it fun?" This sounded a bit gauche so she added. "Sorry to sound so awe-struck but the thought of being able to study a subject like the human body excites me. I probably sound rude."

The woman laughed. "I love your enthusiasm." She reached across the table and shook Calista's hand, "I'm Elizabeth—and you are?"

"I'm Calista Waterman. I'm up here on holiday. My father lives in Quake City and I'm supposed to be learning about life on the outside." Her thoughts again rushed out in a rattle of excitement.

"As compared to the inside—where?" Elizabeth raised her eyebrows.

Damn, she'd let that slip. Too late now, and who cares anyway? Only men and boys, and she'd had enough of them for a while. She lowered her voice, checked there was no one within hearing range and whispered "I ran away from the tunnels. My father came and guided me out."

"Good on you!" Elizabeth thumped the table with glee, totally ignoring Calista's attempt at secrecy. "That's what I like to hear. Another escapee has decided to join the real world." She grasped Calista's hand, turned it over to look at her palm, ran her fingers over her wrist and held it lightly for a few moments. "You seem to be healthy. Lucky you. I can see you've had a good diet in the last few years. Your hair is shiny and your eyes are clear. Things must be better in the tunnels than we are led to believe."

Time to confess. "I'm a breeder, and I've had the best of everything. I've been very lucky."

"Lucky? To be bred from? Inseminated?"

Calista nodded.

"Have you had children already?" Elizabeth's voice softened.

"Two," and for the first time in her life Calista didn't feel proud to say this.

"You poor thing, you only look about seventeen."

"I'll be nineteen next week," and she added, "They're lovely children. My mother is looking after them while I'm outside."

"I don't doubt they are beautiful and well cared for, my dear. I shouldn't have let my shock show. That was very unprofessional of me. I apologise."

"There's no need to apologise. Truly. I'm just delighted to be able to speak to someone who isn't my mother's age. Not that Mother is bossy. She's a darling, I just long for some female company."

Elizabeth maintained the grip on Calista's hand, holding her gaze. "I'm going to be here for about another week. You can talk to me at any time. I'll be in the library every day."

Calista retrieved her hand and her heart lifted. This woman could be a friend, but what did she mean by 'unprofessional'?

"Thank you. Are you a professor of something?"

A laugh erupted, high and brittle, cutting the air in the library as her new friend enjoyed the joke. "Nothing so grand. I'm an itinerant doctor. I qualified this year and I'm wandering the land, helping people where I can, hunting out new knowledge," she indicated the pile of books at her elbow, "And trying to put my qualifications to good use."

"That sounds very grand—and generous," Calista said. "Are the books helping?"

"Yes, I'm particularly interested in Māori remedies. We only have sulphur powder available as an antibiotic these days so anything else that can ease pain or cure ailments is worth its weight in gold." She sighed. "The next thing I have to do is to find these plants and use them, and find people who know where they're growing."

To Calista it sounded like an amazing life to follow and with a promise from Elizabeth that she would definitely be there the next day, Calista checked out the books she'd selected. With a lighter heart, she set off back to The Plains Hotel to help Betty prepare the midday meal, and catch up with Mathew.

It was too early to go to bed, and the warmth of the kitchen held them in its embrace. Betty had locked the house up and bid them good night, and as the only guests they had the downstairs to themselves. After the midday meal, Mathew had glanced through the books she'd brought from the library and it seemed he could read most of the basic words. Only the higher level of children's book had interested him. Although tempted to race back to the library, she'd resisted and helped Betty bottle some peaches, but tomorrow she'd get him more books at the young adult level, and see Elizabeth again.

But for now, she'd decided it was time to face the truth. Dwelling on it wasn't helping.

"When were you going to tell me about my father's second family?" He looked up from the book he was reading and the momentary surprise in his expression turned into one of relief.

"So you know," he said. "Who told you? Had to be Betty."

She nodded. "She told me this morning because she realised I didn't know, and at least she thought I was grown-up enough to handle the news." She could hear the bitterness in her voice and tried to bury those emotions. "So tell me, Mathew, when were you going to tell me?"

"It really wasn't my responsibility." His gaze flittered around the room before returning to hold hers. "Your father should have been the one to explain it."

"Explain what? That he couldn't help himself? That he was lonely? What about my poor mother, who probably doesn't know a thing about it?"

"It's not that simple. Life is different now. There are too many widows and men still have their needs."

"If I hear that expression again, I swear I will spit." Her voice rose and her throat ached. "What is there so special about men's needs? Tell me." She stood and pushed the chair away from the kitchen table. The same table she'd heard the news this morning. "What about women's needs? Don't they get a say?"

Mathew stood, knocking his chair over, and moved to her side, his arms outstretched to hold her but she stood firm, back erect, head high, furious with the state of the world and men in particular.

"No Mathew, I don't want a hug, I want an explanation."

He stepped back, shrugged and returned to right his chair and sat again. "It's not my fault." His tone off-hand and casual.

He had a point. She was unfairly blaming him for the state of the world—her world at this moment. "True. I'm sorry. It's not your fault at all, but I thought Carbonites didn't tell lies."

"They don't. You just have to ask the right questions. If you had asked your father, he would have told you."

"But I didn't know that day at Ferrymead fair. A little girl called him 'daddy' and he ignored her. I can't get over that."

"He was protecting your feelings, because he hadn't had a chance to explain. He feels bad about doing that to Belinda." Finally, her half-sister had a name. "So it's been discussed?" He nodded. "Then tell me my half-brother's name and the name of my father's mistress. I might as well know everyone's name, in case I ever meet them again." A half-laugh escaped. It had to be funny, otherwise, it was just too sad.

"The boy is Colin, and the children's mother is Angela. She's not your father's mistress, she's his common-law wife. They've been together for seven years."

Since before the day she saw her father on the train. Already, by then he'd found comfort on the outside. Did this make him any less of a father? Did it lessen his desire to get her out of the tunnels to learn how to live? He had come for her because he loved her and wanted what was best for her, so he said.

She sat again and her gaze wandered the kitchen then came to rest and she studied the grain in the tabletop. How many years had the tree grown before men felled it and made into planks? Nobody asked its permission. Was her life any more important than that tree? Her palm smoothed the wood, her fingertip followed the grain to a large knot, bevelled and worn. If everyone had their own journey, then this was hers and she'd better make the most of it before she too was cut down, like the tree that made the table.

She wasn't sure about this 'being a leader'; the reason her father had used to bring her outside. He didn't really know her as a person, only as his daughter. She would have to think about that. He talked about the Carbonite Council wanting her, but from what she could see, he was in charge of all of them unless the council was his name for the group? It didn't really matter anymore. Whatever the reason, here she was, and she was going to make the most of every day, starting now.

"It's still light. I'm going for a walk." She would walk until her anger eased. Just the pleasure of walking in the fresh air would sure help. She slipped her cape from the back of the chair, and threw it around her shoulders then hurried outside. Almost tripping on the uneven path made her more careful when walking on the broken surface of the road, where the grass was winning the war against the bitumen coating, cracked and disintegrating from years of neglect.

With long strides she set off, glad of her strong boots. The smell of dried grasses, ti-tree oil from the manuka bushes and even horse dung, all pleased her. The twitter of the birds as they settled for the night in the surrounding trees reminded her not to go too far. Night was falling. She reached the crest of the rise and looked back onto Cheviot with its ramshackle houses, big old civic buildings and an untidy arrangement of fences and hedges. It didn't look much in the sunlight, but dusk softened the edges and she felt a fondness for it that no other place had evoked.

Perhaps it was the library, or Betty—or better still, her new friend Elizabeth? This little town seemed like home, and there at the hotel's gate stood Mathew, looking for her in the gloom. She waved. He waved back and hurried toward her. She sat on a nearby tree stump and waited, not yet ready to return to the hotel, and bed with its nightly love-making. How did one say 'no' without distressing the other person? Something else she had yet to master.

"Move over a bit," he said as he arrived panting from the uphill run. "You had me worried. I thought you'd run off."

"I said I was going for a walk."

"But you've never done that before," he said.

He had a point, she hadn't, but she would in future. "I'm going to take lots of walks from now on. They are great fun. I prefer them to cycling."

He reached for her hand and stroked her fingertips before he lifted them and kissed each tip. "That's a good idea, just don't do it alone—please. I like a good walk myself, but not a fast march at the end of the day." His gaze held a plea that tugged her heart.

She'd forgotten, again, of Mathew's fear; of his promise to her father to keep her safe and protect her.

"I'm sorry I flew at you, Mathew. You're right. I didn't ask the right questions and when I see Father again I will talk to him about it." She made the effort and kissed his cheek. "In the meantime, how was your day?"

With visible relief, Mathew smiled and wrapped his arm around her shoulders. "I had a busy day. There's enough work around here for the next two weeks at least. We can stay here for that long without paying a penny. I have the carpentry skills needed to fix the rotting boards and windowsills, plus there are lots of small things that need mending, too." He stifled a yawn. "Betty is thrilled to have us. She loves the company and there are not a lot of travellers passing through, now that autumn has set in."

"Good, because I'm going to the library every day we're here. There are so many books to read and today I met a young doctor. She's travelling the country helping people, just like the Carbonites do. Isn't that wonderful?"

"Don't get too friendly. She might tell someone about you and we are trying to hide, in the open, aren't we?" He tugged her to her feet and they walked hand in hand down the slope toward the hotel.

She didn't tell him it was too late. She'd already given up her secrets to the first young woman she met. In future, she'd be more careful.

Chapter 15

"**I**'m leaving tomorrow."

Elizabeth's announcement hit Calista like a physical blow, her stomach contracted and her chest ached. Her throat tightened so hard she wondered how to get the words out. "Why?" was all she managed, despite a hundred words racing around in her mouth trying to escape, desperate to stop Elizabeth's departure. It wasn't fair. Her new, best friend and now she was leaving.

"Henry Phillips is going home and he's going to show me a stand of native bush that he thinks has kawakawa in it. I can collect some leaves and berries and make poultices and medicine—I hope."

Inspiration hit her. "I could help you with that." Elizabeth nodded, "You could if you are still here when I get back."

"No, I meant I could come with you." The idea jelled in her mind. "I could help with the gathering. We'd collect twice as much with two of us doing it. Plus, I'm a good cook, I could help with the poultice making." Anything to stay with Elizabeth.

"What about your …partner? Won't he mind?"

"He's got heaps of work to do for our landlady. Surely we will be back in a couple of weeks, won't we?" In her excitement, she'd forgotten all about Mathew.

"I guess so. Then again, I might decide to travel further north. Depends on who needs me and if there are any settlements inland that Henry knows of." Elizabeth twisted her lips, obviously considering Calista's offer. "It won't be a fun trip, you do realise that? It will be long days and rough conditions. I'll be walking and the tracks will be too steep and uneven for a bicycle.

"I love walking. I've been walking every night in the last week."

Elizabeth 's look of indulgence reminded Calista of how her mother smiled whenever she'd assured her she could do something she'd never even tried. "I have strong boots, overalls and a cape that keeps out the weather and keeps me warm. Truly I have."

The silence stretched, and Calista wondered if everyone in the library could hear her heart beating. It echoed in her ears as her hope, strong as a child's desire for a treat, hung on Elizabeth's answer.

"Alright, you can come, but you will need to get Mathew's approval. I don't want people saying I kidnapped you, and tore you away from your husband."

Of course, the pretence needed to be maintained, especially as now several of the nearby readers had given up pretending to read and were openly watching them, and listening.

"I'll ask him tonight." Tell him more like it. He'd developed quite a bossy attitude which had begun to irritate her. "It's a wonderful opportunity for me to learn as well." She couldn't help herself and stood and hugged her friend, "Thank you, Elizabeth."

Elizabeth's strong laugh bounced around the room, "You mightn't thank me when we are knee deep in mud, or shivering over a campfire, but I can't fault your enthusiasm. You're right. It is a great learning opportunity, especially after your upbringing." And that was all that was said on the matter, especially with their audience, a few of whom then clapped, as if they had just been entertained. Hopefully, they were agreeing with Elizabeth's decision.

By the time they parted in the late afternoon, arrangements had been made, this time in whispered tones. They'd leave at six in the morning, with dawn breaking, as that was when Henry Phillips planned on starting his journey home. He was sharing lodgings with Elizabeth, further up the road, and his packhorse grazed in the paddock behind the hotel. He'd warned Elizabeth not to be late. He 'couldn't abide women who dawdled', had been his actual comment. He didn't sound like an enjoyable travelling companion, but nothing mattered to Calista, as long as she could accompany Elizabeth on what would be a real adventure—not something planned by her father, or Mathew.

All she had to do now was break the news to Mathew, who would not be pleased. However, it didn't really matter what he

thought. She was going to do it anyway.

⟶ ⟡ ⟵

"**Y**ou're what?" Mathew's voice rose in disbelief.
"Shhh, you don't have to tell the whole village."
He shook his head. "I can't believe you're serious. You're going to hike off into the interior with that young doctor, gathering leaves and things that might be useful in the future." He'd been sitting in bed, reading, but now he got out and stood at the foot of the bed, staring at her. "You are not going, Calista. I won't allow it."

Talk about red rag to a bull. Her mettle rose. How dare he give her orders? "Well, I've news for you. You, Mathew Althorp, have no say in what I will or will not do. I have told Elizabeth I'm going with her, and I'm going. She's depending on my help."

"Total rubbish. She's been doing this for a year. You told me that yourself." He walked back and forth. The room was quite small to pace in and he looked quite funny, being angry and trying to look as if he was in charge. "She's used to being on her own. She doesn't need your help any more than I do to fix up the broken things around here."

That hurt. She'd offered to help him. He obviously didn't think she could do anything useful, unless it was in the kitchen. She'd packed her backpack before he'd come up to bed and it sat beneath the window. Her boots and overalls were folded beside it, with her cape safely packed away. She would leave her two dresses here. As much as she loved wearing them they would be impractical in the bush and on muddy tracks.

"She's probably only humouring you, knowing you will want to come home by the end of the first day."

She held her jaws together to prevent a nasty answer creeping out. Did he think it hadn't taken determination and stamina to survive in the tunnels? Did he honestly think her life had been easy up to now? There was no way to explain what it felt like in the tunnels. The dim lighting, the claustrophobia of small rooms and the overpowering odours of people jammed together. Add to that the total lack of privacy and free will. Think conception without love—and she shuddered.

"Are you cold?" he asked, his tone soft as he paused his pacing and stood at the end of the bed.

"No, just a nasty thought passed through my mind."

He spread his arms, "Let's have a cuddle and see if leads anywhere. That'll warm you up," he said, a shy smile lighting his face and erasing the worry lines on his forehead.

A reasonable enough suggestion, but it irritated her. "I'm not cold and I don't want a cuddle, or anything except a good night's sleep, because I'm leaving early in the morning." A silence followed and the temperature of the room seemed to drop. "I will be back, you know. It's not like I'm going away forever. Elizabeth reckons two weeks at the most, more likely only ten days."

"I still think it's a stupid idea—and risky. Anything could happen. You could fall over, slip down a bank, break a leg—anything." His grip on the iron bed-end tightened and his knuckles whitened.

"Anything could just as easily happen to me here as well. Besides, learning about medical remedies and how to heal people could be very useful to the Carbonites. Then I can use my knowledge to help people. Isn't that what you all do?" She studied his face, seeing his resolve wavering.

He nodded in defeat and returned to the head of the bed and climbed in beside her. "Yes, that's a good reason to go, but it doesn't ease my worries. You know what I promised your father."

Not that again. "Really Mathew, don't bring that up all the time. I'm going with a doctor. Nobody will want to hurt her?" She rolled over away from him, tired of having to defend her decision.

"Do you know where you're going?"

"I don't know, exactly. It's somewhere inland," which sounded a bit unrealistic, but did it matter? "Elizabeth knows the man that is taking us. It's an area with lots of bush near to his block of land. I don't know what it's called."

"What's the man's name?"

She wanted to roll over and smack him on the leg. Honestly, his interrogation and resistance to her adventure was seriously irritating her. He didn't need every little detail. This was her adventure. She wanted to keep some information to herself. "I don't know," she lied. "He's staying at the same boarding house as Elizabeth. That's all I know." And that was all she was going to tell him.

"Total madness," he muttered as he sighed. The bed moved as he lay down, his husband-like performance over, she hoped.

She lay with her back to him, facing the window. The blind was up, but there wasn't a moon tonight. A few stars showed through the scudding clouds and she tried to imagine sleeping under them with the bush as a canopy like they'd done on their way here. It had been quite nice. Did Elizabeth have a tent? She couldn't carry anything more. Her backpack seemed heavy already. No use worrying. Elizabeth had been doing this for a whole year. She must be equipped with some sort of protection.

Mathew rested his hand on her hip, as if asking permission to proceed. She lifted it and dropped it behind her. Moments later he stroked her arm with a feather-light touch and she moved away and his hand lifted away. "No," she said. "Not tonight." He turned, giving a snort of frustration or anger, but she didn't care. Sometimes a girl had to have a rest and get a good night's sleep.

Despite this intention, it took a while for sleep to come. Long after Mathew's breathing had settled into a quiet rhythm and a gentle snore, her mind continued to roam her memories. Images of her mother and children distressed her but she pushed them away and concentrated on what the next day might hold. This, she was sure, was what living was all about; learning, travelling and helping people. Perhaps she could be a Carbonite eventually—just not yet, especially as she still told lies.

A fitful night's sleep meant she woke before dawn and slipped out of bed as quietly as she could. After dressing, she folded her nightdress and slipped it under her pillow. Not a practical garment to take camping and it would be waiting for her when she came back. She thought about kissing Mathew goodbye, but then once he was awake he'd probably want to talk her out of going, all over again. She didn't need to start the day with an argument and after a quick wash and with excitement tensing her spine, she tiptoed down the staircase.

The lock made a loud clonk as she shut the front door behind her and paused at the top of the steps to inhale the cold morning air. A soft mist had settled over the town and it parted and swept around her as she walked up the road to where Elizabeth and Henry stayed. A few lights winked on as early risers stirred. In her haste to leave she'd forgotten to eat so she sat on the back doorstep of the boarding house and ate some dried apples Betty had given her.

At least Betty had thought it a good idea to go with Elizabeth. It had been too hard not to share her excitement and Betty was such a good listener, and sensible too. She'd insisted Calista take the fruit, along with some hard-boiled eggs, all in her pack. The large canister of dried oats weighed a lot, but they would be so welcome at the end of the day, along with a pinch of salt from a small container and an even more precious tiny pot of honey.

Just as doubts began to niggle, Elizabeth's grin of welcome eased her inner turmoil.

"Good morning, Callie. You're nice and early. Good girl."

Of her own accord, Elizabeth had shortened her name to a familiar one. Up to now everyone outside had been very formal and called her Calista.

"Henry's in the horse paddock. He's loaded the horse and is waiting. Let's go."

Elizabeth took her hand and together they walked through the long damp grass, through the gate and joined Henry. He looked them over as if assessing a couple of prize beasts and grunted. Calista presumed it was approval, as they were early and dressed appropriately for their journey.

"You'll do," he said. "Follow me."

"I love your boots and overalls," Elizabeth whispered. "Good choice."

"Thank you," Calista replied, pleased she'd done something right. They walked single-file, Henry, his horse, Elizabeth and then her, through the straggly seed heads of the autumn grass. Henry opened the gate into the wide world and after she closed it she hurried to catch up. The thin dirt track worn into the hillside by many feet and hooves wound upward out of the mist into the morning's thin sunshine. As yet the mist hadn't burnt off down the valley but it signalled heat to come. Already the smell of grass and dung drifted on the morning's breeze.

The climb continued and her throat dried. She sipped some water, knowing she needed to conserve it. She wouldn't ask for a break, wouldn't puff and pant, nor would she complain. She might have over-committed her enthusiasm for walking but no matter what lay ahead she was determined to enjoy it.

Mathew straightened and leaned on the shovel. The wind caught his jacket and lifted his hat, which he jammed on again, his residue anger still evident in his furious digging of the neglected garden. Three days had passed and she still hadn't returned. His hope that Calista would find the trek too hard and return to him had been in vain. He scanned the pastures to the west. No sign of her still, and now the weather was deteriorating. A storm, blowing up from the south, promised heavy rain and wind, and his darling Calista was out there somewhere, unprotected, unprepared and possibly cold. His heart ached and he wondered if he could have handled it better. But what could he have done, except physically tie her to a chair? And still she probably would have trailed after that damn doctor when he finally freed her.

The need to get the seed in and covered before the rain meant he worked fast, broadcasting the lupins over the soil and raking them in. He stood, savouring a sense of satisfaction and didn't notice the two men until they spoke from behind him.

"Mathew Althorp?"

He turned and viewed the strangers taking in their pallor, their many layers of clothing, and then his gaze rested on their well-made boots. *Tunnellers.* "Who wants to know?"

"We understand that you are staying here, in this boarding house, with a young woman."

"Says who?" His heart raced but for the first time he was glad Calista had gone.

"Says everyone we talk to, so let's stop messing about." The taller man stepped closer, his breath reeked of tobacco and possibly rotten teeth. "We know who you are and we aren't interested in you. It's Calista Waterman we want." He spat on the ground. "She's needed back at home. Her mother's ill, her kids need her and the father of her children is most insistent she comes home immediately."

"She doesn't know the father of her children, so you're lying." He smiled to hide his apprehension. "Also, why would she want to return to the dark, dampness of the tunnels?"

"Oh, we've got a smart one here," cursed the second man. He hitched up his trousers and curled his hands into fists. "What you think, sonny, doesn't matter. You're nothing. We only want the girl."

"You're going to be disappointed, because you can't have her." Mathew swallowed and took a deep breath. "She's my wife and I'm not letting her go."

"Listen here young fellow, married or not it doesn't matter what you want. We know she's here. We know she's had her hair cut and we know the two of you have been here for over a week. Just tell us where she is and we'll collect her and be on our way."

"What if she doesn't want to go?"

"Pity that, but we will be taking her anyway." The taller man side-stepped and the shorter man took his place. "You really don't want to mess with us, boy, we're serious. Now, just take us to the girl and we'll be on our way."

"You're totally crazy, both of you. Do you honestly think for one moment that Calista would go with you—or that I would let you take her against her will?" His voice rose. "She ran away from the tunnels. Why would she return?" He lifted the shovel, wondering if he'd need it as protection.

Both shook their heads, implying he was stupid. "Something bad could happen to her kids, perhaps." the taller one murmured. "Or her mother," the other suggested.

Thank heavens she wasn't here to hear this. Their story eased his tension, even he knew that life was too precious to purposely harm any residents of the tunnels. He stood taller. "You're both wasting your time, and your threats, she's not here."

"She was here a few days ago. She was seen at the library." The smaller man raised his fists. "Don't mess with us, sonny, we're serious."

"I'm not lying. She's not here. She's gone." His voice cracked. "I'm glad she's gone, even if it broke my heart. At least you can't get her now."

The blow caught him by surprise. His head turned with the force of it and an explosion of pain consumed his mind. The shovel almost slipped from his grasp as he staggered, trying to regain his balance. His sight blurred from the blow, but with his feet planted apart he swung the shovel with a will filled with defiance. It moved in a low arc and connected with a thud to something or someone. Not the result he'd hoped. His assailant must have moved. Before he could blink his sight clear and step around, another blow hit his skull from behind. With that, he fell, his shoulder hitting the ground, his head following. His ribs screamed as a boot connected and then dirt flew into his eyes and mouth. He rolled on his knees, hoping to stand but a blow connected with his buttock, sending him face-down in the dirt. Choking with earth in his throat, spitting lupin seeds mixed with the metallic taste of blood, he retched, ashamed to hear himself whimpering.

"Where is she, boy?" A voice screamed in his ear.

He spat and managed to say "I don't know," before his hair was pulled and his chin lifted, only to have his jaw hit. Darkness descended and the pain disappeared, to return moments later when he felt himself being raised from the ground and stood on his feet. Someone supported him under his arms. He couldn't see. Dirt stung his eyes each time he tried to open them. "One last time—where is she?" The man's rotten breath assailed his senses, his spittle landed on Mathew's cheek and slid down. He wanted to wipe it away but he couldn't move, his arms were pinioned behind him. Two against one wasn't fair.

"Answer me!" His assailant screamed…any pretence of civility long gone.

"I don't know," he managed to whisper, hoping the darkness would return and take away the pain. Another blow landed, his ribs buckled. The world went dark and the pain receded to a tiny point in his brain, and then blinked out.

He had no idea how long he lay there but the pain woke him; that and the low murmuring of female voices. He groaned, desperate to make them stop moving him, wanting them to leave him alone in his misery. Now so cold he shivered, his body shaking, his legs jerking. He flailed with his arms, trying to push them away until they held his limbs down. Fearful someone would hit him he whispered "I don't know," time and again. They ignored his pleas. When they tried to sit him up he screamed as a red-hot iron stabbed into his side. If this was torture then he'd rather die. His last conscious thought was of Calista.

At least she was safer, wherever she was, than being here with him.

Chapter 16

"Home, sweet home." Henry Phillips sighed and wore a broad smile, something Calista had not seen in the two previous days and nights. It softened his looks, and for the first time she saw relief in his relaxed shoulders and joy as he spread his arms wide and said, "My kingdom. Look at it ladies, isn't it beautiful?"

They both nodded, but to Calista it just looked like more of the same scenery. Rolling grass-covered hills with scattered clumps of manuka and gorse. The steep hillsides were laced with thin meandering stock tracks, giving them a striped look in the afternoon sun. During their journey, the landscape had been split by the occasional deep gully, requiring them to follow paths worn deep by a multitude of travellers with two and four legs. Any downward track was followed by an equally difficult climb back to the rolling pasture, but the valley below them was a gentle curve in the land. Below them, tucked in against the hillside, the roof of a house could be seen, with a thin trail of smoke from one of the two chimneys. A narrow path, like a thin ribbon, ran to a small bridge and across be a meandering creek. Here and there, light glinted on the bends where the willow trees had left a space and allowed the afternoon sun to shine through.

"Is the stream your only source of water?" Elizabeth asked.

"There's a small spring further along the hillside from the house, which we use for drinking water, but for bathing and washing we cart from the stream."

"It's a fair way to haul water," Calista commented, wondering why the house hadn't been built closer to the stream.

"It is," Henry agreed, removing his hat and scratching his head,

"But when it rains up in the hills," he pointed toward the dark bush-clad horizon, "the stream becomes a roaring torrent, thirty yards wide at times. When that happens, we're glad we're living halfway up the hillside."

"And the bush you are taking us to, is that it…way in the distance?" Elizabeth's voice carried the weariness of their trek and echoed the despair Calista felt at the prospect of many more days to reach the promised source of medicine.

"Oh, no," Henry laughed. "It's just over the next hill." He pointed past the creek to the opposite rise. "There's a lush valley of bush there. We can go tomorrow. I thought you would both enjoy a night in a bed and a good home-cooked meal before we go looking for kawakawa and koromiko."

"Sounds wonderful," Calista said. The previous two nights had been far from fun and despite beds of bracken she'd been glad of her cloak, which had stretched and tucked around her. At least she'd been warm. Elizabeth used a sleeping bag that looked many years old, but was designed for snow, according to Elizabeth. Her gentle snoring, heard whenever discomfort disturbed Calista's sleep, confirmed its marvellous qualities.

"Come on, ladies, in half an hour we will be sitting down to a nice hot cup of tea." Henry set off with a spring in his step, and as had been their practice in the past few days, Elizabeth and Calista followed the horse, far enough back to avoid any of its natural functions, which to Calista's puzzlement came without warning or reason.

Later, with a hot mug of fresh tea enclosed in her hands and several warm scones nestled in her stomach, she struggled to stay awake. Smothering a yawn, she shook her head and paid attention to the discussion around the table.

"So…are we truly going to collect leaves tomorrow?" Elizabeth raised her eyebrows.

Henry nodded. "Of course, I promised, didn't I?"

"You did," said Elizabeth. "But I feel you have more pressing things on your mind."

"I do. I had an ulterior motive to get you here."

"I wondered about that." Elizabeth's smile took the edge off her statement.

Kayla, Henry's wife, laid her hand on her husband's arm. "We are grateful you are here, Doctor, whatever your reason for coming." Her gaze caressed her husband's face, but a sadness draped around her shoulders. "We have two healthy sons, but our daughter is poorly. We would be so grateful if you could look at her. Perhaps make a diagnosis? Hopefully tell us how we can improve her health."

"Of course, I will. If she is fed as well as you have fed us, then surely it can't be from any lack of nourishment." Elizabeth's smile seemed to cheer Kayla and she left the table to work at the bench.

"The children will be home from the neighbour's later. They go there once a week for schooling and company. I'd be grateful if you could be unobtrusive in your initial examination, Elizabeth. We try and make light of her complaints of aching bones and general lethargy."

Calista collected the mugs and plates, and offered to help Kayla with the evening meal but was shooed away. "Nonsense, go away with you. There're two beds in the spare room. Go and pick a bed and lie down."

She needed no further encouragement, and once she'd removed her boots, she slid onto the patchwork quilt with a sigh. The low murmur of voices lulled her to sleep and only the bright gabble of the children arriving home dragged her back to the present. That and the divine aroma of roast lamb. Would she ever get enough? She doubted it.

The evening passed with talk of rustlers taking stock, the network of neighbours, and the primitive party line they had established using the old telephone poles and wires. Already the phone was ringing with families wanting Elizabeth to visit them. Promises were made that after the collection of bush medicine, the doctor would do the rounds of all the families in the hamlet. Kayla was happy for them to use her kitchen to prepare the leaves, the bulk of which they would dry, and some they would steep in boiling water and use as a tonic. An early night to prepare for tomorrow's bush tramp was mooted and everyone went to bed.

A hand squeezing her shoulder woke Calista's and she sat up with a start. Her cry of exclamation was cut short by seeing Elizabeth beside her, a lit candle in her hand and her finger to her lips.

"Don't wake the children. I want to look at them in the dark. Henry will take us to their bedrooms. I want you to come with me. You could learn something from this."

Such craziness, creeping around in the dark. Why not examine the children in the daylight? But she slipped out of bed and padded after Elizabeth, with Henry again leading the way up a long hall that had many doors leading off each side. First they stopped at the boys' room, where Elizabeth insisted both candles be blown out. More craziness as they stood in the dark for many minutes before she was satisfied and gently nudged Calista out into the hall once more. Henry then led them to another door.

Again, they stood in the dark, and Calista had to swallow a gasp as a pale glow appeared around the sleeping child's head. Elizabeth grasped her elbow and ssshh'd in her ear. In the faint light, she could make out Elizabeth bending over, peering down at the child's hands and stepping back to Henry's side. At a tug on her gown, Calista followed them to the door, but paused to steal a backward glance at the faint halo of soft green light. Unbelievably beautiful, yet seemingly menacing at the same time.

Henry reached around her and pulled the door closed. They followed his candlelight held aloft, back down the hall, around the corner to the kitchen where he lit the lamp and turned to the ever-warm kettle on the back of the coal range. He poured hot water into three mugs and added a splash of something from a bottle kept high in a cupboard. With them all seated, he turned to Elizabeth and said, "So tell me. What's wrong with my little darling? It has to be something bad to cause her hair to glow like that." A tremor in his voice betrayed his fear, despite his wry smile. The candlelight cast even deeper shadows in the lines on his face and Calista's heart twisted in sympathy for the man's despair.

"It's called 'Angel's Kiss.'" Elizabeth paused before continuing. "As you saw, in the dark their hair glows like a halo and in severe cases, fingernails can also develop a glow." She gripped Henry's hand. "I'm sorry, Henry, but there is nothing I can do, except to give her medicine to keep her comfortable and take away any pain. I can't cure it—and while she may live for many years yet, she will probably be infertile—which in this day and age is not such a bad thing," she offered as if in comfort. "It's the curse of today—low radiation sickness. Some people seem to absorb radiation more readily than others. We all absorb it. There's no escaping it...but when it reaches a certain level within the body it becomes visible in the dark."

Calista sipped her drink and the alcohol content warmed her throat. Henry took several swallows before he spoke. "Will the medicine we make help?"

"Hopefully, yes. If it eases her discomfort, then she will want to eat more and will sleep better. You will know how to make more as she needs it. The kawakawa plant's leaves are good for all sorts of things, according to the books I've read. The plant seems to be an all-purpose panacea, plus koromiko is especially good for digestive and bowel problems, so I would think both will help her."

He nodded. "Then we will pick plenty, and I will nurture the bushes so we never run out."

"You will need to keep their location secret, or the trees could be stripped. I haven't been able to find any further south."

"I think this could be the most southern stand. It prefers a warmer climate. I know there's a lot in the Tasman Forest., further north." He sighed, a sound so sad that Calista's eyes prickled and she fought back her tears.

"Such a lovely name for an insidious sickness," Henry said.

"It is, and it's sometimes hard to diagnose because you need utter darkness to see it. Often in cities, there is light pollution from neighbour's houses and fire hearths in bedrooms and kitchens. Out here, it's easy to see." Elizabeth turned and asked, "Have you seen it before, Calista?"

She shook her head. "Never, but then in the tunnels we always have light; dull orange light everywhere, even in our apartments. It's never completely dark. Who knows how many people have Angel's Kiss there."

"Tunnels?" Henry said, "You are from the tunnels?"

She nodded.

"Dear God, you poor thing. You must be so glad to have escaped."

"I am," she said, but guilt gnawed at her soul. She'd left her mother, her children and now Mathew as well. She really was not a nice person. She needed to change, but not just yet. If any good was to come from her selfishness, it had to be this. To recognise this illness and help alleviate the symptoms.

Henry stood. "Goodnight, ladies. I'll go and break the news to Kayla. Thank you, Doctor Elizabeth. Tomorrow we will all pick leaves, a thank you from my family to you."

The following days were a blur of picking, drying, crushing and sorting. Calista and Elizabeth made poultices of healing manuka honey with dried kawakawa mixed in. They selected and packed the best leaves for tinctures and for seeping as a tonic. The large quantity they had picked was reduced to the cloth bags...now packed in their backpacks, after leaving some for Henry and Kayla. A few precious glass jars filled with the honey ointment were the only real weight added. Henry's bees had gifted him a surplus this year, and he refused to take any form of reimbursement except Elizabeth's promise to visit every household in their network, to check each family's health.

Feted like royalty, they traversed the countryside. Each family hosted them for one or two days, before sending them on to the next, usually guided and delivered by the eldest child so they didn't get lost. Elizabeth ran her clinics wherever it suited: a spare room, in the shade of a nearby tree, on the porch out of the wind, or down by a stream where the sound of the water gave her the privacy to talk to each family member for as long as needed. Calista wondered at the lightened mood of each family as they left. Whatever Elizabeth did, it certainly helped. All Calista could do was to dress wounds if asked and mix up tinctures and teas.

They were resting in the corner of the Pendegrast's porch, slumped in old deck chairs, sipping honey mead made from the family's hives. Sheltered from the southerly which carried with it the chill of the snow-capped mountains, the afternoon's watery sun warmed them into a drowsy state. Elizabeth yawned and refilled her glass.

"I shouldn't," she said. "This is my third. I could go to sleep. What bliss."

"Back to Cheviot tomorrow," Calista said, her feelings confused about their return. It had been such a wonderful break. The sound of a horse approaching mingled with the loud cackle of from one of the family's hens. She loved these sounds. Their peaceful solitude was abruptly torn apart with shouts from the other side of the house and heavy footsteps running up the passage toward them.

Maria Pendegrast flung back the screen door and called. "Dr Elizabeth, please come. The neighbours have brought their son. He's badly hurt."

Calista followed them out to the kitchen, where sprawled on an old couch laid a young boy; at the age of being gangly, nearly a man but not quite. His left leg was propped on a chair to keep it high, and a blood-stained cloth wrapped it from knee to ankle. His thigh above the wound had a tourniquet of rope tied tight. Whatever had happened he'd lost a lot of blood, his pallor almost grey.

Elizabeth kneeled next to the boy, her fingers unwinding the cloth and the iron-like smell of blood wafted to Calista as she stood nearby.

"It's all my fault," the boy's father said, despair etching deep lines in his face. "He was riding a young colt I've been breaking in. I truly thought he'd be able to hand him, but that horse has a nasty streak. It decided to get Alex off his back—took the bit between its jaws so Alex had no control and he ran the boy along the fence line." The father shuddered at the memory. "It's an old fence and the top wire is barbed wire, rusty as hell." By now Elizabeth had peeled the bandage away. "You can see the mess it's made." A hitch in his breath stopped the man from speaking.

Elizabeth turned to Wally Pendegrast. "Have you any alcohol, other than honey mead?"

Wally nodded. "I've some from a friend with a still. We add juniper berries and call it gin."

"Sounds ideal. Bring me a small bowl of it, and a couple of nips in a glass." She turned to Calista. "Please bring my medical bag, and then get a bowl of boiled warm water. Add salt to make a saline solution. I'll need my tweezers first before you make the saline up." Calista and Maria hurried off to complete their given tasks. By the time she returned with the saline solution, the doctor was picking bits of rust and debris from the jagged wound. It had been three hours since the injury and already the flesh looked proud and swollen. The bleeding had stopped and Calista noted the tourniquet gone. The tweezers were being dipped into the bowl of alcohol between retrievals and the young lad was sipping on the rest.

"Drink up, young man," Elizabeth ordered. "And when you've finished, your father will get you another."

"Are you making him drunk?" Maria said, her voice rising in disapproval.

"I want to numb his brain enough so the stitching of the wound won't make him jump. Do you have any better ideas?"

Maria shook her head and retrieved the gin bottle from the dresser and topped up the young man's glass. "Drink it all," she instructed him.

Finally, Elizabeth seemed happy and she pressed the edges of the wound together where she could, gently lifting torn flaps and matching them to their previous edges. In places pieces of flesh were missing. Calista watched, memorising everything she could see until Elizabeth looked up and said, "Right, young lady, your turn. You can sew it up."

"Me?" Calista's stomach clenched with both apprehension and excitement.

"Yes, because you haven't had three glasses of mead, and I have. Your hands will be steadier. Maria has sterilised the silk yarn and you will find the needles in my bag. I'm going to hold the skin together for you."

While she cut a length of yarn and threaded the needle she asked, "Any particular stitch?" A small attempt at levity.

"No, as long as each one is knotted and there is a sufficient slack between each stitch for the thread to stretch as skin heals, Ideally each stitch should be individual, but it's too late now to teach you the proper way. I should have thought to do it earlier."

Calista thought for a minute, then decided. "I'll do a knotted blanket stitch and leave a loop between each stitch."

Elizabeth nodded. "Fine, now let's do this as quickly as possible."

Their patient by now had his head lolled back against the couch, his mouth slack. He gave them a lopsided grin. "Good to go," he offered. "I might sleep through this."

"I doubt that," Elizabeth muttered as Calista took a deep breath, shut all sounds out of her brain and concentrated on making the torn flesh the neatest seam she'd ever mended despite sudden jerks and the occasional yelp from the patient.

When she was done, they soaked a strip of cotton in Kawakawa infusion and spread it with a thin layer of manuka honey. They eased this along the zig-zagged injury then wrapped the leg in fresh bandages.

"You will have a scar to go with you story," Elizabeth said, patting the young man on his arm and to his father she said, "Keep the leg elevated. Change the dressing every two days. I'll give you some ointment. Take the stitches out in a week, but if there are parts of the wound still healing leave those stitches in for a further few days."

The father, whose name it appeared was Harold, pumped

Elizabeth's arm, holding her hand so tightly she winced. She patted his shoulder and retrieved her arm.

"How can I repay you? If you hadn't been here, he may have lost his leg from infection, or worse, his life."

"Well, he didn't, and he won't," Elizabeth said pragmatically. "But if you have spare honey, I'd love some to use in my travels."

"Would you like a horse as well?"

The doctor laughed. "No, thank you. That would be just another thing to look after and feed. I'm happy to use my legs to travel—at least I know they won't bolt away on me."

After the injured lad was loaded onto an old trotting sulky that doubled as a wagon, they stood and watched the high-wheeled trap bounce its way down the farm track.

Elizabeth slipped her arm around Calista's shoulder. "You did a fine job, Callie. You should be proud. The scar should only be a fine white line in a year or so."

"You can thank my mother for that. Finally, the hours of unpicking she made me do has paid off." Pride lifted her spirits. She'd made a difference today, a big difference, to one young man's future. Elizabeth must feel like this most days.

The next afternoon, after twenty days away, they stood on the hill above Cheviot, looking down at the jumble of old houses. To Calista it seemed as if she had arrived home after an exhausting journey.

"I feel like Henry did, when we stopped above his house that day. 'Home, sweet home,' he said…and now I know how he felt."

"Good," said Elizabeth. "Because I'm leaving you here."

"What?" Calista swung round, staring at her friend. Surely, she'd misheard. "You're coming with me to Betty's, surely?"

Elizabeth shook her head slowly. "No, my lovely, I'm not. Young Christopher here will take you down to her back fence and see you safely over it, then he's coming back to take me north." She stepped close, wiped the tears from Calista's cheeks and hugged her. "You have a fine young man to go to and your whole life to lead. It's been a privilege knowing you and thank you for all your help."

Calista breath caught in her throat, her heart a cold stone in her chest. She'd assumed too much, yet again. "It's me who should be thanking you. I've learned so much and I know there's so much more I could learn. I'd really love to come with you." She choked back her tears and held Elizabeth's hands. "Please come, just for one night. Please. Why go north so soon?"

"There's more bush further north. Christopher knows the way—and more families to serve." She held Calista at arm's length. "Go now. Hurry down the hill. Go to your young man, and use what you've learned. Isn't that what the Carbonites do? Help people? That's why you came with me, to learn these things." Her smile creased her cheeks, her hair wisped around her gentle face. Calista gave her one quick kiss and whirled away, blinded by tears, pushing the branches aside roughly, hearing Christopher following but not daring to look back as she stumbled down the worn path toward Betty's hotel. She fixed her mind on all the exciting things she would tell Mathew. He'd be so proud of her now, and what she could do to help him and her father's band of men. She didn't love Mathew—yet, but he was the dearest of men, kind and thoughtful, and she really liked him. It was important that he admired her as well, and didn't just desire her. One day she hoped to know what true love felt like. What she'd experienced up to now, she guessed, was probably lust and curiosity and not love at all.

Until they met again, she'd think about Elizabeth at night in the dark when she could polish her memories, hide her tears, and be grateful for the days she had with the young doctor, not pine for the days she had not. She hadn't lost a sister, simply mislaid her.

At the back fence, she stopped and thanked Christopher. The boy nodded shyly and turned away. Within moments he'd disappeared into the scrub and she climbed the fence to pause on the stile and look at the garden plot, now covered in a carpet of new shoots. Mathew had been busy. There were new boards along the back wall and even the chicken run seemed to be standing taller on its corners. She imagined his face when he saw her and with a lighter mood she hurried up the back steps and opened the door into the kitchen.

Chapter 17

"Hullo?" she called. "I'm back. Anyone here?" Silence. She walked into the foyer and called up the stairs: "Betty, Mathew... I'm home." Some of her delight trickled away. This wasn't as she had imagined her homecoming to be. The house seemed too quiet.

Then Betty's head appeared over the top banister and a moment later she hurried down the stairs, across the foyer and threw the lock on the front door, then raced past Calista, through the kitchen and bolted the back door. Only then did she turn and smile. "Welcome back, girlie. I've been worried about you." She pointed to the table, "Take a seat, I'll make us a drink. You can tell me all about your travels."

Calista gripped the back of a chair and glanced around the room, wondering at the tension in the air and Betty's fluttering hands. "What's wrong? Why have you locked the doors? I'm not going to run away?" Then another thought hit her. "Where's Mathew?"

"Sit down. I'll make us a cup of tea." Betty turned away from her gaze.

"Something's wrong, isn't it?" Dread rose in her throat like a sharp stone. "Please, Betty, tell me."

The woman's shoulders slumped. She sighed and stepped close to take Calista's hands. It must be worse than she could imagine. Tears welled. "He's dead?" she whispered.

"No. Almost, but no...he's alive. He was badly injured."

"He fell off the roof?" It was the best guess she had. Again, Betty shook her head.

"What? Oh, please, just tell me." She slumped into the chair, faced Betty, her back steeled for the worst news possible.

"He was beaten, kicked unconscious. We found him in the back yard. It was three days before he could speak. His ribs were badly broken, he'd lost several back teeth and I suspect his jaw might have been cracked too. It was terribly swollen."

Calista stood, she had to get to him. "I can help. I've got medicine with me. Things Elizabeth taught me to make, herbal medicine that will ease his pain. Where is he?"

Betty tugged her down to sit once more. "He's back in Quake City. I put him on a cart two days ago, on a mattress, wrapped up warm. I sent him back to your father, because I didn't know where you were, or if you were safe. He needed more nursing and needed to be kept safe. A trusted friend took him, covered from prying eyes." Betty's fingers interlocked and twisted. Her brow furrowed as she sat, silent, appearing to wait for Calista to respond.

He was alive and safe. Her panic eased. "But who would beat him? He's such a gentle soul. Why would anyone do that?"

Betty chewed her lip, looking to the back door and into the foyer before catching her gaze once more. "It was you they wanted. They beat him to find out where you were. They'd been asking questions in the town and had identified you as being with him. If you hadn't gone with the doctor they would have taken you. He didn't tell them where you were. He kept telling us that."

"He couldn't. He didn't know, because I didn't tell him which direction I was going. It was a childish thing I did, to keep that information to myself—but perhaps it was a lucky thing as well. He couldn't tell them what he didn't know, no matter how much they beat him."

"That's what he said too, once he could talk."

Calista pointed, "And the doors? You've locked me in?"

"You're wrong, I've locked everyone else out," Betty said. "Did you see anyone when you arrived?"

"No, I came down from the hill. A young man came with me, then he went back to Elizabeth. We saw no-one. I climbed the back fence, to surprise you and Mathew." The enormity of it hit her. Men wanted her. They beat Mathew to find her. They were still out there, somewhere. Was it the Mic's or Casper's men? Fear gripped her. This time there were no Carbonites standing guard. Now Betty was at risk also. Somehow she had to get back to the stockade. But how—and when would it be safe to travel?

"You're to stay hidden until I work out how to get you back to your father."

She nodded. She was used to being inside. It wouldn't be a new experience, just living like she used to, all the time. At least it wasn't dark this time and there were no hideous sodium lights in this house.

"I could cycle back, quickly." She could do it alone, surely?

"No chance. I sent the bikes back with Mathew. We had no idea if you'd even return. Plus, they were too valuable for me to keep here. I hid them under the blankets, with Mathew. The Carbonites needed them."

Betty's warm hand squeezed her shoulder and a light kiss landed on her head. It eased her despair. "Don't worry, sweetie," Betty said, "I'll sort something out. It might take a few days. I'll get a radio message to Aaron that you're safe. He's been worried sick."

Calista curved her arms on the table top and laid her head on them. After the excitement and satisfaction of her trip with Elizabeth, her return revealed only fresh fear. It was like she carried a plague that infected everything she touched. Poor Mathew. But if she could get to him she could help him heal. Koromiko helped to heal bones, the book said. Perhaps she could get Betty to bring the book from the library so she could study it while she stayed hidden. At least she'd be doing something useful while she waited.

Ten days later, she dressed in the dark before dawn, climbed under the covers on the back of a cart, on to the musty smelling mattress and nestled down for the long trip back to Quake city. Betty's friend had agreed to do another trip, but it had taken all the coins in Calista's money belt to convince him.

It was a bouncy, hard trip with a cool welcome at his cousin's place overnight, with scant hospitality. The next day, once they reached the city's limits, she climbed onto the seat beside him, a scarf tied over her head to hide her blond curls, and an old checked blanket converted into a cloak, made her look like an old lady as long as she hunched her shoulders. An easy task as she was bone-weary from the journey.

The cart stopped at the end of the street. She could see the stockade's high gates and the lights on the top floor. Her heart lifted. What a welcoming sight.

"My horse is knackered. I'm going straight on. You can walk the rest of the way." The driver's surliness hurt. He'd been well paid, but she accepted that this was his one show of power—to make her walk the last little way.

One hundred yards from safety. She could do that easily, she could run that distance in a few minutes. In the darkness, she shrugged off the blanket disguise and climbed down from the dray, then with murmured thanks and her backpack held in one hand she broke into a run for home.

She nearly made it.

"Calista!" A man's voice called out and she stopped and turned, expecting to see one of her Carbonite friends.

"Calista Waterman?"

"Yes, I'm back." She peered into the murkiness, fog swirling now around her feet. "Who is it?"

Arms wrapped around her from behind. An odour of unwashed clothing and coal dust assailed her senses as a hoarse voice said, "Miss Calista, we've come to take you home. You're sorely missed by your children, and your mother is unwell. You're needed at home, not wasting your time consorting with the Carbonites."

"No! I'm not ready to return yet." She struggled against the man's grip, but he forced her to walk forward past the stockade's high gates and down an alleyway, where another man grabbed her by the wrist and dragged her into a shed.

She screamed, "Help me. Someone please help me!" Her cry echoed in the dark as it bounced on the shed's walls. A rough palm slapped her face and she gasped.

"Stop it." She yelled. "Stop dragging me around. I'm not an animal." She grasped her pendant and pressed it, hope flaring briefly before a gag was shoved roughly between her teeth and tied behind, catching her hair in the knot.

Surely now she would be rescued, this close to the stockade?

"You're not an animal, but you're worth more than a prized heifer, young lady. You'll bring us a lot of money when we get you home," one of her assailants said, triumph filling his voice with satisfaction as he grabbed her flailing arms and held them while the other man tied her wrists together.

She struggled against their efforts to tie her, kicking out, hitting something soft. The following curse gave a moment of satisfaction.

If you continue to kick, we shall tie your legs together as well."

The threat enough to stop her kicking but she continued to writhe, hoping to break free.

In the darkness, the smell of animal manure wafted and nearby the thud of a hoof and the frightened squeal of a horse bounced around the walls, followed by the creak of wagon wheels.

One man held her by her bound wrists. The other could be heard harnessing the horse and cursing against the wayward shafts of the wagon. Outside somewhere in the dark a child's cry broke the silence. She couldn't scream with a mouthful of rag, the taste threatening to make her vomit. Her muffled protests were ignored, except for a punch on her arm. "Be quiet. We won't hurt you if you keep quiet. Scream and yell anymore, and we might be forced to knock you out."

At least her legs were free. If only she could grab a moment and run—anywhere, as long it was out of this building and into the street. She twisted, trying to catch her captor unaware, but when he moved off she realised she'd been tied to something. The two men murmured together, throwing things onto the wagon base. She could hear the thumps as things landed. How many minutes had passed? She bent down over her hands, low enough for her fingers to find the pendant and press the back of it again and again. Her sight was adjusting to the dark and at the sound of footsteps she straightened, frightened they would see the pendant and take it away.

Moments later she was manhandled onto a wagon and guided to a mattress.

"Lie down there and keep quiet. Once we're clear, I'll remove the gag. If you keep struggling it'll stay there." At that sickening thought, she calmed her movements, breathed deeply and fumbled with her tied hands to ease down. Her body ached from the day's journey and her struggle to be free. Weariness swamped her as a blanket fell over her. The mould and dust made her cough behind the dirty cloth. Her backpack arrived with a thump beside her and she reached to pull it closer. At least she had her medicines.

They said they wouldn't hurt her. Surely, she'd be rescued at any minute. This close to the stockade they would all know she needed them. With both hands, she clasped her pendant and repeatedly pressed its underside, whispering, 'Please Father, please William, please Mathew…someone please, come and get me."

But no one came. The wagon lurched onward under the night's dark cloak, travelling at a steady pace, pulled by a horse that seemed in a hurry to be somewhere else. With each bump in the road and turn in direction she knew she was beyond rescue. No-one had heard her distress signal.

The vibration of his pendant dragged Mathew from a deep slumber, and he sat up, his ribs protesting at the sudden strenuous requirement. He gasped, his arm against his ribs, one hand wrapped around his pendant, while he fought the pain blurring his thinking. Calista! She must be close. His heart filled with hope for an instant, then a band of fear gripped it in a vice—she must be in danger. That's why his pendant had vibrated.

He swung his legs out of bed, paused to gather his strength the limped across the wooden floor to the door and along the mezzanine passageway. Calling out "Mary, Mary," he descended the stairs, gripping the banister for support, cursing his injuries and gulping great breaths as panic swept through him. He had to get outside. He must go to her, wherever she was. Damn his broken ribs, bruised body and weak legs.

The kitchen was empty, only the enticing aroma of their evening meal filled the space. He turned around and using the wall for support hobbled along the hall to Mary's room calling out. "Mary! Mary! Anybody? Help me. Calista needs us."

Mary Sutton came out of a room and hurried toward him, rubbing her eyes, and running her hands over her hair, pushing stray strands behind her ears. "What is it, boy? I was having a wee lie-down. You should be resting too. I gave you a draught to ease the pain." She held him by his shoulders, held his gaze and her very presence calmed him. He took a deep breath.

"Calista is nearby. She's in trouble. My pendant woke me, vibrating. She must be very close. We have to open the gates and look for her. Where is everybody?" Tears prickled at the back of his eyes and he blinked rapidly. The last thing he needed was to be distracted by stupid tears. Ever since the beating, he'd had to fight to control his emotions.

"Yes, you and I can do that," Mary said and helped him back up the hall. Once in the main foyer she grabbed a large key off its hook and helped him down the steps, out into the yard.

"Where is everyone?" he kept asking.

As she unlocked the small door next to the high gates she explained, "Aaron is at home for the evening with Belinda and the children. Benjamin and Simon are away getting the final load of coal before winter strikes. Now…where's Kyle? I remember, he's at the hospital this evening and William will be back from the gardens to share our evening meal any time now… so, there's just you and me here."

With the doorway open, she ushered him through, and they stood outside the stockade, peering both ways along the road, as the fog thickened, and the velvet dusk spread.

His pendant vibrated again and then once more, fainter this time as if moving away.

"Calista!" he shouted, "Calista, we're here! Where are you?"

In the stillness, the sound of a horse's hooves clip-clopped faintly then faded to silence. He stared at the heavens, his mind pleading for any god to help him, but the light from the stars winked out as the fog wrapped them in its damp grip, as if the gods were ignoring him.

"She's gone, Mary." His breath guttered as despair swept over him. "She was here, and the gates were locked. Someone has taken her. I know it. I just know it."

Mary hugged him, strong arms around his frail shoulders, and he leaned into her ample bosom. "Those damn tunnellers," he swore. "I bet they were waiting for her; waiting to catch her when she came home."

They stood outside, calling, then listening, until the cold seeped through their clothes and chilled them.

"Enough," Mary said. "We've lost her." She guided him back through the small doorway, "They desperately want her returned, so she will be safe. No harm will come to her, Mathew."

"If only I'd been awake. I should have been waiting at the gate."

"You will be more useful to her when you are healed. Besides, we were waiting to hear from Betty that she had found a way to get her back—and we hadn't heard." She led him into the house, sat him at the kitchen table and began to lay the table for their meal. "She's a strong lass. She'll be fine. At least we know we can get her out of the tunnels. We've done it once. We'll do it again."

Mathew stiffened his back, ignoring the pain in his side. He held his fists up. "I'm going to learn how to use these. I'm tired of being a pacifist. I'm going to rescue her, Mary, just as soon as I'm well enough."

"I know you will. I'm sure the others will help you any way they can, but in the meantime, you need to rest, eat well and then you can concentrate on learning the skills you'll need to fight for her freedom."

With that, she placed a large bowl of chicken broth in front of him, as well as several thick slices of bread on a plate. "Now, eat that up, and then there's meat pie to follow." She ruffled his hair. "I'm determined to get you strong again. We all want her back here as much as you do. It's just plain bad luck there was no one on duty." She sat opposite him, waiting for him to start. "I always think that bad luck is followed by good luck. How else would we know when bad luck strikes without a comparison? I'm sure things will work out."

He nodded. Mary had a point. Their time in Cheviot had been wonderful, a dose of good luck. Tonight's events were bad luck, very bad luck. But good luck would come again. He'd make it happen if it was the last thing he did with his life. He'd bring Calista back to Quake City, to him and to the Carbonites, where she belonged.

Chapter 18

"**I** see you've got your breeder back," Aric Sanson tapped the agenda in front of him. "I bet that cost you a pretty penny and a bit more."

Wallace Howe gritted his teeth and took a deep breath. He wouldn't rise to Aric's sarcasm. "Yes," he said, "It wasn't a cheap exercise, but it was worth it. She's back looking after my children as she should be."

"I also see further in the report that she has fomented unrest among the workers. Talking about her little adventure and telling them we are all subject to radiation, even here in the tunnels." He pointed his finger at Wallace. "It's not a good look, Wally. You need to have a word with her. Much more of this and we'll have to take action."

"Like what?" Wallace challenged. "You know how valuable breeders are, regardless of whose sperm we use, and she's due for another insemination. I have her booked in for her preliminary visit with Dr Webb at the end of this week."

"I suppose after all the expense, you expect your sperm to be used. Have you spoken to Dr Webb? Booked yourself in, along with a couple of sexy magazines?"

"Stop it, you two." Peter Pengally rapped the table with his gavel. "I'm fed up with the continuous sparring. If you can't get along, then I shall call an extraordinary meeting of the colony and vote two new members onto the committee. There's no shortage of willing volunteers." He glared at both men and after a pause, continued, "We are here to discuss the running of this community, not bicker over who has the most children." He held Aric's gaze.

"And you aren't pearly white either. How many children have you sired? And don't be tempted to lie because I can access the records if I doubt your answer."

"Four," Aric mumbled, his gaze dropping to the papers in front of him.

"Then I think we will drop the subject, except for the matter of Calista Waterman causing unrest. That's a serious matter. I will take up with her personally, neither of you needs to be involved."

"Threatening to throw her out of the tunnels is probably just what she's wanting," Wallace said. "If we can get her pregnant quickly, that should settle her down; female hormones and all that. It usually makes them more biddable, so I'm told."

"We are not discussing insemination any further today. She requires an examination before we take any further decisions. However," Peter now fixed Wallace with a steely gaze and sniffed. "Your report of how she was returned successfully would be appreciated."

Wallace had anticipated this moment and prepared his report which he now read. He delivered it in a flat tone, eliminating any of the relief he'd experienced or any mention of the huge dent it had made in his private savings. "Further to my previous report, my scouts lost track of her north of Quake city in the town of Cheviot. They returned to the headquarters of the Carbonites reckoning on her eventual return to base. Once settled into the area, they made themselves useful to the neighbours by carrying out repairs on homes and stables, always watching for her return and listening to local gossip. As luck would have it, she returned one evening when all the Carbonites were away, except for one."

He took a breath and hurried over the next bit. "Luckily, the young man was still incapacitated from his visit to Cheviot and in no position to give chase. With darkness on their side, they were able to take her by surprise and transported her directly to Arthur's Pass rail station. From there the two scouts accompanied her on the next returning train to Erewhon Station, where they reported to me personally. I then took her to her living quarters where she was reunited with her mother and children." He didn't add it gave him an excuse to spend time with the children and observe their healthy development.

"I also instructed her to report for work the next morning at the hydroponic gardens. She's been back a month and is working well. Except for spreading lies and telling stories about her adventure, as she calls it, she has settled back in. I don't think her time outside has caused any permanent damage."

"You hope," Aric muttered.

"One query," Peter said. "How did your men know the remaining Carbonite was incapacitated and wouldn't be able to follow them?"

Wallace had hoped to skip over this detail. The over-eagerness of his scouts to earn their bonuses would now be revealed.

"Did your men have a spy within the stockade?" Peter's interest was piqued.

"No, the locals constantly chatter about the Carbonites, probably because they are the local charity."

"That doesn't answer my question. I suspect your men were involved in this Carbonite's injury. How else would they know he was in no position to give chase?"

Wallace squirmed in his seat and added, "Unfortunately, my men were rather over enthusiastic in their questioning of the young man, when they caught up with him in Cheviot. He couldn't tell them where Calista had gone to. I understand their frustration caused them to leave him rather injured." Peter's intake of breath didn't auger well. "Also, they saw him being returned to the stockade in a wagon a week later," Wallace added, which in retrospect wasn't a wise thing to say and didn't improve Peter's mood.

"Rather injured? Returned to the Stockade on a wagon and several weeks later he's still incapacitated? I thought I said I wanted no violence in retrieving her?" He banged the table. "I abhor violence! It seems to me we have imported nothing but trouble by dragging her back. It would have been better to leave her to return of her own accord. It's not as if her father doesn't know how to get in and out of here." Peter Pengally twisted his lips in disgust. "You are on a short leash, Wallace. One more stupid move like this, over one young breeder, and I'll be holding that election meeting."

Wallace's heart thumped and his stomach turned. He'd pushed his luck to the very edge with this. He'd have to step right back if he wanted to have some control over his children's future. Now was certainly not the time to approach Peter with his appeal for another child.

"Now, on to more serious matters," Peter said, sniffing loudly and blowing his nose into a grey rag, "like the water supply to the gardens and do we have sufficient coal imported to see us through the winter?" The lights flickered and dimmed. After a moment of near darkness, they regained their eerie glow. "Plus, we have to get the damn generators repaired. The last thing we need is a blackout."

With that, the three men turned their attention to the rest of the agenda. Wallace hoped Peter Pengally would have more serious matters to hold his attention in the immediate future than Calista Waterman; mother of Wallace's two children, escapee returned and now trouble-maker. Perhaps he should have left her outside after all.

In the hydroponic gardens, Calista was able to briefly pretend to be outside, surrounded by climbing beans, telegraph cucumber vines and the sprawling tomatoes. Especially near the tomatoes, as their smell overpowered the used ozone odour of the tunnels. At least here in the gardens the air seemed fresher as the plants filtered and cleaned it. Lost in thought, working on auto-pilot she checked the nutrient flow, ensured each plant received sufficient food and searched for insects. It amazed her that even here bugs seemed to find a way in—and managed to breed.

A cough behind her caused her to turn around, expecting to see one of her co-workers, but instead, Mr Pengally, chairman of the community committee stood there, twisting a small rag in his fingers before he pushed it into his trousers' pocket and put his hand out.

"Miss Waterman?"

"Yes, Mr Pengally, that's me." She shook his hand and resisted wiping her hand on her overalls. *What could he want?* The committee members didn't generally mix with the residents. Probably because they didn't want to hear the constant complaints. Everyone said finding a repairman to lodge a request with was like looking for gold in the tunnel walls. "How can I help you? Would you like a tour of the gardens? Are you on an inspection tour?"

"No, I've come to see you."

This set her heart pounding. *What now?* It was bad enough being back and trying to find a way out. Was she about to be punished for her escapade? She stood tall and although her jaw ached, she held her silence. She would not offer an excuse. The scouts had proudly told her the committee had sent them to retrieve her. She held his gaze and thought about her father, the stockade and Mathew — all the good things she'd experienced. The man seemed to be embarrassed for some reason. Perhaps he wasn't used to having his gaze met and held. Eventually he spoke. "It's good to have you back. I'm very pleased. The whole committee is pleased that you've returned."

"It wasn't my idea. I'd rather have stayed where I was." Her thoughts rushed out. "Are you aware that I was virtually kidnapped, bound, and returned here like a criminal. At least that's what it felt like at the time." Anger heated her face and she flicked her hair off her forehead.

"Sorry about that, but we considered it a necessity. You are a valued member of this community and we needed you to return."

"Why? My children were being well looked after by my mother. Working in the gardens isn't a specialised skill. There wasn't any great need for me to hurry back." She took a step back and turned to examine a nearby plant.

"But there was—and still is." Pengally followed her as she moved further up the row. "You are scheduled to have another child." When she didn't acknowledge his statement he added, "We have invested much time and effort into your well-being. You've had the best of food and comfort, not to mention your spacious accommodation. We feel it's time you did your part by returning the favours." He sniffed loudly. "Accordingly, you are scheduled to see Dr Webb tomorrow morning at ten. You can visit him before you come to work."

She continued to move along the row, ignoring his words, and he followed, his tone now hardening. "While you can rudely ignore me, you can't ignore your responsibilities to the community. I expect you to see Dr Webb and if you don't there will be consequences."

He'd resorted to threats? She swung around to face him. "What consequences?"

"You might find your family is moved to other accommodation, not as spacious. "

This made her snort. "It can't get much smaller than it is for the four of us, let alone adding a baby."

"Other people have less room," he snarled, "and perhaps you

won't be given as much food. Your mother may have to return to work…and your children will be placed in childcare."

She inhaled a deep breath to calm her thudding heart. "Are you threatening me, Mr Pengally? Is this the way the community committee works?"

"We always consider the community's wellbeing is our priority. You having another child is in the community's best interests. We need more workers for the future." He sighed and his tone changed as if she were of low intelligence. "As I pointed out, if you resist then your living standards could suffer."

"I've never been threatened before, in all the years I have lived within these walls, but then I'd never been outside before—and tasted freedom. I don't like being threatened. Why pick on me? There are other young girls here of breeding age and good little mothers. Why can't they increase their birth rate?" He broke their gaze, looked away and scanned the gardens, but didn't answer her. She tried again. "Why just me? I've already had two children. I don't want to be inseminated again." Her voice broke and she swallowed hard to regain her composure.

"It's the wish of the father of your other two children that you have another."

"Then let him have it—whoever he is."

"You don't know?" Pengally's eyebrows shot up so far his brow creased.

"No, I've no idea who the father of my children is, except it's the same person. I presume it's one of the younger members of the community."

Pengally shook his head slowly. "Why do you think you get special treatment? Surely you are not so naïve that you haven't worked it out?"

Now it was her turn to shake her head. "I've no idea," she murmured and plucked the leaf off a nearby capsicum.

He let out an explosive sound of exasperation. "Well, I'll tell you who it is. Wallace Howe is the father of your children, the man who gave you your wonderful cape. A cape many residents would love to own."

She remembered Mr Howe's visit after Caleb was born, and recalled how he often dropped in to check on her and Mother's health. Of course! He probably really wanted to see his children.

"That old man?" She couldn't suppress a shudder.

"He's not that old. In his early fifties, about the same age as me." Pengally's face reddened, and he stood taller and tucked in his belly.

Memories roiled through her mind, of Wallace Howe visiting their rooms, stopping her in the tunnels to enquire after her family. His forced smile whenever he met her. It all fell into place and she gagged. "Excuse me, I have a bit of nausea at present and I need to keep working. I have more rows to check before I can go home this evening."

"Of course," he backed away. "Then I can expect you to keep your appointment with Dr Webb in the morning?"

She nodded. She'd go, but there was no way she would be inseminated again—ever. Dr Webb was in for a surprise.

If only she had a map of the tunnels and the service passages. Somehow she had to get out of this place, with her children and her mother.

The back of her eyes prickled and she fought back tears of rage. "He threatened me, Mother. He said he'd put us into smaller accommodation. That you'd have to go to work and Caleb and Vanily would go into day-care. You know that's a poky place where the children all exchange illnesses, colds and nits." She paced around the small room as her mother pointed to the speakers on the wall. "I don't give a damn if they listen, I'm not going to be inseminated by sperm from an old man."

She followed her mother into the small bathroom and once the toilet had been flushed her mother whispered beneath the noise. "You mustn't make trouble. It will cause bad things to happen to us."

"You are too compliant, Mother," she hissed. "You need to go outside and smell freedom. It's hard out there, but it's also wonderful in between the hard bits. Haven't you ever wanted to go out with Father? Why didn't we both go with him the first time he left?" She'd wondered about this in the past weeks. Perhaps if her mother had gone then her father wouldn't have started another family. And, worst still, how would her mother react when she found out? Because she would eventually find out, not that Calista intended telling her.

In a low tone, her mother said, "I've always been frightened of large spaces. I was born in here. I know nothing else. I'm frightened of the outside. Just the thought of it makes me stressed."

"Well, you'd better get your head around it, because as soon as I can find a way out you are coming with me and the children, I am not having my children grow up in half-light, like white slugs under a barrel. I want them to run and roll in the grass. Climb trees, learn to swim, all the things normal kids do—and you're coming with us." As she opened the door and turned to walk into the lounge she caught the slow shake of her mother's head in her peripheral vision. She hoped her mother was expressing despair, not refusal to join her.

Once they were together at the kitchen table, sharing a cup of tea, her mother asked, "Are you going to see Dr Webb in the morning?"

"I am," she said firmly. "But I'm telling you now, I won't be inseminated."

Chapter 19

"Good morning, Calista." Dr Webb's smile was genuine. He looked truly delighted to see her. "Take a seat while I catch up on your notes."

She sat beside his desk, scanning the various charts on the wall of muscles, bone structure and various organs of the body. A bit like other people would put up posters of landscapes or hang pictures of old family members on their walls, Dr Webb educated his patients with graphics of his favourite subject—medicine.

He finished reading and looked up. "Well, young lady...I see you've been busy—and having a real adventure by the sound of it. Off in the night with your father and out into the big wide world. Did you enjoy it?" He seemed genuinely interested and as most people had murmured for her to be quiet, or stop telling lies, she smiled in return to his query.

"I did. I had some wonderful times—and a few awful ones. Like being captured and taken away from Quake City on the back of a wagon; tied up like a criminal, pushed in and out of overnight houses, sleeping on smelly beds, and finally bundled onto the train at Arthur's Pass to be marched off here at Erewhon Station and told to go home and get back to work. That part wasn't nice at all." Dr Webb didn't speak, so she continued. "It's all so different out there from what we are told. Yes, people are poor, and often hungry...but they are happy to be alive and busy getting on with life—getting married and having children."

"Mm, and that brings me to why you are here." He checked the file. "I have received notice that you are to be assessed to ensure you are healthy enough to receive another insemination." When she didn't say anything, he checked his notes again. "That will make three children for you."

"I'm not having any insemination. Not now. Not ever again."

"Please don't make my job any harder than it is, Calista. You look to be extremely healthy. Your hair is lovely short by the way. I like how it curls around your face. It's a good cut. You had a good barber do it?"

"I did, In Cheviot. It needs doing again. The curls are growing out into waves."

"I know Cheviot. I grew up around there," he said.

"What are you doing in here, then?" Her thought blurted out before she could stop it.

"Doctors are needed everywhere and I had a calling to come into the tunnels. An old family friend persuaded me that I could do more good here than I could outside." He sighed. "I thought I'd just stay for a couple of years, but I can never find the right time to leave, so I'm still here fifteen years later."

"So you know how to get out?" Her hopes rose only to fall at the shake of his head.

"Sorry dear, I can't tell you that. It's something you need to work out yourself. The Mics would not be happy if I told you the route."

"So you call them the Mics too. That's what my father calls them: 'Men In Charge'. He doesn't like them."

"They do the best they can with what they have. Remember the original settlers came into the tunnels to work here, establish the communities up and down the train line, and to keep safe from the radiation. They were volunteers. Many fought to get here."

"But you and I know that was a false hope. There's as much radiation in here as outside."

"It's not proven. We could easily be better off." He closed the file with a snap. "Come on young lady, up on the examination couch. Let's see how your body is. I need to examine you thoroughly."

"You might be surprised with what you find," she said, as she slipped out of her outer clothes, down to her underwear and climbed up on the bed.

Dr Webb prodded and pushed, kneaded and sighed. Examined her eyes and ears through his instruments and had her stand on his scales before he noted her weight on a small pad and returned to his desk. "You can get dressed, Calista, then come and sit down again."

She dressed and sat quietly, waiting for what she knew he was going to say. She was so sure of her diagnosis—and secretly delighted.

Eventually, he finished making notes, closed the file again and sat looking at her, a small lift at the corner of his mouth, a half-smile. "You know what I'm going to say, don't you? She nodded. "After having two children, you must know all the signs." She nodded again, waiting for him to say it. Once he uttered the words, she would know it was true.

"You're pregnant already. I'd guess you are about eight weeks gone. Not enough to show yet, but I presume you are experiencing nausea and bouts of tiredness."

"Yes, I'm getting very sleepy in the afternoon, but it was the morning sickness that aroused my suspicions. I'd had such an eventful few weeks that I'd lost track of my periods."

"Well, congratulations, young lady. Your adventures obviously involved a sexual experience." He smiled broadly. "I hope it was worth it."

Keeping as formal as possible she said, "It was very educational, thank you."

"And this time you know the father of your child?"

"I certainly do. He's a young man, quite good looking in a rugged sort of way—and very kind and thoughtful. He says he loves me."

"Do you love him?" His eyebrows rose with his query.

"Not yet, but I might in the future. I need more time with him, to fall in love. This is why I must find a way out." She twisted her hands in her lap. "Please, Dr Webb, help me get out. He doesn't know he's going to be a father."

"I can't do that. I'm sorry. My job is to look after your health and that of your children." He pointed at her stomach, "Including that little one, so I need to you eat well and rest when you need to. Shall I give you a note to your supervisor explaining why?"

"Oh no, please don't do that." Fear ran like iced water down her spine. "I don't want anyone to know yet, especially not the community committee. I've just found out that one of them is the father of my two children. He might restrain me somehow. Stop me from leaving by taking my children away. Mr Pengally has just told me Wallace Howe wants me to have another of his children. What is he going to say when he finds out I'm pregnant already?" Tears welled and slipped down her cheeks.

Dr Webb reached and patted her hand. "Patient confidentiality will cover all that, for the moment. I'll tell him I examined you and you are exceedingly healthy. There are other things I can arrange to create delays before a date is set for insemination. Not that it would work. It would be unfair for him to believe you are carrying his child and time-wise the birth would reveal the error." He thought for a moment. "I can understand why you need to leave the tunnels again, so leave it with me and I'll see what I can do. Others know all the exits down the mountain."

He stood and she knew the appointment had ended. She rose and hugged the kindly man.

He held her at arm's length, holding her gaze, his eyes twinkling. "You'll be fine. Remember the oath I took when I became a doctor: 'First do no harm". You will be safe in my care, child. Just carry on as normal. We will find a way out of this muddle; just try not to fall asleep at work. Someone might get suspicious."

At the door, she paused and turned to ask, "Dr Webb have you ever heard of Angel's Kiss?"

He nodded. "We were taught about it in medical school, but I've never seen a case."

"I have. I saw it with Doctor Elizabeth when we went inland hunting plants for Māori remedies. A young girl had it. You need complete darkness to see the hair glow—and the nails in severe cases. It's a beautiful sight for something so deadly."

"There may be cases in the tunnels," he said. "But we never have complete darkness, so I wouldn't know if any of my patients have it." He smiled, "Don't you go worrying your head about things like that. I'm sure you and your children are fine."

She hadn't been thinking of her children, rather concerned more for her mother, who had lived inside all her life. Since she'd returned she'd noticed how frail and tired her mother seemed, and her guilt weighed heavily for leaving her mother to look after the children for months. It had been a selfish thing to do, even if her mother had never complained, not once. One thing was certain; when she left next time her mother would be coming. They were a unit and she wanted her whole family to be free.

"Thank you again, Dr Webb." Calista raised a hand in farewell and shut the door behind her. Only then did she allow the joy she'd been holding down for days to bubble up. She laughed out loud and set off down the passage, fitting in a skip now and then. She was carrying Mathew's baby. She wasn't imaging it. It wasn't the result of the stress of being kidnapped; she truly was pregnant.

This child would be born outside, with its father nearby if possible. Somehow, sometime soon, she was going to leave these cursed walls once and for all.

Aaron Waterman leaned against the veranda post and gazed with admiration as the two men stepped and twisted around the centre of the courtyard as if in a dance; their long batons cracking like rifle shots as they collided. They whirled, sparred with thrusts, batons meeting, clacking, then withdrawing to circle again. Each thrust calculated and executed with grace. It wasn't a whirling dance, more of a slow waltz with a bit of tango thrown in. He smiled with satisfaction and nodded his approval.

The two stopped, stepped away from each other and bowed low. Their mock battle finished, their war over. No winner here today, simply master and student, though which was which was becoming harder to tell.

"Great display," he called and clapped softly, then put his arm around young Mathew's shoulders and pulled him close. "So good to see you healed and agile on your feet. How are your bones and muscles holding up?"

Mathew wiped his brow with his shirttails and lightly punched Aaron on the arm. "Watch out old man, I'm fighting fit, thanks to Winston and his lessons."

Aaron turned to his faithful friend. "And where on earth did you learn those moves?"

Winston, a large man not known for speaking unnecessary words, thought for a moment. "I learned Kenpo from my father, who learned it from his father. I've no sons, so I've designated Mathew to carry on the family tradition."

"Not really," Mathew protested. "I asked him if he could teach me. I once saw him disarm a beggar who tried to steal from us. It was over in a flash and I knew it had to be a learned move, to act so quickly." He raised his baton. "Winston gave me this staff. It's hardwood, really strong and with my bo, as it's called, I'm going to rescue your daughter from her dark tunnels." He grinned at Aaron. "I'm off to have a shower, see you at lunch."

Ah yes, his daughter. A thread of guilt stabbed his conscience. The child he'd brought into the light and then not looked after properly. How could he have got it so wrong? To be away with his other family on the very night she returned, no doubt hoping to reach safety. There were a lot of 'ifs' about the whole sorry affair. If only Betty had been able to get the message through that Calista was coming. But the man with the ham radio had been called away to help an ill relative and Calista had already left. If only he'd stayed at the stockade that night he would have received her distress call on his pendant and rushed after her. If only the others had been home too. He wished he'd never sent the two of them north, thinking they'd be safe. Then Mathew had been beaten so badly all the poor lad could do was to stumble down the stairs to Betty that night, too late to save her. Enquiries among the neighbours narrowed the suspects down to a couple of men who'd moved into the area, made themselves useful and were now, suddenly gone. It must have been them. His shoulders slumped as despair swept over him yet again. He was getting too old for all this.

He felt a hand on his arm. Winston loomed above him. "It's alright Aaron. I know you feel bad. We all do. I wasn't here that night either. But I'm teaching young Mathew all I know and I reckon he's now strong enough to go and find her." They walked into the house and through to the kitchen where Mary had a pot of stew and fresh bread ready. While Winston washed his hands, Aaron ladled out the meat for the four of them and cut the bread into slices.

They sat in communal silence, each with his thoughts until Aaron had to ask, "When do you think you'll leave, Mathew? Are you taking someone with you?"

Mathew looked to Winston, who nodded. "Yes, Winston says he'll come. Perhaps not into the tunnels, he's a bit large." A quick smile was exchanged and Aaron guessed this had been well discussed. "But he'll bring the wagon with Buster and wait at the bottom of the mountain. I'll go in alone."

This didn't sound like a very good plan and Aaron opened his mouth to protest.

"I know what you're going to say. I shouldn't go in alone. But I have to, Aaron. I've studied the plans of the tunnels, the ones you brought out with you, and I doubt they've changed. It's hard rock. Not like slapping up another passageway in a house. I'm sure I can find my way to your apartment."

He had the confidence of youth. A self-belief that Aaron had once had; the confidence to drive you through the worst of situations.

"What of Eleanor and the children? Do you intend to bring them out too?" A pit yawned in his stomach. Another problem he'd created, something else to solve.

"Of course. Why wouldn't I? Surely Calista won't leave them again. I know she pined for the children terribly, although she tried not to show it. Anyway, there is no way I would leave Eleanor there on her own." The boy raised his eyebrows. "I'm not sure how you are going to cope with having two wives in the same city, but I will be bringing her if she will come." Mathew's neck reddened, but he held Aaron's gaze.

The boy had certainly grown into a man over the past few months and Aaron knew he deserved the comment. He didn't know how he was going to cope either, but he'd have to tell Eleanor himself— which is what he should have done with Calista. She now knew, according to Mathew; another embarrassing moment to navigate with her, when she returned.

"I'll get Henry Pope to make a copy of detailed plans of the passages and living areas that are pertinent once you get inside. There are a few exits anyway," he added. "Some easier to walk through than others. If you are bringing my grandchildren you will need to use the wider passageways. We can look at the plans this evening and make a decision on which would be the best to use— the closest and the widest to the apartments." In the pause, only the sound of them eating broke the silence until Aaron added, "You may have to defend their decision to leave. There could be guards on the nearest big exit to the sleeping quarters."

"That's what I'm training for," Mathew said. "I'll sneak in through the water and air ducts…and march them out through an exit. It's not supposed to be a prison."

"And I'll be outside the exit," Winston said.

"But it might as well be a prison. Leaving is not encouraged. We know that from the very fact the Mics sent men to take Calista back."

The discussion died for a while but unable to help himself Aaron added, "It's winter, it's damn cold. There could be snow on the mountains. Why not wait until spring? In three weeks' time the sap will run and the trees will begin to bud."

"I'm not waiting a day longer than I have too. It's three months since I came back. I'm well, I'm fit again—and now I know how to fight. I'm going as soon as we've packed the wagon." Mathew looked at Winston.

"Yes, we'll pack tomorrow and leave the next morning."

"It'll probably take you three days. I'll radio Castor Seville and he can put you up overnight. The next night you'll need to spend in the shed we left the bicycles in, at the bottom of the mountain. You'll need blankets as well as food."

For the first time, Mary joined the discussion. "I'll worry about all that, Aaron. Just leave it to us. We'll work on bringing Eleanor, Calista and the children all out. I'll make sure there are supplies and enough warm bedding." She pointed her spoon at Mathew. "This young man has done us all proud. He's worked like mad to get well and fit. I have every faith in him and Winston bringing your family home."

Tears bit at the back of his eyes. He blinked, blew his nose loudly hoping they wouldn't see his tears. What had he ever done to deserve such loyalty from this small band of followers? Such kind, like-minded people, who cared about him—and forgave him his weaknesses as well.

Chapter 20

"We're going to be late," Calista said to her mother as they hurried along the passage toward the communal exercise rooms, the only space large enough to hold the monthly resident's meeting.

"Since when have they ever started on time?" Eleanor commented. "In my lifetime that's happened just once." And she tugged at Calista's jacket. "Slow down, you're puffing me out."

Calista slowed and waited for her mother to catch up and they walked at a leisurely pace from thereon, along the twists and turns, down the narrow passages and into larger ones, always following the arrows on the walls. Even after a lifetime, Calista could get lost in the maze of tunnels if her destination wasn't indicated on the walls.

The babysitter had arrived late, and had initiated a game with the children. This, in turn, excited them so much they were reluctant to go to bed. It was a small delay but enough to annoy Calista to the point where she had to bite her tongue to prevent a sharp comment to the teenager, who was no doubt practicing being a mother for when her turn came. They were lucky the neighbour's daughter liked the children enough to look after them for a couple of hours.

She stood aside and followed her mother into the room, already filled with residents. The collection of people had a smell of its own—coal dust and boiled cabbage, and the only seats available were in the front. No one wanted to sit in the front row and draw attention to themselves. This was the night when they had the chance to complain, but would have to listen to the obligatory pep talk from the Accommodation Manager, and the Health and

Safety Officer first. Dr Webb also sat at the top table, to answer any questions residents had. Rumours were always going around about contagious conditions that could be circulating through the air conditioning.

She and Eleanor took their seats at the end of the front row and waited for the low murmur to cease. Only a rap with the gavel by the Health and Safety Officer stopped the buzz of conversation, and the meeting began.

The general health of the community was analysed, the cleaners and cooks were praised, even the gardeners were mentioned tonight. Several births were announced, followed by scattered applause. It promised to be another boring evening, but was the only chance residents had to mingle with others, other than hurried conversations stolen in the tunnels.

Calista hoped she would be asked to speak, but all that was said was "Calista Waterman has returned from her short visit to the outside. We are grateful she has returned unharmed," and the Health and Safety Officer carried on to other mundane affairs. Dr Webb flicked a smile her direction before his gaze returned to the front.

Finally the meeting opened for comments from the residents and once the complaints were over and notes taken the Manager of Accommodation queried, "Any other business?"

Calista stood. "Yes. I'd like to talk about my journey to the outside."

"Shut up," a voice yelled from the back of the crowd.

"Yes, sit down. We don't want to listen to any of your lies," called another.

"You're just a trouble maker, Calista Waterman. Sit down and be quiet."

She knew there might be some resistance. The outright aggression silenced her but she didn't sit. She stood tall and answered. "You can't judge if you've never been there." No one answered that. "How many others here have been outside and returned?" She looked around the room. "Go on, hands up if you've been outside." No one moved.

"Well I have, and I'm telling you there is no reason to stay in here, in these dim conditions, breathing each other's air, queuing for meals, working in muggy, stifling conditions." She took a deep breath. "Outside is hard. Yes, there's poverty and illness, but no more than we are struggling with inside these walls. The only thing we have here is constant comfort from the air conditioning. It's cool in summer, warm in winter and every day it circulates the illnesses that we suffer from. Did I mention the lack of vitamin D that weakens our bones? We have that too."

"But we're protected from the cancer the sun can cause—and from radiation."

The scorn in the voice cut through her determination and she faltered. Could she stand the wave of dislike that washed against her? If not now, then she'd never do it. Her courage rallied. All she needed was one deep breath and to go on.

"Yes, the radiation. The very reason we are all in here is to be protected from it. The main reason the original residents fought to be in the ballot to live here. The one thing they would be protected from." She paused. This was the opportunity she'd been waiting for. A scornful resident had brought it up, not her. "I'm telling you, there is no escaping radiation, either outside or in here."

"I don't believe you," a woman shouted. "My children are safe because I live and work here."

"No-one is safe. It's everywhere." Above the protests, she raised her voice and continued. Her throat ached from the strain of making herself heard. "It's in the air we breathe. It's in the water we feed to our plants. It's in the snowmelt we use for irrigation. It's in everything we eat."

"No, it isn't" someone shouted. "Our drinking water is from an underground spring."

"Lies. Pure lies. You're just a troublemaker."

Pelly from the gardens jumped out of her seat and yelled, "You should listen to her. What she says makes a lot of sense." Only to be pointed to by a woman at the back, her face twisted with dislike.

"You're nothing but a troublemaker as well, so be quiet. We don't need your sort telling us what to do." Pelly sat, her brief effort of support shouted down.

"Sit down and shut up," another man called out.

The gavel rapped. "You've no proof. Show us some proof, Miss Waterman." This request came from the Health and Safety Officer.

The crowd began to get restive, several people stood to leave. The aggression was palpable. It tainted the air. How could she prove something you can't see? Knowing she was losing the battle, she turned in despair and sunk to her seat…then the lights went out.

For a facility that was never completely dark, the inky blackness stunned the crowd to silence. Moments passed and then the murmuring began, chairs scrapped on the rock floor but people couldn't leave. No one could see where to go without light.

Beside her, a faint glow appeared and she turned, her stomach clenching in horror as her mother's hair began to glow. Angel's Kiss! If her mother had Angel's Kiss, were there others? She stood and looked into the blackness and there, and there again, dotted about, more glows were appearing. It was now or never.

"Look." she shouted above the buzz. "Look around you. There are people here with hair that glows. See the beautiful pastel green." A stunned silence swamped the room and before the noise rose again she added. "Even my mother, who was born here, has it… and she's never been outside." Her voice broke. "That's the effect of radiation. It's called 'Angel's Kiss'. Once your body has absorbed a certain amount of radiation it shows in your hair, like a halo, and in your fingernails too. Look at your hands. Are your fingernails glowing?" The murmuring eased, then rose again.

Nearby a woman screamed, "No, not me. My poor babies." Another man howled, "My wife. Look at my wife's hair."

In the light of the dotted examples of Angel's Kiss, Calista stepped to the top table and touched Dr, Webb's arm. "Please support me. Here's your proof, Dr Webb. Now you've seen it."

He nodded and stood. The sound of his chair falling back and hitting the floor, like the crack of a rifle, bounced off the walls and the babble of consternation ceased.

"People, listen to me. This young lady is telling the truth. Until tonight, I'd never seen it before, but I learned all about it in medical school. Only the accidental breakdown of the generators tonight has allowed me to confirm Calista's claims." You could have heard a pin drop. The crowd held its collective breath. "She has discussed this disease with me and here tonight is your proof. I'm convinced. You should be too. The evidence is here before us." He spread his arms, "The sad truth is, we are no more protected from radiation in the tunnels than if we were living outside."

The noise rose once more, beyond a murmur to shouts of disbelief.

People who displayed the glowing hair began to move through the crowd as if to get away from their diagnosis. Calista looked to where her mother sat and the realisation of how ill her mother was hit her like a sledgehammer. She moved to her side and wrapped her in an embrace, murmuring assurances that she would be alright, that she would look after her always and not to be afraid.

The lights flickered on and steadied, and within seconds the glow of Angel's kiss disappeared. You'd never have known it had been visible. Fear still circulated the room accompanied by its odour; but normality was winning.

She stood again and called out. "I'm not telling lies. Why would you live in the dark when you can live in the light?"

No one answered. Many looked away, while others stood and headed for the exit. She stared at the retreating backs, feeling she had lost their attention and the halos had been a beautiful mirage. Then, here and there, a head turned, a smile reached her and arms rose to display a thumb raised above a fist. There was support out there after all; other residents who might consider leaving this prison.

They were among the last to leave. She supported her mother, holding onto her elbow, taking her time to walk out the door. What a shock she'd delivered to her. How dreadful to find out your whole life had been lived on a lie. Her mother's tiredness now explained, her frailness not due to her age at all. Angel's Kiss had appeared right beside her, into the core of her family unit. All the more reason to get her mother and children out of this place.

As they turned into one of the lesser tunnels, toward home, a touch on her shoulder stopped her thoughts. She whirled, arms spread to protect her mother, frightened someone would curse her, or worse, but it was Dr Webb and the band around her chest eased.

"That was quite a performance," he said.

"It wasn't a performance. I meant every word of it," she said, preparing to defend her stand.

He bent and whispered. "Thank you for your bravery tonight. Come and see me tomorrow morning. I think I can help you," and he hurried past them, ducking into a side passage and disappearing from sight.

After a broken night, listening to her mother's restless sleep, Calista knocked on Dr Webb's office door. It was early, before breakfast, but he must be in because light showed in a thin ribbon under the door.

The door opened and he beckoned her in. "We are safe here. There're no listening devices as I've said before; patient confidentiality and all that." He opened a drawer in his desk and withdrew a large rolled of paper which he spread out on his desk. "What I have here is a portion of the plan of Erewhon's residences and the nearest large exits doors and service aisles."

She leaned over to study them. It would take more than a few moments to absorb the detail, but it was just what she needed. "Can I have it?" Hope rose in her chest, her voice high.

"Not this one."

A rock fell into her stomach. "Can I copy it?"

"I've saved you the trouble." He grinned and from a lower drawer pulled out a thick roll. "Here are some copies. I suspect there are others who would leave with you...myself included."

She grasped the roll, gratitude bringing tears to her eyes. "Would you come? Really?"

"I would," he said. "I feel my work here is done. As you've proved, radiation is within these walls. I may as well be outside, helping people who probably need me more." He walked her to the door. "Hide those. Hand them out to people who you genuinely believe want to leave—and please tell me when you decide to break out. I may be of use on the night."

Again she hugged the kindly man. "Thank you so much. I will, I promise. You'll be the first to know."

"Don't leave it too long." He pointed to her stomach. "This one will begin to show soon. Not only will travel be harder for you, but the Mics might want your child. I can't delay your insemination date much longer, and then the truth will be out."

Bile rose in her throat as fear washed over her. Her muscles stiffened and she couldn't move.

"Don't panic, my dear. I'll keep you safe," the doctor said and gently eased her to the door. "Now run along to work, and when you set a time and date, excuse yourself from work and come and tell me. I'll be your deputy. I'll handle the group who decide to follow you. I hold a position of power—and now's the time for me to use it."

Encouraged by the doctor's support Calista passed copies of the map to the several family leaders who approached her over the next few days. Even a couple of her fellow workers broached the subject and wanted to escape. The support, while sparse, buoyed her spirits and she promised to let them know when she was ready to go. She would need their physical presence when they got to the exit, with strength in numbers.

When a timid knock on their apartment door sounded, a few evenings later, it stopped their conversation. Calista looked at the children and held her finger to her lips. They giggled and exchanged glances, thinking it was a game. Her mother raised her eyebrows and whispered, "I'm not expecting anyone. Are you?"

Calista shook her head, rose and walked to the door just as the knocking sounded again. Perhaps someone wanted to talk about going outside? It wasn't an official-type knock. She left the safety chain on, and eased the door open to the chain's limit. The outline of a man showed in the tunnel's lighting, too dark to see his face. It seemed familiar, but it couldn't be.

"It's me," the figure said, "Mathew. Quickly, let me in."

She had to shut the door to unlatch the chain, but quickly opened the door wide, beckoned him in, shut it and latched the door once more. Only then did she let her heart have full reign. He stood smiling and nodding at her mother and the children; tall, handsome and tapping a long stick on the floor. She stepped in front of him, cupped his face in her hands and kissed him. A longing like she'd never known poured from her heart. Did he feel it? He did. The stick clattered to the floor and he embraced her, squeezing her so tight she ran out of air. She broke their kiss, suddenly embarrassed in front of her mother. Wrapped in his arms she leaned on his chest and whispered up to him,

"I've missed you so much."

"Me, too." He stroked her hair until she stopped trembling and calmed. Only then did he turn her around and with his hand wrapped around hers he took the few steps to the where her mother sat and bowed low, "Mrs Waterman... Eleanor, I'm Mathew. I love your daughter and I've come to take you all outside to be with Aaron."

Her mother didn't reply. She seemed to be beyond words but

pointed to the bathroom and Calista understood. She tugged Mathew into the small room, flushed the toilet and then kissed him again, not stopping this time until each of them needed to breathe properly.

The toilet had filled by then, so she flushed it again, murmuring under the sound, "I can't believe you're here. I'm so sorry I left you and went with Elizabeth. It was stupid of me; childish even. You should have come too, you'd have loved it." She gulped, the words tumbling. "Then when I got back Betty told me you'd been beaten. I was so ashamed that I'd caused you to be hurt." She ran her hands over his shoulders and arms. "Are you recovered?" She stroked his jaw where a red line ran from his ear to his chin. "You were cut?"

"No, a boot sprig did that. It's healed but my jaw is still tender. I think it was fractured."

Her hands flew to her mouth. How dreadful! Guilt stabbed her again, but he took her hands in his and kissed them. "It doesn't matter. It's over and gone and I truly think I'm a better person for it. I know exactly what I want in life, and that's you. To be with me forever, to marry, to have our children—but first we have to get out of here."

Should she tell him now? No, not yet. Instead she changed the subject. "How did you find us? Is Father here?"

He shook his head, "No, but Winston is. He's outside waiting, with Buster and a wagon." He sat on the side of the small bath and pulled her onto his lap. "Aaron gave me a copy of a detailed map, and I was able to memorise the passages to get here. I know how to get out as well, by the nearest exit. It's just a matter of when we go." He hugged her tight. "Can we go tonight?"

Her thoughts whirled. "No, there're things to arrange. I have to let Dr Webb know. He wants to come with us, plus there are families I've given maps to. I need to let them know, so they can join us. The more of us in a group, the less chance any guards will have. We'll outnumber them. Besides, Dr Webb says most of the guards are young men. It's something for them to do in the evenings to keep them busy, instead of fighting their raging hormones." She giggled a little, remembering Mathew's own desires. "That's what the doctor said."

Another thought occurred. "How did you pass through the tunnels without being stopped?"

"I just strode through, looking official, stopping here and there to peer into any box on the wall. No one said a word to me. I wasn't nervous. Winston has spent many weeks training me in a form of martial arts, Kenpo, and I have my bo with me. I can disarm and defeat anyone who dares to threaten you." He kissed her again.

Practicalities distracted her and she broke their embrace. "You will need to sleep on the couch tonight and tomorrow morning early we'll go to Dr Webb's offices. I'm sure he'll keep you busy for the day while I go to work. I'll spread the word, quietly." He nodded. "When do you think we should leave?" she asked.

"I've arranged with Winston for him to be near the chosen exit at ten each night, until we leave. It was the only way I could assure he'd be there, not knowing if you were here, or whether I'd have to go to another community to find you."

"You were prepared to do that? To leave, travel further down the alps to find another entrance and to search all the communities, for me?"

"And why not? I've told you, I love you and I promised your father I'd bring you back."

Her heart filled and her throat ached with longing. Yes, she loved this man too, more than anything in the world. Together they could accomplish any of their dreams. All they had to do first was... get out of here.

Chapter 21

"So…you're the young man Calista had adventures with?" Dr Webb pumped Mathew's hand with enthusiasm. "Fine specimen, Calista. Good height, strong grip, nice smile."

She laughed, "Stop it, Dr Webb, you're embarrassing both of us. Yes, this is Mathew and he has a plan to get us out—tonight."

With raised eyebrows and an incline of his head, Dr Webb encouraged her to go on. "He has a friend, with a horse and wagon. Winston will be waiting outside Exit E5 at ten each night until we leave, but we thought we should go tonight. The longer we leave it the more the news will spread." He nodded and she hurried on. "I've handed out the plans to three families and several young people. They may have told others so I don't know how many will turn up, but I will pass on the leaving time today."

The doctor looked concerned. "Will the wagon carry the children?"

"Yes," said Mathew. "And anyone else unable to walk a distance, or needs to rest. I want us to get to Castor Seville's by the following night, where everyone can rest for several days. It'll be a mad rush, but I don't think we should stop if we can help it."

"Food and water?"

"In the wagon, plenty of everything."

The frown on the doctor's head disappeared. "You seem to have it sorted. Let's hope there's only a couple of young men on guard, and that they're asleep." He looked at Calista. "But what are we going to do with this young man all day?"

"I thought he could spend the day with you." She smiled her best. "He's very good at looking official and perhaps if you had a clipboard he could wander around with you and pretend to take notes."

"Great idea, we can do that. I even have a spare white coat he can wear." He pointed to a door. "If you go in there young Mathew you will find several hanging up. Try them on and take the one that fits best."

As soon as Mathew left the room, Calista spoke, her voice just above a whisper. "He doesn't know about the baby, yet. I don't want him thinking I have to be molly-coddled. He needs to focus on getting us all out. He's been learning self-defence and reckons he can disarm the guards."

"Good idea," Dr Webb agreed and then said in a loud voice, "I hear you do martial arts?" to Mathew as he returned, looking the part in a white medical coat. "Just a minute and I'll get you what you need." Within moments he had placed a clipboard in Mathew's hand, and several pens were sticking out of the coat's top pocket. "Now you look the part. I'll introduce you to anyone who seems nosey as a supply technician, taking an inventory of the community's medical stocks. That way we can open lots of cupboards and check out the exit we intend to use."

Calista moved to Mathew's side, pecked his cheek. "See you later," she said. "If you get home before me, try and convince Mother she is going to be alright outside. She's very nervous about the journey."

He nodded and she slipped out the door, leaving him in safe hands.

Calista looked around at the assembled group. The passageway was full; in the dim lighting stood three families, five single youngsters, plus her family of four. The tiniest two children were carried, one a babe-in-arms, one six months old, each asleep. She carried Vanily on her hip and her mother held Caleb's hand. The remaining children stood with their parents, wide-eyed at this late-night adventure. A quick head count totalled twenty-two souls ready to start a new life tonight. Too late for second thoughts now. Mathew and Dr Webb stood at the front ready to lead them.

"Anyone missing? Anyone who said they'd come but hasn't turned up?" There was a general shaking of heads and a murmur of 'no's.

"Good, no tattle-tales either," and he smiled. Without the doctor, this would have been so much harder. When this was over she must thank him in some way.

Dr Webb raised his arm and beckoned everyone forward. In a quiet shuffle they headed down the route chosen. The narrow winding passages forcing them into a long winding trail, like a line of ants Calista thought, carrying meagre belongings, one bag per adult. After fifteen minutes of quiet progress they reached the junction to the wide tunnel that led to the exit. The air seemed fresher already.

The group paused and in soft, firm tones Dr Webb said, "If we are challenged at the exit door, you are all to stand quietly while Mathew and I negotiate with the guards to open the door. Understood?" Heads nodded and a child's voice rose in query before being hushed by the parent. The surprise element would be over the moment they turned into the tunnel unless the guards had already heard the high-pitch of the child's query. "We are hoping to avoid any violence," Dr Webb added then nodded to Mathew.

"Everyone ready?" Mathew's cheerful smile and air of confidence seemed to calm the atmosphere, already permeated with the odour of perspiration. Fear does funny things to people and Calista knew this moment was one that many had dreamed of but had never had the chance to pursue. Her heart swelled with pride as Mathew held his bo aloft and beckoned them all to follow.

She offered a quick prayer to any god that happened to be listening and turned to grin at her fellow residents, checking that her mother stood nearby with Caleb. She did.

"Let's do this," she whispered to the young people who were gathered at the front with her. They turned into the wider passage and formed a united cluster, filling the width, and then following Mathew and Dr Webb they walked purposely toward the large iron door that stood at the end of the tunnel.

Beyond that door lay the freedom they all desired.

"Halt!" yelled a guard, his armband stripes reflecting brightly in the light that flicked on, probably triggered by their arrival. The whole passage filled with a bright glare and in the moments while their eyes were adjusting Calista thought all was lost. Except, after several blinks, she could see that Mathew had stepped forward, his stick held upright, and he announced with confidence.

"I have with me a group of residents who wish to leave this

community. We wish to pass through the door to the outside. We will not return, just simply leave. You may shut the door behind us." The guard stepped closer but Mathew stood firm. "Please allow us through."

"And who the hell are you?" the guard asked, "And on whose authority are you asking me to open the door?" The man stood square and heavy, his chest stuck forward, his expression severe.

"On my authority," said Dr Webb and stepped to Mathew's side. "I say we can leave."

A second guard had appeared from a small room at the side of the door. "Do we have trouble here?" he asked, his voice behind his face shield betraying his youth, his query totally ignored by the adults.

"Sorry Dr Webb, your position is not high enough. No one leaves without a written authority from a member of the community's council. This entrance is for goods and services only." He chuckled, "You all need to take a train instead." The suggestion seemed to amuse him.

"Then I say we are leaving for medical reasons. As the sole doctor in this community, I consider that is sufficient reason. My diagnosis should over-ride any minor regulation."

Uncertainty flickered on the guard's face. "I might have to check on that," and he turned to lift a communication phone off the wall.

At this Mathew stepped forward, muttered, 'My apologies, but we can't have you doing that. We're leaving, tonight—now."

"Like hell you are." The guard lifted his fist and swung it, only to meet Mathew's rod before his fist could contact with Mathew's face. The bo twanged as it met flesh, the phone clattered against the wall and swung back and forth on its cord. Mathew stepped close, pushing the man back, the staff across the guard's chest. He resisted with shouts of anger and flailed arms trying to get back the advantage but the thrusting bar pinned him against the rock wall.

"I really don't want to hurt you," Mathew yelled above the curses. "All we need are the keys off your belt and we'll be outside and gone from your life."

"Never," the guard shouted. "Tonkins, ring central."

The young guard took several tentative steps forward, but Dr Webb stayed his progress with a raised hand.

"Don't, young Tonkins. I know you and your family. You don't want to get involved with this dispute. Go back into the office. Stay out of it."

The older guard struggled against the bo. His arms pinned down, and Mathew leaning at sufficient an angle that he couldn't reach his clothing with his flailing hands. With a swift movement, Mathew dropped the stick and as the guard leapt forward from the wall, Mathew grabbed his body, swung him around and locked him in an embrace. A quick side-kick followed and Mathew had the guard's feet flipped from under him. He collapsed against Mathew's chest.

Quick as a pouncing cat, Mathew had the guard in a headlock and moments later the man slumped to the floor, unconscious.

The watching crowd stood silent.

"Fine sleeper-hold," Dr Webb muttered, and moved quickly to retrieve the bunch of keys from the guard's belt.

"He'll only be out for a minute or two," Mathew said, and stared at the young guard, now close by but wavering with indecision. "Want to join him?" The lad shook his head. "Would you like to come with us instead?"

Tonkins nodded, "I'd love to. Don't want to be around when they find you lot have all gone," and he slipped into the group, merging with the small crowd among friendly back-slaps from his fellow teenagers, who were now excitedly chattering about the last few minute's developments.

Calista felt a tug at her skirt and looked down into Caleb's excited face. "A real fight, Mummy," the four-year-old said. She looked to find her mother. Why had she let him come to the front? There were two tall men behind her. "Where's Mother?" she asked, standing on tip-toe looking around. Pelly stepped up to stand beside her, now holding Caleb's hand so tight the child was protesting.

"She gave me Caleb. She said to tell you she can't do this. She's gone back." Pelly's tears told the truth. "I hate telling you this, Calista, but your mother was shaking all-over, terrified of the door opening. I truly don't think she could help herself."

For a moment Calista's world became a black void that she seemed to be falling through. How could her mother do this to her? It was too late now to run back and drag her out with them.

"She slipped away the moment the guard appeared. She'll be long gone now," Pelly added.

Vanily seemed a weight she could no longer carry and she thrust her at Pelly. "Please carry her for me. I'll take Caleb—and thank you Pelly. Thank you so much for holding on to my son." Imagine if her mother had taken Caleb with her. She shuddered, bile rising in her throat.

A cheer brought her out of the void and into the real world. Her mother had made the decision. A well-chosen time to retreat, and possibly thought about previously; unless her terror had overwhelmed her when the exit door loomed in front of them.

That door now stood open. The night air rushed in as a cool breeze that ruffled their hair and swirled among them. There were gasps as Winston's large figure stood framed in the doorway, until he and Mathew hugged and Winston boomed out, "Hello everyone, welcome to the outside." He beckoned, "Now hurry along, we need to get down the mountainside as quickly as possible." Winston passed a lantern to Tonkin, "Here young fellow, you look official. You can lead the way. Turn left outside, take it slow and follow the path down. You can't get lost. There's a horse and wagon at the bottom. Wait there for the rest of us."

Chapter 22

Tonkins disappeared, followed by the rest of the teenagers who rushed out the exit. The families followed, filing past Calista, all holding tight to their children.

"Step carefully. The path is narrow," Mathew told the adults as they passed him at the door. "Just take it quietly and you'll be fine. We'll come up at the rear." He'd been busy because as Calista approached the door, she noticed the elder guard now sat on the floor, trussed up and leaning against the wall, his expression a mixture of anger and dismay. She stopped.

"Would you like to come with us?"

He shook his head. "You're bloody idiots, the lot of you. The radiation will get you."

"It will get you in here too," she said. "Ask around about Angel's Kiss. See what the residents have to say about that." She patted his shoulder. "I'm sorry we had to tie you up, but we need time to clear the mountainside. You'll be found in the morning." And with that, she turned her back on her existence among the rock walls and stepped out into night, Mathew at her side, with Caleb riding on his shoulders. They left the door wide open in case any stragglers turned up, late for the departure.

The stars winked their delight, the breeze stroked her hair, and she paused to inhale the sweet smell of the earth. A morepork called.

"Winston?" she asked, but Mathew smiled and replied, "No, I think that's a real one this time. Winston is down with the group. A young girl is carrying Vanily. We're the last to leave."

He touched her shoulder and put Caleb on the ground. "Just stand there like a good boy," he said. "I need to talk to your mother."

She waited, wondering what he wanted to say that needed his arms free, but he hugged her, kissed her briefly and said, "Well done, my love. You did it. You lead them out." He hugged her tight to his chest and whispered in her ear. "I see Eleanor has left us." She nodded. "It was her decision. You can't live her life for her—and it does solve one problem; your father's other wife."

"I know," she said. "And I feel so guilty for being relieved about that."

"I want to go," Caleb said, "Now, Mummy. We are getting left behind."

"Quite right," said Mathew, and swung him up again onto his shoulders, then grasped Calista's hand and they hurried down the track to catch up to the others.

Following the light from the lamp held aloft in front, they all slowly navigated the path downward. There were trips in the dark with curses attached, but the children exclaimed in delight at the moon glimpsed now and again between cloud breaks. The sky finally cleared and the moonlight lit their descent. By two in the morning they had reached the wagon. The children, a total of seven, were quickly nestled among the blankets and mattresses. A set of grandparents climbed up as well and the bags of precious memories were tucked around them all. The six teenagers whooped and raced in wide circles frightening the horse, and after a stern word from Mathew, were taught how to stroke the horse's nose, under Winston's guidance. Their delighted gasps at the clear sky and the smell of the night air, made everyone smile.

An air of joy and celebration energised the group and they set off at a slow pace, extending their distance from their former home. Winston slipped an apple from his pocket into the horse's mouth and the frothy juice that dripped from Buster's warm soft lips made Calista forget about her sore feet and aching back as she walked beside him, inhaling his horsey aroma. How she'd love to climb onto the wagon as well but she hadn't told Mathew why. She plodded on, picturing their destination and the barn at Castor Seville's place, with blissful hay to sleep on.

She forced one foot in front of the other, eyeing the ground in the dim light, looking for holes that might twist her ankle or shrubs that would pull at her clothes. Only the sound of their feet, crunching the gravel and grit underfoot, broke the night air. A ground fog, only inches high, swirled here and there in the hollows. After the tunnel's regulated temperature the air nipped about her ears, but everyone had dressed for the trip.

After what seemed an age of stumbling blindly, following the horse-drawn wagon, dawn lit the horizon in the eastern sky. The mountainside behind them became a high menacing shadow no longer able to influence them.

"Breakfast time," Winston called and halted the horse, this time feeding Buster a carrot before he climbed up to the driver's seat and retrieved a large basket which he handed down to Mathew. Two rugs were spread out, and the children were marshalled to sit down. Winston and Mathew handed them buns, filled with cheese, dried fruit, and some sort of salad, which in the faint morning light could have been anything Calista decided. There would be lemonade to finish, they were promised. While the children ate the adults helped themselves from the back of the wagon.

Now would be a good time to tell him, and Calista moved away for a bit of privacy, to stand by Buster's head and beckoned Mathew to join her.

"I need to tell you something...something really important, Mathew."

Before she could continue, a rumble began in the distance. Thunder? She looked south. No, the sky was clear. The noise grew louder, and louder again as if a train was coming. But there were no trains around here. The ground began to tremble beneath her. It was hard to keep upright. She staggered, grabbing Buster's reins to steady herself and pointed to her children. Mathew raced to comfort them. The horse's ears flattened and his legs stiffened, his flanks trembled in the shafts. She held his bridle until Winston arrived to hold the other side, murmuring soothing words. She turned to see Mathew had Caleb and Vanily, his arms around them, his grin making them smile. The ground rolled; wave after wave. The wagon bounced, and the babies that had been asleep howled in protest. The earth shrieked as if in agony, its voice mixing with the screams of terror from the newly released tunnellers.

"Just an earthquake," Winston shouted above the roar. "You're quite safe here. Lie down, everyone. Just lie down on the ground and ride it out. There's nothing to fall on you." The other parents had already reached their children, and before she could take a step to reach Mathew the ground slammed up to meet her. She rolled away from the horse's hooves, now stamping in terror as Winston braced himself under the horse's chest to prevent him from bolting with the wagon with its precious cargo.

And still, the earth screamed, lifted them high and dropped them down. Threw them sideways and rolled them back. Her breath had been knocked out of her. She heard Mathew's voice. "It will pass. Stay calm, everyone. Ride with it, don't fight it. It will pass," he shouted, and then her children plopped down beside her, giggling about another bumpy ride. She stretched to embrace them, as Mathew lay down behind her and wrapped her in his arms.

They rode the quake for what seemed ages but was probably only minutes. Even when the noise stopped and the earth calmed, it trembled ever so slightly underfoot. Putting on a brave face the adults stood, dusted themselves down, and checked their children over.

"All good?" Mathew asked and everyone agreed. "Great. Well done, folks. That was probably your first earthquake. There could be more tremors, there usually is, but as long as you are in the open, just lie down before you get thrown down, and wait for it to stop." There was a lot of nodding within the group. "Then let's finish our breakfast—and there's lemonade of course, for the children."

The mood lightened, frowns disappeared and an air of festivity emerged.

"Now, what were you going to tell me, before all that happened?" Mathew whispered in her ear. She moved away from the crowd and held his hands in hers, holding his gaze. It took her several deep breaths to start, because their relationship would change from this moment on. Surely he would be happy? Perhaps he wasn't ready for parenthood? She'd never had to do this before. Just as Mathew opened his mouth to speak, she blurted it out. "I'm pregnant."

His face softened, "Oh, you poor darling, have they done it to you again?" He wrapped her so tight in his arms she could hardly breathe. "Don't worry. I'll love the child as if it's my own, just like I'm going to look after Caleb and Vanily."

She struggled free of his hold and cradled his face, her heart swollen with love, "No, it's yours." His brow creased as he looked down at her.

"Really?"

For a moment her stomach fluttered that he dared to doubt her, and then she laughed "Of course, I'm sure." She lightly punched his arm. "Don't you remember Cheviot?"

"I'll never forget Cheviot." He swung her off her feet and whirled her around, his smile lighting her life like a beacon. "God, I'm a lucky man," he said with a whoop, and she saw Dr Webb give a quick smile at their antics.

Then the earth trembled again, stronger this time. They both called to the children who were playing a game of running through the tussock clumps.

This time they didn't need to sit down, but stood and watched the distant mountain still towering nearby, close enough to watch the patches of snow slide down deep gullies, to see rock faces break away and career earthward, creating huge clouds of dust when they hit the level ground. The faint line of the path they'd descended split and pieces vanished. Clumps of stunted trees slid sideways, toppled and fell over, tumbling down the slopes. There were gasps as a line of trees bent, touched the ground and stood again as the mountainside rolled under them. Even at this distance the screech of rock on rock, like the crack of breaking glaciers, echoed out over the plain to the watchers.

Dr, Webb moaned. "My poor friends. The living quarters will be destroyed." He moved as if to walk back the way they'd come, but Mathew reached and held his arm to still his despair.

"You can't go back. Even if you could, you wouldn't be able to get in."

"I have a responsibility. People need me." Tears rolled down his cheeks.

"People need you here too. We need you." Mathew put his arm around the doctor's shoulders. "There is a huge need in Quake city."

Calista slipped her arm around Dr Webb's waist and rested her head on his shoulder. "Will this kill people?"

He nodded. "Almost certainly. Not much of the infrastructure will have survived that quake. Water supply, electricity, lighting will all have been damaged."

"Surely some will survive." She couldn't believe that everyone would die. Perhaps her mother would survive, even with her fragile health. "What about Queenstown and the Dome?"

Dr Webb shook his head. "Possibly, they're in the open on the lake's edge. Then there's the Wanaka settlement too. The dome may have cracked. It was anchored at Wanaka." They stood in silence, feeling the tremors beneath their feet, waiting for the next jolt.

"We may never know how many have been killed," the doctor continued, "until survivors straggle out of any exits they can find." His voice rose in anger. "The Mics were told the Alpine Fault was overdue to move. Nine hundred years overdue in fact." His breath shuddered, "Nothing would dissuade them. They went ahead with the internal railway, determined to build their utopia, then dared to ballot the accommodation. Even when Quake City tumbled for the third time they wouldn't take any safety measures."

Images of her mother, crushed, perhaps drowning in water or trapped unable to get air and food, swamped Calista's mind and her knees weakened. But she stood firm, breathed to calm her panic and concentrated on watching her children, once more running around chasing the others. It had been her mother's decision.

"Perhaps some will escape?" Mathew sounded hopeful.

"The path down has been destroyed," Dr Webb muttered.

"But down is down. They can always slide. It's going up that's been rendered almost impossible."

The doctor nodded and moved from their embrace. "Is there really a need in Quake City?" Hope caressed his tear-stained face.

"A massive need. We have spare rooms at the Stockade, but I promise you I'll build you a clinic of your own. I'll personally do this for you if you'll come with us—a thank you for looking after my darling for me." He hugged Calista to his side.

"And I'll help you," she added. "I can make ointments and infusions. I have some native leaves in my bag…and I know where to get more. I helped Dr Elizabeth. I learned a lot." The idea of being his assistant filled her with excitement. "I'm good at sewing up wounds too."

Dr Webb looked pointedly at her stomach.

"I can help for a while, and then I can help again after the baby comes." She grinned, happy to be able to openly boast of her condition.

"We'll see. First, we need to deal with any survivors of that disaster." He pointed at the distant mountain where the clouds of dust were settling, slowly revealing the scarred cliff faces. The occasional boulder dislodged and rolled, a rumble travelling toward the spectators. Looking like tiny pebbles from this distance, they must have been the size of a double-storied house or larger.

"Okay everyone. Show's over, let's move on." Winston chivvied the group into moving once more and they turned their back on the Southern Alps, now fractured, its spine broken.

The Dome and Queenstown may have survived the destruction and even if the Dome had cracked, did it matter? It had all been a lie. She wondered how many people there had Angel's Kiss? She doubted anyone would have checked. Another secret the Mics had hidden.

Calista took one last look at the mountain range, her final look she decided. She would turn her back on it…and her previous life. If it meant anything to her in the future, it would simply be where her mother probably lay buried, and nothing more. The future lay ahead, inviting and promising. She had all she'd ever dreamed of, and instead of having to make a decision on whether to breed or lead, she'd done both—her way.